READER PRAISE FOR THE ESSIEN SERIES

"A real page turner"

"Love the Essien family"

"My new favourite author"

"Excellent"

"Great series"

"Fantastic"

"I want to be like Felix Essien when I grow up!"

ALSO BY KIRU TAYE

The Essien Series
Keeping Secrets
Making Scandal
Riding Rebel
Kola
A Very Essien Christmas
Freddie Entangled
Freddie Untangled

Bound Series
Bound to Fate
Bound to Ransom
Bound to Passion
Bound to Favor
Bound to Liberty

The Challenge Series
Valentine
Engaged
Worthy
Captive

Passion Shields Series
Scars
Secrets
Scores

Men of Valor Series
His Treasure
His Strength
His Princess

Others
Haunted
Outcast
Sacrifice
Black Soul

Riding REBEL

First Published in Great Britain in 2018 by
LOVE AFRICA PRESS
103 Reaver House, 12 East Street, Epsom KT17 1HX
www.loveafricapress.com

ISBN: 978-1-9164755-4-0
Also available as ebook and audiobook

DEDICATION

To all families who stand together in times of turmoil and in times of celebration.

You don't choose your family. They are God's gift to you, as you are to them.

~ Desmond Tutu

CHAPTER ONE

"Mr. Petersen will see you now."

Heart thumping in a heavy gallop in her chest, Rita Dike straightened from the wooden frame armchair and rubbed clammy palms down the sides of her black trousers.

The secretary, Calista, who spoke to her, a dark-skinned girl not much older than her own twenty-four years, wore black platform stilettos, a grey pencil skirt, and a black and white striped fitted shirt, face made up and blemish-free, tresses of long dark hair almost to her rounded bottom.

How much do secretaries earn? She stared with envy, lips slightly parted, as Calista manoeuvred around her maple-finished modular desk and sashayed across the red-carpeted floor.

Surely, the girl didn't take home that much more than she did. But Rita had already done the mental mathematics and no way could she afford the expensive hair extensions or designer shoes with red soles. Not with a mother in the village and a university undergraduate sister who depended on her for financial assistance.

Calista turned the metal door handle and pushed back the oak slab. Rita swallowed the lump in her throat and relegated worries about her finances to the back of her mind. The faint scent of tobacco reached her before she saw the occupant of the massive, modern white-walled office. A new concern churned her gut.

Why had she been summoned to her boss's office? Not five minutes into the start of her work day and she'd received a phone call from Calista asking her to come up to the top floor.

Her tentative, "Why?" had received, "You don't ask why when the owner of Zen Media invites you to his office. If I were you, I would get up here *ozugbo*." Pronto.

Rita had abandoned her work and taken the lift upstairs immediately, her insides quivering. She'd never been summoned to the boss's office alone before.

Now she stood at the threshold, sucking in regulated breaths to keep the worry at bay.

"Good morning, sir." She gripped her hands at her back to hide their trembling.

A head full of dark, curly hair lifted, and enquiring amber eyes pinned her.

"Ah, come in, Miss Dike."

Nodding, she walked further into the space, cold air from the air-conditioner kissing her skin. The first time she'd heard Mr. Petersen say her name, and surprisingly, he used the correct two-syllable 'de-kae' pronunciation instead of the one-syllable 'dyke' that some other non-Nigerians used.

Then again, he seemed to be more Nigerian in his appearance than most, especially since she'd read he'd been raised in South Africa. Like now—he looked almost regal in a silver caftan and trousers with white embroidery around the collar and edges as he strode across the room from the large beech desk to the cream sofas at the other end.

Stacked beech wood shelves lined one wall. The other side showed floor-to-ceiling tinted glass and a view of Lagos Island, the bustle of the main commercial district, and the Marina. Bumper to bumper cars and buses, as well as crowds of human traffic, milled on the congested street level.

She hovered next to the sofa, hands held rigid behind her.

"Sit." He waved her to the seats before he relaxed into one, legs and arms spread.

Obeying, she sat on the edge, though the cool, buttery softness urged her to lean back into the leather. She couldn't loosen up until she knew the purpose of the meeting.

Calista lowered an aluminium tray of bottled still water and two tall glasses onto the light wood coffee table. The scent of her sweet perfume lingered in the air after she had retreated.

"Help yourself to the drink," Mr. Petersen said.

The sharp scrutiny of his gaze made her swallow hard.

Glad for the distraction of opening the metal cap and pouring water into a glass, it occurred to her this would be her first time of drinking water from a glass bottle. In Nigeria, these were the most expensive waters and an obvious sign her boss liked to enjoy the finer things in life.

Clearing her throat, she said, "I hope there's no problem, sir. Have I done something wrong?"

She prayed not. She couldn't afford to lose this job in a climate where most recent graduates were unemployed.

"Not at all," he replied in an even tone. "I have a very important assignment for you. Are you up for it?"

Head snapped back, she stared at him, mouth agape. A rush of excitement flowed through her body at the welcome words, and she sat up straight.

Her job as a junior reporter amounted currently to no more that of a glorified clerk. When she'd done her degree, she'd had dreams of travelling the country and the world, reporting on life-altering events. Instead, she found herself stuck doing the occasional birthdays and obituaries for the Sun People Newspapers.

Now, it looked like her fortunes could be changed.

"Of course I'm ready, sir. Anything you have for me, I can do it." Eagerness made her rush her words.

Surely, it had to be something wonderful. He'd used the word 'important'. Perhaps a sting operation to find corrupt civil servants, or some investigative work on the spate of attacks and kidnappings from Boko Haram. The possibilities were endless.

"You are going to help me take down the Essiens."

"The Essiens?" She leaned back as her brows puckered in confusion, her brain in overdrive. Only one family came to mind. "Do you mean that of Chief Aloysius Essien?"

"The very same one," he replied, his tone still even and almost nonchalant although he watched her with hawk-like eyes.

Mouth dried out, she swallowed a hard lump in her throat as her heart thudded in her chest.

"B—but...isn't he in his sixties, and one of the richest men in Africa?" And she barely had two Nairas to her name. How the hell was she supposed to help take down a powerful man like that?

Blood rushed in her ears as panic rose.

Petersen's shoulder lifted and fell in a blasé manner. "Perhaps. But I had a different member of his family in mind for you."

What? She worked for a media company, so she knew the Essien brothers as well as anyone who read the tabloids or business pages. They lived on a different stratosphere from her—financial aristocrats. They were known as the kings of finance in the money markets. She had nothing in common with them.

Her boss lifted a folder from the small table next to him and withdrew a photograph. He pushed it across the coffee table.

Rita picked up the picture and stared, mouth agape.

Mesmerising eyes, amber as the sun, stared back from the glossy surface. Her body flushed with heat.

Probably photographed during a glitzy event due to the well-known young actress in a shimmery black dress hanging on his arm, the man in the image had dressed in less formal attire—dark blue denim trousers, double cuffed white dress shirt, and light grey jacket made from some shiny fabric that could have been silk.

Toffee-coloured skin showed beneath the undone top buttons of his shirt. She licked her lips as she followed the trail of skin up to his face.

Damn. He's hot.

With high cheekbones and a perfect Nubian nose, he had a catwalk model's presence. But the compelling eyes and day-old dark stubble on his chin gave him a dangerously masculine edge.

And she hadn't even focused on the lips yet. Oh, his full lips curved in a sensual tilt. What would it feel like to have them pressed against hers? She traced one index finger over the smooth gloss as she imagined being the woman in his arms.

"I need you to get close to Tony Essien."

Amusement tinged Petersen's voice and had her remembering where she was. She lifted her gaze and met glinting eyes.

"I'm sorry, sir." Her cheeks heated up, and she dropped the photo on the table as if she'd been caught trying to steal it.

"No need to be sorry. He is quite a handsome young man," he replied with a hint of pride in his voice.

The way he sounded, he could've been talking about himself or his son, even.

"I don't know Tony or any member of his family, or anyone that knows them very well. How am I supposed to get close to him and why would I?"

"You will get to know Tony and his family very well in the next few months. I'm going to arrange for you to meet him. As for why..." He reached across and passed her a manila folder. "This is for you to read. It contains details of the investigation Ifeoma Ejiofor was doing on the Essiens before she tragically passed away. I gather she was your friend."

"Yes, sir." Her voice broke, and her shoulders drooped as she remembered her friend and colleagues who had died as a result of a car accident three months previously. "Ifeoma was two years ahead of me at the University when she became my friend. When I graduated, she helped me get this job."

"I see. I'm sorry about her death." He sounded genuinely sympathetic.

She nodded, afraid her voice would break again if she tried to talk. The past year had been tough on her in general; she would suddenly start crying with little prompting. Inhaling deeply, she blinked a few times, so the tears building up behind her eyes wouldn't spill. After a moment, she could read the words in the sheaf of papers tucked in the folder without blurry vision.

Each of the Essien brothers including their father had a dossier sheet with information like date of birth, schools attended, relationship status, employment status, various photos, and even people they had dated or married. But most of the information seemed to be on their business dealings, and apart from a list of girlfriends and wives, she could see nothing in there that wasn't in the public domain.

When it came to Tony's file, she discovered an addendum attached where her friend had scribbled a note.

I have reason to believe that Tony Essien is not an actual Essien. Attempts to obtain an original copy of his birth certificate have proved abortive, and the copy that I received shows signs of being doctored.

From my observation of this Essien, he shares little traits with his brothers. Although his complexion is close to Mark's, which reflects their mother's fair skin, his eyes neither match his brothers' nor his parents.' And his behaviour and attitude is also far removed from his brothers. He has no involvement with Apex Holding businesses except as a shareholder, although he part owns the Reams Bar & Restaurant with his brothers.

The only way to gain more information will be to get closer to the Essiens. I'm an already established journalist who has had dealings with them. Every time I ask a question during an interview, they clam up and only give canned responses.

I will need to find someone on the inside who can provide relevant information. But it's been difficult finding any disgruntled ex-employees let alone family member or friends who will spill the beans.

Ah. I have an idea. Rita is also an actress, and Tony is a movie producer. She could go undercover as an investigative journalist acting in one of his movies to get closer to him.

I will have to talk to her about it.

Rita looked at the date scribbled at the top of the note. A day before Ifeoma's fatal car crash. Her chest tightened.

"Ifeoma was working on this with you?" She looked up at her boss who had been watching her calmly as she read the contents of the folder.

"Yes. She'd been investigating for a few months, but she'd hit a dead end and needed another way of getting into the Essiens' camp. As she couldn't do it herself, she suggested you. She was going to have a chat with you about it. Unfortunately, that never happened."

Rita glanced at the note again. "According to this, she wants me to pose as an actress?"

He nodded. "I understand you've acted in a few Nollywood movies."

"Yes, sir. But those had been mostly walk-in parts. Nothing major. It was just a way for me to earn some money while I was at University. I loved acting but my parents wanted me to follow a different career path, and I chose journalism."

"Now, you have an opportunity to do the two things you love." He bared white teeth in a smile.

He had a point. Acting and investigative reporting were two things she enjoyed. She'd never imagined she could do both at the same time. Seemed like it would be possible.

"Yes, it's an excellent opportunity, sir. But what exactly do I have to do, and why is finding out about Tony Essien's paternity so important? You said something earlier about bringing them down."

As much as doing the things she loved would be good for her, she couldn't go prying into people's privacy without a valid reason.

"The Essiens have been involved in some shady business dealings for a while and it is rumoured they are mixed up in bribery and corruption at the top level in Nigeria. We are dedicated to rooting out all that is rotten about Nigerian politicians and elites. But we haven't been able to make any mud stick to the Essiens' squeaky-clean image. They use their power and influence at the top to shut down any investigations we carry out.

"If we put someone on the inside who can find out some of what goes on behind closed doors, we can expose it and hopefully, it will have a domino effect. Tony's paternity is just one of the things that would rattle them enough to reveal themselves."

She nodded and stiffened her spine as she absorbed the information. A corrupt, powerful man had destroyed her family unit, so she certainly understood about taking down one.

"I also heard that one of their companies was involved in the recent collapse of several government pensions' schemes."

"What? No!" She jerked her head back and her nose flared as a spark of anger ignited in her veins.

"Yes. And they have no qualms about leaving thousands of families with no income while they carry on driving sports cars and jetting around the world."

Like fuel to a flame, his words ignited her rage. Despite the air-conditioner, sweat beaded her forehead.

How could they? She'd lived with the effects of having the solid ground ripped out from beneath. Her family had lost everything. Despair had gripped her father and left him with a stroke which eventually killed him.

"My dad lost his job because of that pension scam." She pushed back the bile in her throat while clenching and unclenching her hands. She rocked in place, her voice choking with emotions. "We lost everything. My father died, and we had to move back to the village. We had to start again from scratch."

She remembered the body of her father lying in the morgue and how they'd had to go cap in hand to beg relatives in order to pay for his funeral. Jaw clenched, her hands curled into fists on her lap. The back of her throat hurt as the anguish she'd felt for months since her world fell apart returned.

The Essiens had destroyed her life and left her with nothing. She stared at the pictures again and focused on Tony. Suddenly, his image appeared smug and arrogant. She transferred the hatred she'd initially felt for her father's bosses to the Essiens.

She wanted to see that smirk wiped off his face. To see him taken down several pegs. Have his world ripped apart.

"If this is too raw or close to home for you, I can find someone else to do it," Mr. Petersen said in a warm voice that conveyed sympathy.

"No way, sir. I'm going to do this. I'm going to be the best damn actress. I'm going to get close to Tony Essien, and I'm going to enjoy bringing down both him and his family."

CHAPTER TWO

Tony Essien stretched and rolled onto his side. His arm hit a warm body, and he peeled drowsy eyes open. Grey dawn light filtered through the curtains and dappled a feminine form covered in bedding.

Screwing up his forehead, he studied her pretty face and tried to remember her name.

Bukky? Rukky? Some name that ended with 'ky' or shit like that. He couldn't bring himself to care as his temples throbbed with a dull ache. He massaged the sides of his head and sat up.

Traces of her makeup smudged the azure Oxford pillowcase where her face had been pressed against it last night. Tresses of black hair spread out behind her.

Memories of the past night replayed in his mind. Him yanking on her hair while he fucked her doggy style on the mattress. *Mehn*, she'd been a screamer; her moans had echoed off the walls, and he'd stuffed her red lace panties into her mouth to muffle her cries of delight.

By the time he'd spilled into the condom, she'd come so many times he'd stopped counting after the third.

Some people would consider his sexual proclivities debauched. He didn't care. At twenty-five, he was young and a long way from settling down. And as long as there were women willing to take his brand of pleasure, it shouldn't matter.

Money solved everything. And Lagos girls would let you do anything to them as long as they got well compensated in return. A handful of zeroes added to numeral digits on a check guaranteed no one ever discussed their encounters with him outside of the bedroom. Just as well, really, since his family courted scandal like skaters on thin ice.

As he swung his legs over, his feet sank into the soft pile of navy blue carpet, and he stretched out before heading toward the en-suite bathroom, navigating around the furniture in the still-dark room.

Time to dismiss this one. He didn't want her still on the premises when the rest of his family awoke. Although he had his self-contained house, he lived in the main Essien family estate, which meant he shared the same gated entrances as his parents.

His brothers had moved out and bought their homes, but his mother was reluctant to let him move away. So they'd compromised by refitting the two-bedroom house which had previously been used as guest quarters for him, instead.

"Come back to bed, Tony."

The sultry invitation had him rotating his head to look back.

Silver light from the window showed the girl leaning on her right elbow, her other hand pushing down the blue sheets, revealing a slender body of chocolate skin, dark nipples peeking at him in invitation. A coquettish smile curled her full lips.

He pictured those lips wrapped around his dick, and his half-awake erection turned to a full-blown morning wood. He should take up her invitation and return to bed. A glance at the bedside clock proved he still had some time, if they were quick.

He racked his brain again for her name, but it only aggravated his headache.

Damn! Why couldn't he remember?

"I have things to do this morning," he said in a gruff voice, instead.

His irritation hiked up, for some reason. It shouldn't have bothered him. Not the first time he'd forgotten the name of a girl with whom he'd had sex.

"Starting with this body. You should definitely do this body."

She winked at him, and he had to smile. She was forward. Truthfully, he liked his girls this way. To hell with all that 'playing hard to get' bullshit. Any girl who tried that crap with him never got a second chance. He never liked second-guessing what they wanted.

Life proved complicated enough without getting sexual signals mixed up.

This morning, it wasn't working, however. Perhaps it came down to seeing the girl in the cold light of day without the fuzzy influence of alcohol. Perhaps it amounted to the fact that he couldn't remember her name. Whatever. He wanted her gone. Fast. Still, she was fine, and she knew how to use her mouth. She gave head like a champ, enthusiastically and with a helluva suction.

But he had other priorities right now.

"I've already been there, done that," he replied in half-amusement.

"Oh, come on, Tony. I'll make it good for you. I'll let you come in my mouth again. And it's still dark outside, anyway. We have time."

Did she just use the collective to describe both of them or what they'd done?

"*We?* There is no 'we'," he snapped, his annoyance rising even more because he'd thought about inviting her into the shower so that he could come all over her face.

But not now. Not if she thought there existed more to them than just sex. He couldn't go there again. Couldn't let any girl think he wanted more or could give more.

"I didn't mean—"

"I know what you said. Get dressed," he ordered and reached for the wall switch, turning on one of the lamps. Soft yellow light filled the room. "Freddie will take you home or wherever you want to go."

"You're dismissing me?" Her head jerked back, and her mouth dropped open.

He didn't respond as he picked his phone from the dresser and sent a text message to his bodyguard. A response came back almost instantly.

I'll be there in two minutes.

Freddie shared the house with him, so he was always on site. At first, Tony had hated the fact that he couldn't have any privacy. But having his bodyguard around twenty-four-seven had its advantages, like right now.

In addition, the man had become more than security to him. Freddie had saved his ass more than just once. Tony didn't mess with the guy. Freddie had seen him at his worst, had been by his side when he'd dropped to his lowest.

Just as if someone flicked a switch in his mind, despair curled his shoulders and bent his spine. His mind hovered on the edge of darkness.

Sucking in gulps of air, he balled his fists and closed his eyes as he fought the gloom threatening to pull him under.

It had been years since he'd felt the desperate emotions, and he'd thought he'd got them under control. But there were moments when something would trigger them, and he would be back in that dangerous place again.

When he had his composure at a reasonable level, Tony lifted his eyelids and met the girl's gaze. She hadn't moved from the spot, scrutinising him as if trying to figure him out.

Yeah, she could join the rest of the universe that hopped on that lost cause. Even he couldn't figure himself out. He was who he was. People just had to take him or leave him. Didn't matter, either way.

"You are not dressed." He stated the obvious for emphasis as he pulled on his discarded pair of dark blue jeans. He had to wait out here for Freddie to reach them before he went into the bathroom. No way was he leaving the girl alone in his bedroom.

Some of these girls could be light fingered. He'd learned the hard way after he'd lost his laptop and some money. He'd caught one riffling through his drawers once. They just couldn't be trusted.

"Are you seriously dismissing me?"

The disbelief in her voice would've amused him if she weren't currently disobeying his instruction. He didn't like people who didn't comply with his demands, especially when it delayed him from doing what he wanted to do—getting in the shower and dressing for the day.

"Yeah." He raised his brows and crossed his arms over his bare chest. "What the fuck are you waiting for?"

A knock sounded on the bedroom door. The girl startled and yanked up the sheet to cover her naked body.

"Who's that?" she asked in a suddenly meek voice, her eyes like saucers.

"Come in," Tony said, ignoring her question. In his house, his rules applied, and she had to learn to comply.

The dark wood frame pushed in, and Freddie stood at the threshold, already dressed in a pair of black jeans and a white t-shirt that contrasted with his almost sooty dark skin. Sometimes, people referred to Freddie and Tony as Ebony and Ivory because of their contrasting skin tones.

Tony had found it amusing and had jokingly said "Ebony is a chick's name" while he laughed at Freddie, to which he got the response in Pidgin English, "I no know wetin dey make you laugh, boss—" his bodyguard knew that reference always annoyed him, "—but Ivory no be man name now." They'd both burst out laughing.

On the best days, his bodyguard always had a battle-ready, difficult-to-read expression. But as he glanced at the girl still on the bed, Tony could have sworn he saw something flicker on Freddie's face. A weird cross between anger and adoration, gone so quickly Tony couldn't be sure. But the fact that Freddie had shown some emotion in the presence of a woman still made Tony take notice. He would talk to the man about it later.

"Take her home," he said. "You know what to do."

Freddie nodded and still didn't say anything; another thing of note. Freddie was a talker, at least in Tony's company.

Tony turned his attention to the girl who looked like she'd sprouted roots into the mattress. "Get dressed in five minutes or Freddie will bundle you into the car naked. Your choice."

"You bastard," she screamed.

He shrugged. "I've been called worse."

She glared at Freddie and back at Tony, tilting her chin up. "I can't get dressed with him standing there."

"You had the choice to get dressed in privacy. Too late now," he said in an amused tone.

"You can't do this to me. My father is a senator." Fury remained on her face as she pulled the sheet and tugged it around her body. But she hopped off the bed and grabbed her clothes from the floor.

He rolled his eyes heavenward. "Who gives a shit who your father is? But if you really want to compare parents, then mine can buy yours ten times over," he replied with a smirk. He always found it amusing when someone tried to give him the 'Do you know who my father is?' routine.

She huffed as she pulled her red dress on over her head. She'd looked hot in it last night with her killer heels. This morning, she wasn't looking as hot with her hair in disarray and her smudged make-up. Usually, he allowed the girls to freshen up in the morning before they left. Then again, the girl usually did as he said and got dressed when he asked her to. This one had pushed the wrong buttons today.

She grabbed her bag and pulled out a hair clip which she used to pin back her hair; then she slipped on her shoes.

When he thought she would leave quietly, she turned to face him.

"Can I call you?"

A bark of laughter escaped him. After everything, she still wanted more of him? Lagos girls!

"I'll call you," he replied with nonchalance. He had no intention of doing so but if it made her happy to hear it, so be it.

"But you don't have my number."

"Give it to Freddie." He didn't know why he said it, but it sounded good once it came out.

She nodded and smiled, her eyes bright and expectant. "You know, I thought you were one of the good guys. Well, compared to some of your friends last night."

This time, laughter burst out of his throat in a low and harsh sound.

"You couldn't be more wrong," he bit out angrily. "I am the kind of guy your mother warned you to keep away from. If you were looking for a good man, you should've gone to church instead of a night club."

He turned around and walked into the bathroom, dismissing the girl and Freddie with his actions and words. What was it with these girls, anyway? One night of sex and they thought they knew everything about him.

Glad for the silence and seclusion, he stared at his reflection in the mirror. Amber irises surrounded by whites tinged with red stared back at him. A week filled with late nights must have finally caught up with him.

Not that he partied every night. Managing the Reams Restaurant & Bar meant he kept late nights. The business was a joint venture between him and his brothers.

While his friends lived off their trust funds from their wealthy parents, as an Essien, he'd been made to earn a living as soon as he'd graduated from University. At first, he'd refused to get involved with their various finance businesses. As much as his brothers loved wearing suits and going to an office every day talking about financial forecasts and economic climate, he'd hated the idea.

So when Mark had suggested they get into the restaurant business, Tony had jumped onto it as it provided him with the opportunity to be his own boss and pursue his dreams of building a movie business on the side.

The downside was that he had to find time during the day to write. He wrote the scripts for his screenplays. And he'd been working on a new idea this past week so he could meet a deadline he'd set himself.

Yesterday, he'd been out celebrating a friend's twenty-fifth birthday. Usually, the event would've been at Reams but Tony had asked Ray, the birthday boy, to choose another venue. He'd just wanted somewhere he could let loose after a hectic week without feeling as if his actions would be reported back to his family.

He didn't have anything bad to say about his family. They loved and took care of each other. His two older brothers were closer in age, so they got along very well. Because of the six-year age gap between him and Mark, he always felt like everyone else was up in his business.. So he always pushed back and rebelled. It was in his nature.

In such a close-knit set-up, everybody knew what everybody else got up to most of the time. It made him feel smothered, especially when his mother wanted to know what he was up to while he wanted to cut loose and run.

As an Essien, running was never an option. He just had to find his way of dealing with things.

He understood some of his mother's dilemma. Being the only woman in a household of men, he knew she sometimes wished she'd had a girl so she could have someone to chat with regularly. This was partly the reason she wanted Tony close to home so she wouldn't lose all her children at once.

Sighing, he dragged himself into the shower and stood there while the water washed away the scent of the girl and sex.

Feeling refreshed, he towelled off and pulled a new pair of jeans and a t-shirt from the closet. He walked barefoot into the kitchen.

"Good morning, *oga*," his housekeeper said as she went about her duties in the kitchen. She was a middle-aged woman with a congenial smile.

"Good morning, Kudirat. How are you?" he replied as he took a plastic bottle of water out of the fridge, removed the cap, and drank it all.

"Fine, sir," she replied. "I see *Oga* Freddie leave. You want me to bring your breakfast now?"

He tossed the empty bottle into the bin. He usually had breakfast with Freddie but since the man was on an errand for him, he couldn't wait. He needed to get on with his day.

"Yes, I'll eat now. Freddie can eat when he gets back."

"Okay, sir."

Tony returned to the bedroom and grabbed his laptop. In the open-plan living room, his meal was already set up at the dining table when he came back out.

He ate his omelette and toasted bread while he got to work.

CHAPTER THREE

"Relax and stop staring," Petersen said with a charming smile on his face as he extended his hand.

Rita swallowed a deep breath and snapped her mouth shut as she tossed her hair over the right shoulder. After placing her hand into Petersen's as she stepped out of the car, she walked with him through the automatic sliding doors.

She wanted to say, "I'm not staring, just admiring." But she would be lying. Wide-eyed, she gazed at the golden luxury of the hotel's breath-stealing lobby. From the marbled floors and walls to the glittering chandeliers hanging from the high ceilings, a wealth of magnificent details surrounded her.

"Tonight is about making the right impression," he said, leaning a little to the right to speak close to her ear before straightening. "And I'm here to help you pull it off. Remember, godfather."

Rita nodded. He had been like a fairy godfather.

After their conversation a week ago, when she'd agreed to take on the Essien assignment, her life had taken a turn for the better.

She'd had to sign a confidentiality agreement that stated she would keep the investigation a secret and not divulge it to anyone. Concern had twisted her insides, at first. Did this mean she couldn't tell her boyfriend or family, she'd asked.

Petersen had convinced her that keeping the secret formed part of investigative journalism. The fewer people that knew about their arrangement, the better. This way, the secret couldn't be leaked to the Essiens.

It also meant she couldn't tell anyone at work what she was doing. Mr. Petersen had signed her off on an extended leave of absence on full pay. She would be reporting directly to him.

The most astonishing thing was that he'd given her a new phone she was to keep with her at all times in case he needed to contact her. He'd also written her a cheque for an enormous sum, instructing her to upgrade her wardrobe. He'd given her a card for a boutique where he'd booked an appointment for her to visit.

She needed to look like the starlet she was pretending to be. So a total overhaul proved necessary from head to toe.

Of course, no way could she have access to that amount of money without making sure that her mother and sister benefited from her sudden buoyancy. She'd sent them some cash, telling her mother she'd earned a pay rise. At least, it hadn't been a total lie.

With self-conscious fingers, she caressed the smooth red satin that fell over her skin like melted chocolate. She had never worn anything so luxuriously decadent or provocative.

In fact, anything decidedly smart in her wardrobe amounted to more functional work wear rather than glitzy ball gowns.

She certainly had nothing in her old rack this vibrant, this sexy. This red.

With a deceptively high neckline, a cut-out slashed diagonally across the chest, showing a salacious hint of swollen, soft, fleshy breasts.

The vivid and bright colour gave the illusion of shimmering liquid crimson pouring down her body. It screamed at people to notice her.

And they did. Heads turned as they walked into the hall holding the ballroom where guests for the movie post-premiere party congregated.

Suddenly the centre of attention of so many assessing pairs of eyes, her grip on Petersen's arms tightened. "Did I really have to come here?"

She tried her best to keep her head up and own her new look. She was an actress, after all, even if she wasn't all that great.

"Of course. How else do you get noticed as a budding star than at an event where the crème of the Nollywood movie industry will be present?"

Petersen guided her to a table that had his name on one of the places. Glad to be sitting down so that she didn't make a fool out of herself by tripping on the tower-high, glittering designer sandals, she allowed the excitement of being in a venue such as this to finally permeate her skin.

She scanned the room packed with guests, women in glitzy outfits and men in expensive black tie tuxedos. Most of them she recognised as major players in the industry—actors, actresses, directors, producers, you name it. They were here laughing, chatting, drinking, nibbling. She had the urge to take out her mobile phone from her clutch purse and take selfies so she could prove she had actually been at the event with all the glamorous people. Her housemate wouldn't believe her, otherwise.

Everything sparkled and appeared gilded. It could have been a trickery of dim lighting and glittering glasses, but the ballroom seemed beyond exquisite.

"Champagne?" A waiter stood before them with a bottle of bubbly in an ice bucket.

"Please," she replied, and Petersen nodded.

The waiter filled two crystal glasses will the light amber liquid, bubbles fizzing to the top.

"Here's to nailing the Essiens," Petersen toasted when the server moved on to the next guest.

"Cheers."

Rita lifted her drink in the air before sipping it. She'd never had champagne before, so the fizzy explosion of flavours of pears and apples on her tongue felt like tasting stars. She loved it.

"I've just spotted someone I need to say hello to. Are you alright on your own for a moment?"

"Of course," she replied a little nervously. She didn't particularly want to be left alone at a party where she didn't know anyone except her boss.

Petersen patted her hand congenially before striding off. She pulled the black, soft shimmer silk pashmina across her shoulders, suddenly feeling lost and cold in the almost freezing air from the air con.

The hotel had played host to dignitaries and celebrities over the years and was magnificent. Who wouldn't want to cosy up to the grandeur of the place? The venue made her feel like a celebrity just by being there. She felt like a Nollywood starlet, even though her claim to fame amounted to a two-bit, walk-on part for a few seconds.

Men stared at her openly, with appreciation. These guys were out of her league, dressed in suits worth more money than she earned in a month. Her boyfriend, though he had a good job, didn't earn enough to buy expensive outfits like those, either.

An unfamiliar thrill shot through her blood. And she had to admit it—she enjoyed the attention. Partly the reason she enjoyed acting so much.

"Not feeling lonely, are you?"

The thick, sexy drawl vibrated through her body and had her rotating in her seat to see who had spoken.

She saw a pair of black Chelsea boots first, certainly not the kind she'd expect at a black tie event, but still fashionable enough to work. Then a pair of dark trousers made from a shiny fabric wrapped around sturdy thighs, not bulky but hinting at lean, corded muscles beneath the fabric. Her gaze paused at the gleaming, studded black belt. Also not something she expected to see at an event like this, but eye-catching.

"Like what you see?" Amusement tinged his voice this time.

Heat flooded her face. He must have thought she was staring at his groin, which invariably she was, and this time, she had to look.

Did his fly just swell a little?

Oh God. Her face heated up even more, and she turned away, reaching for her glass of champagne to cool down.

She took a sip, allowed the cool liquid to flow down her throat, counted down from five before turning back to look at the man and apologise for staring.

Her apology died in her throat, and her mouth gaped.

Sitting in the chair vacated by Mr. Petersen was Tony Essien. She recognised him from the photo her boss had given her.

Except he wasn't the two-dimensional man printed on a piece of glossy paper. He was flesh and bones. Hot and hard. Sexy and arrogant. His lips curled in a killer smile that said he knew what she'd been thinking.

Did the temperature just go up in here? She fought the urge to tug at her collar and fidgeted with her wrap, instead.

"My name is Tony. Tony Essien."

Oh God, that voice. Melted dark chocolate. Why did he have to sound so deep and decadent and yummy?

Breathless, her heart thumped in her chest, and she swallowed hard. She tried to open her mouth to tell him to go away, but she couldn't seem to work her heavy tongue apparently glued to her top palate.

His grin deepened, a dimple appearing on his left cheek. Dark stubble framed a strong jaw and sensuous lips. She could so kiss those wickedly curved lips right now. As if on cue, her tongue finally moved, swiping hers.

"Erm, I'm Rita," she muttered at last. "Rita Dike."

"It's a pleasure to meet you, Rita," he replied, one brow quirked up. "Are you in the industry, an actress, perhaps?"

She gasped, his perceptive query surprising her. "Yes, I've only had a couple of minor roles. What gave me away?"

His hand stroked the stem of the champagne flute resting on the table. The up and down sensual motion captivated her attention until his deep voice had her looking up at his face.

"You've got stars in your eyes," he said and leaned closer as he studied her face. "And they are beautiful brown eyes that remind me of chocolate buttons."

Her breath caught, her body heating up, both from his words and his proximity. His intoxicating scent had to be laced with pheromones or something because her body temperature rose as that of a feral animal in heat. Temptation to lean into him soared.

Lead me not into temptation, she prayed.

"Thank you," she said out loud with a tight smile and leaned back into her chair in the pretence of picking up her glass to gain some breathing space. "I've seen your movie and I enjoyed it."

"Really?" He moved back as if surprised. "It's not exactly a chick flick. What did you like about it?"

With some space between them, her brain functioned again, and she thought about her response when she'd watched his critically acclaimed movie.

"Well, it's very arty and yet cutting-edge. It reminded me of Quentin Tarantino's *Pulp Fiction.* I loved it."

"Wow, you are a little bundle of surprise, aren't you? You don't look like the kind of girl who would enjoy movies about gangsters and hit men. But thank you."

He sounded genuinely shocked and pleased, causing heat to radiate through her chest.

"You are welcome. The production was brilliant. Even the special effects felt real. I know I would love to be cast in one of your movies," she enthused.

"You would?"

"Yes, I think you are one of the best producers in Nigeria. I mean, you don't make a lot of movies but the ones you make are the best. I'll take quality over quantity any day."

"That's an interesting perspective from an actress. Most of the actors and actresses take on several movies at the same time, moving from one set to another, to ramp up their income. Are you saying that if you were cast in multiple roles in overlapping periods, you wouldn't take them?"

"No. I think it's unprofessional and as much as I may need the money, it's more important for me to be known for my professionalism at all times."

"Well, I'm impressed." He dipped his hand into his jacket pocket and withdrew a small gold case, then held out a black business card with gold-embossed lettering.

"Auditions start next week for a new movie in the pipeline. Call that number, and you will be given the address of the venue. It is a closed audition for now, so you will need to show the card to be let in."

"Oh. My. God." She squealed. "Are you serious?" Her mouth hung open as she stared from the card trembling in her hand up to him.

"Absolutely. If you're half as good as you sound, then I'm sure we can find a role for you."

"Of course. I'll be there. Thank you so much." Her body quivered with excitement. There existed an actual chance she would be part of his movie. She had genuinely admired his work before Petersen had told her of the Essiens' involvement in the Pensions scandal.

The dark thought reared its head, and the image of her father's cold body in the morgue popped into her mind. Her happiness dimmed, the smile wiped off her face. Getting involved in this movie should only have one purpose—to get closer to the Essiens so she could find out what Petersen needed to bring them down. She better remember that. She'd been enjoying his company so much, she'd forgotten the reason for being here in the first place.

"Are you okay?"

Tony scrutinised her face, his expression curious. He reached across and tucked her hair behind the left ear.

Involuntarily, her lashes fluttered shut, and she leaned into his soft palm. His thumb brushed the lobe; a light, gossamer touch that ricocheted through her body and made her nipples perk up and chafe against the silk of her dress.

Was that soft gasp hers? Her eyes flew open in dismay. What was she doing? Hardly five minutes in Tony's company and she nearly lost her head. Her wrap had slid off her shoulders unnoticed, and the hard points of her nipples showed through her bodice.

"Yes, I'm okay." Her voice sounded husky as she shook his hand off and pulled the wrap around her shoulders to cover her traitorous body. She forced a smile on her face. "I'll put this away, so I don't lose it."

She tucked the card into her purse.

"I see you are here with Kris," Tony said, leaning back into his seat, one arm on the table, the other on the back of the chair, his legs spread apart in a very confident masculine pose. As if he owned the venue. As if he owned the world.

She caught sight of his fly. Yep. A definite big bulge there. Her cheeks heated, and she glanced away quickly.

"Kris?" she asked, her brain on meltdown, her body inflamed.

How come I'm suddenly ogling man parts?

"Kris Petersen. I saw you walk in with him."

He tossed back his drink and placed the flute on the white brocade-covered table. His fingers drummed on the surface. Long, slender fingers. They'd stroked her skin just moments before. The beats they played matched her thumping heart rate.

"Yes. Yes, of course. I'm here with him." Her voice sounded breathy.

"So you are into Aristos, then." His voice sounded harsh, cold water to her hot skin.

She flinched. "What the hell are you talking about?"

Aristos referred to young girls who dated older men especially for the financial security they provided. Foolishly, she hadn't given much thought to the fact that people seeing her arrive with Petersen would assume she was having an affair with him. Now, Tony had confronted her about it.

"Do you like him because he is older, or is it his money that does it for you?" he asked in a low voice close to her ear, his warm breath whispering on her cheek.

"It's none of your business," she retorted, pulling back as her whole body flushed with embarrassment.

"Perhaps not." He leaned into his seat, his burning, dark amber gaze not wavering. "I don't do love. But if it's money you're interested in, I've got plenty of it, and I can satisfy you in and out of bed, too." His lip curled into a slow smile, and he winked at her.

Her traitorous mind took his words and conjured up an image of her body writhing in bed with him on top of her.

Oh God. I'm so going to Hell. She needed to get away from him. Or she would burn up on the spot. Even that didn't scare her.

"I'm not listening to any more of this rubbish." She shoved the chair back and snatched her purse from the table before heading for the nearest exit.

CHAPTER FOUR

Tony watched Rita walk away, her shoulders stiff, yet the height of her 'fuck-me' stilettos made her broad hips sway seductively even though she seemed unaware of it by the thunderous expression on her beautiful oval face.

Damn! She was hot. His dick hardened just by looking at her. The red dress flowed and shimmered over her slender and curved milk chocolate body like a second skin. That dress acted like a beacon, and as he watched her retreating, it seemed to scream at him, "Catch me if you can!"

Now, there lay a challenge. And while he enjoyed facing challenges in life, he didn't condone it when it came to women.

He liked his women fun and easy. Women who wanted to play hard and fuck hard. Women who didn't play games. Women who didn't give mixed signals.

Not like Rita.

When he'd first spotted her walk in with Petersen, she'd been clinging to the man's arm looking glamorous. Kris Petersen was a patron of the arts, the Nigerian movie industry specially, and as such a regular at these types of events. The man was middle-aged, but each time Tony saw him at an event, he seemed to be with a different woman. He had never paid much attention to any of those women until today. Until Rita.

His gaze had followed her from the time she'd arrived till she got seated. When Kris had left her to go to talk to another movie producer, he had kept watching, unable to look away.

Something about the way Rita had bit her bottom lip in a nervous gesture had him striding across the floor to introduce himself. Clutching her wrap across her shoulders, she'd looked lost momentarily as if she wasn't used to being at events like this.

Maybe she was new to the Aristo game, and Petersen her first catch. If so, she'd scored big for a newbie.

Tony's face puckered into a frown. If she were such a newbie at the game, then perhaps he shouldn't have anything to do with her. But if she was allowing Petersen to fuck her, then why shouldn't he tap that ass, too?

And she did have a fine ass.

In addition, as soon as he'd sat next to her, her brown eyes had blazed first with astonishment at seeing him, then with joy when he'd offered the invitation to the audition. At one moment, he'd seen her lips curl downward at the corners, and he'd wanted to wipe away the melancholy in her expression. So he'd caressed her cheek and ear in the pretence of sweeping her sleek dark hair away from her face. Her eyes had shimmered with lust, her button nose flaring, her soft cheeks flushed, and he'd caught sight of the hard tips of her nipples even as she made a little, gasping noise.

A girl that responsive to his touch he wanted to touch all over. He wanted to take her breasts into his mouth and suck until she moaned in ecstasy.

He still could. He was staying in one of the best suites in the hotel for the night. He could follow her and with a little persuasion, convince her to come upstairs with him.

But that would involve chasing after a woman. He never chased. When he propositioned a woman, she usually agreed straight away, and he was in; a good fuck and then out.

He had rules. No second guessing. No mixed signals. Always be straight up. Give her the best fuck. And move on.

A server walked by and he snatched a glass of champagne from the tray. He could use something stronger, but he'd resolved a long time ago never to drink too much.

At one time, he would've gone looking for something harder and not necessarily from a bottle. He'd been a boy, experimenting with life and love.

His experimentation had blown up in his face. He'd had to scrape himself off the floor, pull himself together, and move on with his life. He had never been the same again. Just fragments of his old self remained.

The new him didn't chase after prickly women even if they were hotter than a bowl of scotch bonnets.

"There you are, Tony."

He looked up at the woman who'd appeared beside him. Bukky Phillips. He schooled his expression. He'd done her already. Last week. It turned out, his mother knew her mum. And his mum had called in a favour. Take Bukky Phillips out. She was a budding actress trying to get noticed in Nollywood. He'd escorted her to the event. Quickly introduced her to some directors and producers, and left her to her own devices. However, she always managed to navigate to him.

"Bukky." He stood up. "Are you enjoying yourself?"

"Yes, it's been great meeting so many of Nollywood's finest," she said and rubbed up against him. "But can we go somewhere more private? I missed you."

He smiled. Nothing mixed about her signal. She wanted him at the earliest opportunity. If he'd wanted to spread her on the table and eat her out in front of the people, she'd let him. Bukky was that kind of girl. His kind of girl.

Still, apart from the fact that they would be arrested for conducting a lewd act in public, he wasn't feeling that kind of vibe at the moment.

A lie. He was, but for a different girl.

"Maybe later," he said.

She chatted about an acting opportunity coming up for which she would audition. He purposefully hadn't mentioned the closed auditions for his upcoming film because he hadn't wanted any more reasons to have to interact with Bukky. Although she did have her uses.

He tuned out the rest of her words and stared across the ballroom. His gaze met Rita's as Petersen slid his arm around her waist. Her expression looked sullen, matching how he felt inside at seeing the man touching her body. Somehow, picturing the guy fucking her had his gut twisting. He shouldn't care. Yet, he did. *Idiot.* She was just a piece of ass.

The way she glared at him with her lips flattened added to his irritation. He knew the jealous expression. Why the fuck would she be jealous because he was with another woman? She'd been the one to walk away from him.

What fucking game was she playing?

"Tony?"

He stared at Bukky blankly and then remembered she was talking to him about some movie role. "Sorry. I'm going to text Freddie to come and keep you company for a while. There's something I have to do."

He pulled out his phone and typed out a message, not waiting for her to respond although she pouted, and her shoulders slumped. *Entertain Bukky. I need her out of my face.*

Sure, Bro. The reply came back from his bodyguard.

He pocketed his phone and stalked over to where Petersen stood with Rita.

"You are hugging the best looking girl at the party all to yourself, Kris."

Despite the man being probably double his age, Petersen has insisted Tony address him as Kris the first time they'd met at his restaurant. The guy didn't seem hung up on deferential monikers.

"Ah, Tony. We were just talking about you." Kris's lips curled into a broad smile as he looked from Tony to Rita. "She is beautiful, isn't she?"

"Very," Tony replied, his gaze intent on Rita as she glared at him for a heartbeat and then lowered her gaze. He should ask what they'd been saying about him. Still, he didn't care. He wanted Rita. "I'm going to have to steal her away—" he paused so his words would sink in and added, "—for a few moments."

"Is that so?" Kris asked, but he didn't sound offended for a man who'd just been told his girlfriend was going to be taken by another man. "There's no need to steal, Tony. She's just been telling me you invited her to auditions and..." his shoulders lifted in a shrug. "I like you very much. So I'll gladly share her with you. Just take care of her."

"What? I don't want to go with him," Rita pleaded in a low voice.

"You'll be alright, my dear. Tony will take care of you, won't you?" Kris took Rita's hand and passed it over to Tony.

"Of course, I will," he replied. Something about the way Petersen had passed Rita off so easily rankled. He'd heard stories about Petersen's sex parties. Two of the girls that worked at Reams had been talking about attending it once. Apparently, Petersen wasn't averse to sharing his women. So nothing new with sharing Rita.

Tony's nose flared, and he glared at Rita, who only returned the glare as he grabbed her hand and strode out of the ballroom.

If Rita belonged to him, he would be punching any man who dared to try to steal her.

Then again, why should he care? She didn't belong to him, and he wasn't about to claim her for more than the night.

If orgies were her thing, he didn't care. *Dammit.*

His grip on her arm tightened, and he increased his pace as they headed across the polished marble floor of the lobby to the lifts. She stumbled. He swivelled, grasped her shoulder, and pulled her to him to save her from falling over. He'd forgotten she was tottering on sky-high-heeled shoes. He shouldn't be such a bastard no matter how pissed off he was at the situation.

His panting breath mingled with hers, their faces only an inch apart. "I'm sorry."

"It's okay," she whispered in a breathy voice, surprisingly subdued.

The urge to kiss her rose, watering his mouth. They stood in the middle of a busy lobby with prying eyes and mobile phone cameras. Tomorrow, their pictures would be splashed all over the Internet. It never bothered him when that happened. However, Rita's artless demeanour indicated she wasn't used to the limelight. Something in him wanted to shield her from the exposure.

So he tamped down his desire and tilted her head up, so she had to look into his eyes. Her soft, smooth skin felt warm, and her beautiful brown irises met his hesitantly. "I'm going to call the lift and go up to my room. It's your choice if you want to come up or not."

"What..." She sucked in a breath as if gathering strength to say what she needed. "What do you want from me?"

"I want to fuck you," he said in a low voice meant for her ears only.

Her lips parted; her breath hitched. The pulse on her neck thundered, and her throat rippled as she swallowed. But she didn't back away, and her saucer-wide eyes turned molten brown with lust.

There. He had his answer. She wanted him. Would she let him fuck her? Because that's what it would be. In his world, sex was about fucking. Wild, animalistic, unrestrained rutting. He would see to her pleasure again and again. Still, it wouldn't be sweet, and it wouldn't be loving.

A lift opened and a man stepped out. Tony released her and walked into the cabin.

Turning, he faced her. Enough game playing. She had to come to him of her volition.

She stood there looking sexy as sin as she bit her bottom lip and her forehead puckered in a frown as if she wondered why he'd left her in the lobby.

"I'm not going to drag you in here, if that's what you were expecting." His fingers itched to do it, however. He didn't want to contemplate that she would turn around and walk away. He had to give her the opportunity. "You have to walk into this lift yourself if you want me."

She glanced behind her and took a hesitant step backward.

His heart thundered. She was going to run. He held his breath and counted to ten to stop from stepping out and grabbing her arm. Instead, he jammed his finger into the door hold button and waited. Seconds ticked by that felt like hours. Sweat beaded his forehead.

She looked up and met his gaze. "Can you make the pain go away?"

"What pain? Are you hurt?" His eyes narrowed, and he wondered what or who had hurt her.

"No, but it hurts here." She settled her palm over her left breast.

He breathed in relief. That kind of pain, he was used to. He'd used sex as a self-prescribed medication to deal with heartache. After a while, the pain dulled in his numb mind. "Yes, I can give you relief for tonight."

She nodded and squared her shoulders. Then she walked into the lift and stood beside him. He punched the button to his floor as relief washed over him. The feeling didn't last long.

"Be gentle with me," she whispered.

Hell, no. He didn't do gentle. He wrapped his arm around her waist and pulled her into him.

"I can't promise you that," he said and rocked his hips so she could feel how hard he was for her already. It took super restraint to keep in check until they got to his room. Something in her pleading eyes made his breath catch and his chest tighten. He softened his voice. "But I'll try."

Why the fuck did he just say that? And yet, looking into her beguiling eyes, he knew he would do what it took to please her. If she wanted gentle, then he had to try.

"Thank you." Her breath fanned his lips.

He couldn't refrain from sealing their mouths together this time. She stiffened in his arms. Seconds later, she mewled as his tongue swiped her soft lips. He took advantage of the opening and delved in. Her flavour of champagne and something else that could be just Rita exploded on his tongue. Letting out a groan, he pulled her tighter until her nipples grazed his chest through the fabrics separating them.

He ate her mouth, drank from her lips. It wasn't enough. He thirsted, hungered for her. He palmed her ass, ground between her hips. She moaned, going pliant and rocking against him.

Next, she was against the cool metal wall of the lift, and his fingers were under her dress, palming her pussy through her lace panties. She was soft and hot. And wet. Slick juices coated his fingers as he slipped under the lace, circled her labia, and tugged at her clit. She arched off the wall and moaned. He slid a finger inside her. She stiffened.

"You are so tight but I know the solution to that." He grinned at her. He would spread her out on the bed and eat her until she was gushing so much that entry would be so easy.

The lift pinged. This time, he took her hand and guided her down the corridor to his suite. Door opened, he flicked on the lights and chucked his jacket.

"Strip," he said as he started unbuttoning his shirt and walking toward the bedroom. He undid his cufflinks and tossed them on the table. Glancing back, he expected to see her in some state of undress.

She hadn't moved from the spot by the door.

"What?" he asked, a little irritated that she hadn't obeyed his instruction.

"There's something I have to tell you," she said and bit her lip.

On the verge of losing his patience because he thought she was about to start playing her hard-to-get-game again, he crossed his arms over his bare chest. "Spit it out."

"I—I'm a virgin," she spluttered the words out.

Back ramrod straight, hands lowered and balled into fists, he stared speechlessly at her. *What. The. Fuck!*

CHAPTER FIVE

After several seconds of just standing there and staring at Rita mutely as she fiddled with the purse in her hands while staring at the floor, Tony turned and caught sight of his reflection in the full-length mirror on the wardrobe doors.

His mouth hung open, his eyes even wider from the shock of Rita's revelation. He looked like a man who'd been smacked upside the head. He scrubbed the stubbly hairs on his scalp and shook his head and then swivelled to face her again.

"Let me get this straight. You are a virgin. As in, you've never had sex with anyone."

Stupid. What else does virgin mean? Still, he had to be certain about what he'd heard. Right now, he couldn't match the words with the woman standing in his room who looked like sex personified in *that* dress. She had to be playing some dumb-ass game. It wouldn't work on him.

"Yes." She nodded and said in a small voice. "I've never had intercourse before."

"Then what the fuck are you doing in my room?" He didn't do virgins. They spelled a whole lot of trouble he didn't have time for. "More to the point, why are you hanging around with a man like Petersen?" A man happy to pass her around his friends like a bowl of M&Ms.

She flinched at his harsh words and her body trembled.

"Answer me, dammit!"

"I'm sorry. I shouldn't have come here." She turned around and stumbled to the door, fiddling with the latch of the lock.

"You are not going anywhere." He strode across the room and grabbed her arm. He had to know what was going on because this was bullshit.

Yanking her to face him, he forced her head back by pulling her hair. That's when he saw the tears. He suppressed a groan. He'd thought his night had been bad when she'd revealed she was a virgin. Now, seeing her tears, his night just took a turn for the worse.

He didn't do tears. No way. If a woman started crying, he ignored it and walked in a different direction. He should just send this one out of his room. For some reason, he didn't do that. Frozen to the spot for a moment, he couldn't let her go.

Sighing, he gathered her into his arms, instead. "It's okay. I'm sorry for shouting."

Her body trembled as she continued sobbing silently, her tears soaking his shirt and shoulder.

What are you doing, man? Stuff some cash into her hands, shove her out of the door, and be rid of her. Remember, no virgins and no tears.

He ignored the voice in his head, scooped her up with an arm under her legs, and carried her to the sofa. She wasn't a heavy girl. He'd lifted heftier weights at the gym.

He settled on the sofa and kept her on his lap, his arm around her as he leaned back.

Growing up in a house full of boys, tears had been a rarity. He'd never even seen his mother cry. And his only girl cousin, Tari, had been such a tomboy growing up. She'd been more likely to be the one inflicting pain on someone else than be the victim. None of the boys who ever came to look for her at theirs would have dared cause her to cry. Not when they knew they had three of her male cousins to deal with, and that didn't count the bodyguards.

So he didn't know what else to do with a crying woman except offer the comfort of his arms.

He would likely regret this later. But something about Rita got under his skin. From the first moment he'd seen her, he hadn't been able to keep her out of his thoughts. Her hot and cold responses to him had kept him unbalanced and out of sorts. Women didn't have this kind of effect on him.

After a while, the rocking of her body stopped, and she fiddled in her purse and took a sheet of tissue out. She sniffled into it and wiped her face. "Can I use the bathroom?"

"Sure. It's that door over there."

It's the only other door apart from the one to the suite, idiot. He stifled a groan. This girl was making him say some stupid things tonight.

She stood gingerly and walked into the bathroom, shutting the door behind her. Rising, he went in search of drinks in the mini bar. He found the small bottle of whisky, opened the cap, and emptied it out into his mouth in one go. He swallowed and the liquor burned his throat. He'd missed the taste and kick of whisky.

There'd been a time when he and his friends would spend the weekend partying and drinking whisky. Another lifetime ago. He no longer spent time with most of those friends. In truth, they'd been more hanger-ons than real friends. When the shit had hit the fan, very few of them had stood by him.

Shaking his head, he dragged his mind out of the past. What was he going to do with Rita? He certainly couldn't fuck her now. His hard-on had deflated as soon as she'd uttered the word *virgin*. Of all the things he'd expected her to say, that hadn't been one of them.

He pulled his phone out and called Freddie.

"Whassup?" the man asked in response. His voice sounded weak and a little out of breath, as if he'd been running. Or having sex.

"Is Bukky still with you?" Tony asked.

"I took her up to her room. She said she was tired."

So who was with Freddie? There were plenty of available women at the event tonight. Freddie was a good-looking man in a rough and ready kind of way. And since Tony had retired for the night, Freddie was off duty.

"Okay." He wasn't sure how to broach the subject on his mind. They'd discussed girls before, but this one proved...different. "Can you come to my room?"

"Sure, boss. Give me a few minutes."

He winced. Freddie never called him boss except when he was annoyed at him. They were more friends than employer-employee. "If you are busy, don't worry about it."

He heard what sounded like a sigh.

"It's okay. I'll be there soon." Freddie hung up.

Tony stared at his phone before shoving it into his back pocket. A prickling sensation on his neck made him turn around. Rita stood at the bathroom door, watching him. She'd tidied up her make-up and wiped the mascara streaks from her cheeks.

Still as stunning as ever, except her gaze flicked to some point on the soft pile grey carpet, and she seemed hesitant.

A string tugged his heart. "Are you feeling better?"

"Yes...thanks," she replied but didn't move from the spot.

"Do you want me to get you something? I can order room service."

"I'm not hungry. But I'd like a drink, please."

"Good." He opened the mini bar. "We have a selection here. What's your poison?"

"Do you mind if I have some of the brandy?" She walked toward him now.

"Of course I don't mind." He took out the bottle and lifted a glass from the table. Opening it, he poured the liquor out and handed it over to her.

"Thank you." She took as sip and grimaced.

He smiled at the expression on her face. She looked adorable.

Adorable? Seriously, man. You are losing it.

"You don't drink brandy often, do you?"

"No. My father used to let me have a sip from his glass," she replied.

"You father sounds like a cool dude."

"He was." Shadows moved across her eyes.

"Was?" he asked, wanting to find out what had changed.

"He is dead."

"Oh. I'm sorry."

Her eyes hardened. "Are you?"

"Sure," he said, caught off-guard by her bristling attitude. "Your father is dead. Of course, I'm sorry about it."

"Why are you sorry? Did you have anything to do with his death?"

"What? It's just an expression of sympathy, Rita. I never knew your father. How could I have anything to do with his death?"

Why the hell were they arguing about this?

She sighed, walked over to the sofa, and sat down with a thump, lowering her head to her hands. After a few seconds, she lifted her head. "I'm sorry. I'm still a little sore about my father's death. It was so unnecessary."

"What happened?" Should he even ask? He appeared to be walking on a keg of explosive gunpowder with Rita. He couldn't seem to get anything right. Except for when she'd been in his arms. It had felt right in his mind and body. *She* had felt good. And he wanted her back in his arms again.

A knock at the door drew his attention. *Freddie.*

"I should go." Rita put the glass on the coffee table and stood up.

"No. Don't go. Please." He'd never pleaded for anything. But he couldn't let her leave. Not yet. "I'll get rid of him quickly."

"Why do you want me to stay? I thought you found virgins repulsive."

He'd never said that. Perhaps his shocked expression had revealed more than he'd said. He rounded the sofa and stood a hair's breadth from her. "I don't find you repulsive, quite the opposite. You threw me. That's all."

"Yeah. Well, I still say I shouldn't have come here. Plus, I have a boyfriend," she muttered under her breath.

"You have a boyfriend and you've never had sex?"

"Some girls like to save it for their wedding night, you know." She glared at him.

"Which begs the question, why did you come up to my room when you knew I was going to fuck you?"

She averted her gaze and bit her lip. "It doesn't matter now."

"The hell it doesn't. I want to know why. Are you some kind of cocktease?" This woman drove him insane.

"What did you just call me?" If her eyes could shoot daggers, he would've been dead on the spot.

"How else do you explain all the mixed signals you've been giving me all night? You let me practically finger-fuck you in the lift and then you walk into my room and tell me you are a virgin. Cocktease."

Growling, she swung her purse at him, and it caught his arm. "You are such an arrogant, pig-headed bastard."

"Yes, I know that. But it doesn't stop you from wanting me. I bet if I stick my fingers into your knickers, I'll find you dripping wet."

"Rubbish," she said and swirled around, turning her back to him as she took a step away.

Grabbing her arm, he pulled her back and kissed her. Hands on his bare chest, she pushed but he didn't let go. Her palms burnt his skin as if imprinting her mark on him. His body ached, throbbed. Hell, he wanted her to put her mark all over him with her hands and her lips.

Wanting more of her, so much more, he tilted his head and deepened the kiss, his mouth ravaging hers while his hands grabbed her ass cheeks. He ground his hips into her. The fingers on his skin curled in as she clutched the seams of his shirt and whimpered her surrender, returning his kiss. They both fell on the sofa, panting out of breath, him on top of her before he resealed their lips together.

Bringing his right hand around, he pulled up her dress until he could reach her panties unimpeded. He dug his index finger into the lace and tore it. Then he found what he was looking for; silky wetness made his digits slide over her pussy.

Breaking off the kiss, they both groaned.

"If you want to go, tell me to stop now." His voice sounded hoarse and raw as he fought for some restraint. Apparently, with this girl, he didn't seem to have any. But for him, choice was a big deal when it came to sex. He would never force himself on anyone no matter how much he wanted them.

And he wanted Rita more than his next drink of water.

Heavy-lidded eyes filled with lust blinked at him, and she swung her head from one side to another.

"If you don't go, I'm going to part your thighs and eat you." He watched for her response to his crass words.

Her eyes widened, blazed with fire, and her body trembled beneath his touch.

Her response served to pour fuel on his hunger. She had so much passion wrapped up in her, and he wanted to be the one to unwrap her. To make her come apart. He nodded. "Yes, baby. I'm going to eat your pussy."

"Oh," she moaned and her body squirmed in a restless action as if becoming impatient for him.

He slid down and pulled the rest of her tattered panty off. Then he spread her thighs, opening her up to his gaze, her dress scrunched around her waist in a shimmer of crimson silk. Below, she glimmered, pink and brown and beautiful, her clit swollen and erect, reminding him of some flower he'd seen in his mother's garden, framed by hedges of trimmed wisps of brown hair. She smelled of musk and sex and Rita.

He looked up at her face and found her watching him as if unsure of what he would do. She didn't move to cover her body, her hands gripping the arm of the sofa as if for anchor. The vulnerability she displayed had his mind reeling. He suddenly wanted to possess and protect her body in equal measures, even if it meant protecting her from him. As surely as the sun would rise tomorrow, he only spelled bad news for her. He didn't want to be the one to hurt her.

What is going on with you, man? Just fuck her already and move on.

He closed his eyes and sucked in a long breath. Her image burned his mind. Her sweet scent filled his lungs. Her skin felt soft and satiny under his palm. His body thrummed, hummed with his hunger for her. In only a few hours, she had become a temptation from which he couldn't back away. And more than anything else, he wanted to taste her right now.

Lowering his head, he swiped his tongue from her slit to her clit. She nearly shot off the sofa. He clamped a hand across her belly, holding her down.

"You taste so good." He licked his lips, savouring her feminine tang before licking her again.

She keened and arched her body, pushing her hips toward his mouth.

Grinning, he glanced up at her. "You want me to eat you, baby?"

"Mmhm." She nodded. Sweat glistened on her forehead, and her long dark lashes fanned her cheeks as she lowered her eyelids. The tip of her pink tongue darted out and licked her lower lip.

Her shyness made him smile. Still, he couldn't let her off so easily. She had to know who she tangled with. For a long time, he hadn't been the type of guy a girl would want to take home to their mothers. Although some girls had tried. They'd been shocked to find out the truth about him. He didn't do sweet. He liked sex rough and dirty.

"Say it."

Her eyes widened like saucers, and she shook her head.

"Not going to work, baby." He leaned back, butt-on-heels, hands resting on her spread thighs. "If you want me to eat your pussy, you have to say it."

"Please don't make me say it," she said in a low, husky voice, the sound whispery feathers on his aching flesh.

Her brown eyes held heat, molten pools of chocolate, and he knew she liked him talking dirty to her. Only her sense of decorum prevented her from using the words.

"Baby, just say the words and I promise I'll make you come like you've never come before."

"I've never had an orgasm before." Her words came in a rushed, breathy sound.

He stilled, studying her again. He couldn't believe she'd never had an orgasm. Didn't she ever masturbate? For some people, masturbation proved abhorrent. Possible that she'd never touched herself sexually. Now, the uncertainty he'd read in her before came to the fore. He realised her innocence must be genuine.

"You haven't? Even more reason you should let me give it to you now. Tell you what, just say 'eat me, Tony'. I want to hear you say my name."

His phone started buzzing in his pocket. He pulled it out, pressed the answer button. "Not now, Freddie. Just wait," he said to his bodyguard in a rough voice. The man must have been tired of waiting for him to open the door and decided to use the phone instead to check up on him.

"I'm still waiting," he said to Rita, who still stared at him as she clung on to the sofa armrest.

"Please, Tony, eat me."

Her voice came out husky and low, and there was no way he wouldn't give her that orgasm.

"Good girl," he said as his lips curled into a smile before he buried his face between her legs and ate her like his life depended on it.

He started off with light teases, licking and swiping his tongue around the lower lips, before trailing down to her slit and tunnelling in with the tip. He might not be prepared to breach her hymen—it didn't mean he couldn't blow her mind. He so wanted to be the first to give her this kind of pleasure even if it would be the last time he did.

Using his left hand to part her labia, he took her clit into his mouth and sucked gently. She moaned, writhed, her body winding tight. He used his right index finger to swipe her juices and slid it down the crease of her ass. He pressed it against her pucker, and she groaned when he worked in and she clamped around him. Her body was wound so tight, her moans getting louder and louder, he knew she wasn't far from her climax.

"Tony. I'm..."

"It's okay, baby. I've got you."

He sucked harder on her clit, and she detonated under him. Her body thrashed for seconds on end as she let out a long scream of his name that echoed in his head again and again. Loads of women had cried his name before. But it hadn't been this important previously. He hadn't been the one to give them their first orgasm. The steel cage around his heart rattled. He slid up and pulled her into his arms before taking her mouth in an intense kiss. She clung to him, returning his kiss with as much passion as he did.

After a long while, he released her to catch his breath. "How was that for you?"

"I—I'm..." she stuttered, her slender throat rippling as she swallowed. "You...you blew my mind. I swear I saw stars."

He couldn't help the smug grin on his face. At least, this way, she wouldn't forget this night in a hurry. "I aim to please."

She laughed, in a soft, tinkly way that clamped his heart and wrapped him in a warm blanket.

What are you doing?

This was about sex, nothing more. He shook off the fuzzy feeling and stood up. He had to let her go. Otherwise, he'd be burying his dick inside her. What would that get him but trouble? If she lost her virginity to him, she would only attach unnecessary sentiments to him. Feelings he couldn't return. She was better off saving her hymen for a guy with a heart who would return her affection. He wasn't it.

Why did that feel like someone was kicking him in the gut?

He picked up her purse from where she'd dropped it on the carpet and pulled her up from the sofa.

"Are you staying at the hotel?"

"No. Why?" she asked, staring at him with still-glazed eyes.

"My bodyguard will make sure you get to where you are staying."

"Oh. Aren't you going to..." She trailed off and bit her lip.

"No, Buttons."

Huh? Pet name? Where did that come from? He stared into her brown eyes. They did remind him of chocolate buttons. And she was sweet.

"I'm not going to—" he was going to say 'fuck you' but changed his mind. "I'm not going to take your virginity. You are better off saving it for a worthy man. I'm nothing but trouble. I will break your heart. Trust me."

She nodded but her smile looked sad. "Am I going to see you again?"

"Of course. You are coming to the auditions next week, aren't you?"

"Do you still want me there?" Her expression gobsmacked.

"What? Did you think I invited you at the auditions only because I wanted to fuck you?"

He was a bastard, but he wasn't such an asshole. Oh, he wanted to fuck her. His erection throbbed painfully and sat like a brick in his trousers. But he would have to find relief some other way. "Your success at the auditions will be based purely on merit and not on whether you had sex with me or not. I don't play around with my business. I only pick the best actor or actress for the role. So you will have to bring your best game on the day to make it through."

He felt out of breath with that speech, but he had to let her know the score. His activities in bed didn't affect his profession.

"Okay. Thank you," she said as he walked her to the door.

He opened the panel to find Freddie still standing there.

"Thanks for waiting, Freddie. This is Rita. Please take her to where she's staying." He would've taken her himself but knew if he didn't let her go now, he wouldn't let her go at all.

"Bye, Tony," Rita said and walked to the lifts.

"Bye, Rita," he said curtly, shut the door, and thumped his head against the wood. He sucked in a breath and her perfume filled his lungs. He wanted to turn around and yank the door open and run across the hallway to beg her to stay.

Instead, he clenched his hands and stared across the room. Something caught his eyes. Her torn black lace panties he'd flung away lay on the floor behind the sofa. He strode across and picked it up, clenching it in his fists.

Dammit. He'd done the right thing by letting her go. So why the hell did he feel like shit?

CHAPTER SIX

Rita sat in church with her head bent slightly forward, her shoulders slumped. All weekend, the sense of shame that she felt had invaded her mind and seeped into every pore of her body.

She couldn't bring herself to look the pastor preaching in the eyes as he droned on about purity of mind and body. About turning the other cheek. About forgiving your neighbours and leaving your anger behind before seeking the face of God.

Unfortunately for her, she hadn't been able to leave her anger behind. It had also become a part of her after a year. She wanted revenge, which was why she'd gone to Abuja on Friday. Why she had allowed Tony to do all those things to her?

Yes, you were getting your revenge, weren't you? While he was on his knees with his face buried between your legs, you were punishing him, right? Who are you deceiving?

Self-disgust made her lips curl as her jaw tightened. The hand that held the pen she used to make notes on her pad clenched.

Okay. She would admit it. She'd been out of her depth. She hadn't expected meeting Tony, sitting close enough to smell his spice and to see all his masculinity so potent and dangerous. She had been overwhelmed.

The instant pull, the attraction to him, had had her heart pounding in her chest and her mouth watering. That he'd approached her and chatted with her, even inviting her to auditions, had blown her mind. When had someone of his calibre ever given her the time of day? Never.

Even when she'd thought she'd escaped him by going to the ladies' first and then keeping close to Petersen, Tony had still managed to fish her out and had convinced Petersen to let her go with him. His exact words had been, "I'm going to steal her," or something to that effect.

Her heart had sunk as soon as Petersen had agreed and handed her over to Tony. She couldn't run or hide anymore. She just had to face up to what she needed to do even if there was an enormous chance that Tony was going to ruin her in the process.

Mind racing and body quivering, she'd followed him as he'd dragged her across the foyer towards the lifts. Then he'd done the strangest thing. Tony had apologised when she'd tripped. She couldn't remember the last time she'd heard anyone apologise to her. Her boyfriend, Anayo, never apologised for anything, one thing about him that bugged her loads. He would twist things around and make it out to be her fault.

But Tony had been quick to apologise, which had surprised her. He was the last person she expected to hear an apology from. He was the arrogant son of a corrupt rich man who had no problem ruining other people's lives just to make money.

Yet...Tony's words had chipped at her hard heart, giving her a glimpse of someone who could very well turn her world upside down again.

And he had.

One minute, he'd told her he wanted to *fuck* her. That 'F' word had ripped through her defences like nothing else he'd said before. She hadn't known she had a thing for dirty talk until that very moment. Her sex had clenched, wept, even, as the rest of her body heated up. She'd wanted to fall at his feet and beg him to take her. To do whatever he'd wanted with her.

Then he got into the lift, tall and handsome and arrogant, giving her the option to walk away. She'd considered walking away, going back to Petersen. But the thought, of leaving him, had made her feel physically ill.

She'd taken a step back, feeling unbalanced more than intending to move.

She'd seen the sorrow and fright in his expression. He'd thought she would leave him. It had been as if he'd felt the same sickness at their looming separation. The connection between them wasn't just a mental thing. It had morphed into the physical.

The ache that had weighed her down for so long had bloomed and made her want to rub her chest. Before thinking, she'd asked him if he could make it go away. She hadn't been thinking correctly. How could he take away her pain? His family had caused it in the first place.

Still, there'd been something in his eyes that had seemed to pull her in and tell her he'd experienced a similar pain to what she felt. And when he'd said he could take it away for the night, she had believed him.

Strangely, the idea, of losing her virginity to him, hadn't frightened her. She'd held onto it for so long, throughout her university days when the girls around her were having sex. She'd never felt the pull to indulge. Her faith had kept her away from playboys. Bad boys like Tony.

And when she'd met Anayo through her late friend, Ifeoma, they'd agreed to take it slow and work towards a life together before getting involved sexually.

And yet, a few hours with Tony had demolished that resolve. In truth, her faith had already been weakened. Since the death of her father, she had been questioning a lot of things about God and faith. With so much anger boiling in her veins, she wouldn't find peace until someone paid for her father's death.

There had been times when she'd wished she could point a gun at the culprits and shoot them. She wasn't a killer, though, and she wouldn't spend the rest of her life in prison. Her boss's suggestion had been the better approach. People like the Essiens thrived on the image they projected to the remainder of the world. If she could dismantle that pristine reflection and make the world see them for the deviant, rotten people they were, then she would have a more powerful victory.

So Tony became just a means to that end, and her virginity would've been the sacrifice that would have brought her closer to the goal.

Now, she wasn't so sure.

Tony had been happy to give her pleasure and her explosive first orgasm. But it seemed the idea, of breaking through her virginity, had disgusted him. And her shame had mounted. She couldn't even convince a playboy like Tony to have her.

If he refused to get involved with her, then it would make getting into the Essien circle a lot more difficult. She still had the auditions to fall back on. But Tony had warned her she had to be at her best to make it through to the next stage.

Rita bowed her head and prayed that she would have another opportunity with Tony. Petersen had warned her not to fail, and she couldn't let her family down. They had already benefited from the extra money she'd been given for this assignment. She couldn't afford to give it back and return to her normal job filing birthdays and obituaries.

"Are you not coming?"

Rita looked up to find her flatmate, Kechi, waiting for her. The service was over, people milling out of the warehouse-style building. She had been so lost in her thoughts, she hadn't noticed the church emptying out.

"Sorry. I was miles away," she said as she stood and walked beside her friend to the exit.

"What's going on with you?" Kechi gave her a side glance. "You've been so distant since you came back from Abuja. Did something happen?"

Guilt pelted Rita's skin, making her body heat up. Kechi was her close friend, and she told the girl most things. But she hadn't been able to unburden her heart since she'd returned to Lagos on Saturday.

"I think I'm just tired. You know this promotion is tougher than I thought it would be."

"*Haba*. Girl, this is something you've been fasting and praying about for so long. To get a job promotion and better pay. Well, it's happened. Or do you want to go back to being a glorified clerk?"

"No way," Rita blurted out.

"There you go, then. You have to be joyful. And just get used to the extra work."

"I know. I know."

"Good. So where is Anayo?" Kechi asked when they got to the car park. "I'm surprised he hasn't come up to you."

"I don't know." Rita scanned the faces of the people around them but couldn't see her boyfriend's face. He was an usher in church, and usually, he would meet them after the service and drive them to his house or Rita's where they would spend the rest of the day. Rita didn't own a car yet, so she and Kechi took public transport.

She stopped another usher, a tall, dark-skinned young man who was also friends with Anayo. "Hi, Rafael. Have you seen Anayo? I can't find him."

"Hi, Rita. Sorry, Anayo wasn't in church today," Rafael replied. "In fact, I was going to call him. Haven't you spoken to him?"

Feeling shame that she didn't know of her boyfriend's whereabouts, she looked away, afraid Rafael would see her guilt. "No. I was away and only got back yesterday. I was expecting to see him in church today."

"Okay," the man said.

"Thank you." She pulled her phone out of her bag. "I'll call him."

She pressed the button for Anayo's number and waited for the call to connect, but it rang, and no one picked up before it cut off.

Kechi stared at her with raised brows.

Rita shook her head. "He is not picking it. I'll try it again later."

"No problem," Rafael said. "If I speak to him before you do, I'll tell him you were trying to contact him."

"Thank you," she said before the man walked away.

"What are we going to do?" Kechi asked.

"We will just have to find our way home."

Luckily, the area, where the church was located, wasn't far from where they lived in Ajah. However, they had to walk from the side street to the busy main road of the Lekki-Epe Expressway before they could find any transportation to take them back. Thankfully, her shoes were sensible enough to walk in, and when they arrived at the bus stop, a bus didn't take long to come.

As they sat in the hot, unventilated bus that reeked of human sweat and odour that made her want to retch, she reflected on the enormous contrast to Friday night as she'd sat in the luxurious chauffeured car of Kris Petersen or the fact she had dined with beautiful people dressed in extravagant jewels and fragrant with expensive perfumes. She thought about how she'd felt to be the centre of attention, having wealthy men ogle her in the red dress.

Now sitting in the bus, she became just one of the masses again. A simple girl with nothing to her name and a family she had to take care of. The area they lived in stood up and coming. All around her, she could see signs of development—works to expand the road, construction of new homes, cranes and heavy machinery on the site of a new shopping mall. Ten years earlier, the whole area had been marshy grasslands.

Half an hour later, they stepped off the bus to walk the rest of the way to the two-bedroom, single-level annex they shared. The roads off the expressway were not tarred and flowed into gulley and humps. In particular sections, the heels of her shoes would sink into the beige sand on a rainy day. Today had been dry, so they had no pools of muddy water to wade through.

They let themselves in through the pedestrian side gate of the high-walled, wrought-iron gated complex. Their landlord lived on the premises with his family in a five-bedroom, two-storey mansion that would have looked at home in Lekki, Victoria Garden City, or any other high-worth locale.

But land in this area proved cheaper compared to those other already established locations. Rita counted herself lucky for securing an accommodation like this as the landlord and his family were kind and although the rent was a little expensive on her wages, it wasn't too bad given she shared the expense with her friend.

They rounded the corner to the back of their building and stopped. Rita recognised the red 2004 Toyota Celica car parked in front.

"Isn't this Anayo's car?" Kechi asked.

She nodded mutely as her heart thundered. Considering he hadn't answered the phone when she'd rung him, she hadn't been expecting to see him at her place. She'd been sort of relieved that he hadn't been at church. She wasn't prepared to confess her actions in Abuja yet.

Ordinarily, the gateman knew him as a regular visitor so there would've been no reason for him not to be allowed into the compound even in her absence.

The expression on Anayo's face, as he stood from the steps leading up to the entrance, said he was upset about something. She remembered when she'd first met him. She'd had a thing for bad boy actor Jim Iyke, and Anayo had reminded her of him but without the ego.

"Anayo, are you okay?" she asked when she stopped in front of him and scrutinised his face. Kechi had already opened the door and walked inside. "We didn't see you in church today. Did you leave early?"

"No," he replied curtly. "I have to talk to you."

"What is it?" she asked, now concerned. Unlike him to miss church. "Is everything all right?"

"You tell me," he snapped.

She flinched. "What's that supposed to mean?"

He glared at her, his face puffed up as if ready to explode.

"I want to know what you did in Abuja." He snatched her arm and dragged her up the steps. His grip on her arm felt tight and hurt.

"Anayo, you are hurting me," she cried out but he paid her no attention as he stomped across her living room.

Kechi, who'd been typing away on her phone, looked at them quizzically, and Rita shook her head and followed Anayo into her bedroom. She didn't have any other choice by the way he held her unless she wanted to air their dirty laundry in front of her housemate.

He dragged her in and slammed the door behind her.

Her heart was thumping and loud in her ears, but she tried to stay calm. "What's gotten into you? Why are you behaving like this?"

She hadn't seen it coming. Hadn't expected it. The next thing she knew, she was doubled over, holding her stinging face as she cried out in shock and pain, her ear ringing from the impact of the slap, her eyes watering.

"I told you to tell me what you did in Abuja and you better start talking if you don't want more slaps." His voice came out loud and filled with menace.

Rita remained in a state of shock, not believing he'd just slapped her, still processing his actions as well as his demand. Why was he asking her this now? She'd told him she was going to Abuja for work, and that had been the truth. They worked for the same firm although he was an accountant and toiled in the finance department.

"I told you I went to a movie premiere and the after-party. The boss wanted me to cover the event as part of my new job." She lifted her head, using the door to hold her weight as her knees trembled. She grew so scared and afraid of what Anayo would do. She'd known he had a temper, but he'd never hit her before today.

He stopped pacing. "Does you new job involve you going up to men's bedrooms? Is the boss now your pimp? Eh, tell me!"

She was going to be sick. How did he know she'd gone up to Tony's room?

"I explained to you I was working on an assignment for Mr. Petersen. He wanted me to interview Tony Essien, one of the movie producers." That was the truth, at least, but she avoided his gaze. "But T—Mr. Essien wanted to go somewhere quiet to chat. His room seemed the obvious place. I went down soon afterward and returned with Mr. Petersen. I never stayed overnight in the hotel."

"So did you get the interview?"

"What?"

"You said you were supposed to interview a movie producer. Did you get the interview done?"

"Yes...yes," she replied hesitantly. "But it's not done yet. I'm supposed to shadow him for the next few weeks. I'm doing an expose on Nollywood movie productions so I've got to go and observe the auditions he is holding this week."

Another lie. But no way could she tell Anayo the full truth, especially when he was in such a raging mood. He would kill her, by the looks of it. He didn't like her acting and called all the young emerging actresses sluts because of some of the raunchy movies in which they acted. Tony Essien's movies were raw and gritty, and there was no way Anayo would approve of her wanting to work in one of them.

She loved acting, perhaps even more than she loved journalism. However, her father had insisted she pursue a different degree than the performance arts she wanted to study, and after acting, writing proved the next best thing.

And while she felt guilty for the things she had done in Abuja, she knew it would never happen again, so perhaps she deserved his slap as punishment for her slutty behaviour. She had learned her lesson.

"You are shadowing this Essien person."

"Yes, Tony Essien. He is an up and coming movie producer and his movies have won critical acclaim. We are running a special feature on him."

"And you are going to be spending a lot of time with him?"

"Yes, but it's just work," she said quickly.

"You say that now. I know these people. The Essien brothers are very popular. Some of the most notorious playboys in Nigeria. And you want to be spending time with them."

"Well, as far as I know, Tony's older brothers are happily married and I think Tony has a girlfriend. He was with a woman at the party on Friday. I mean, look at me. I'm not in the same league as him. He can't be bothered by a simple girl like me when there are flashier girls around."

He eyed her up for a moment before his expression cooled and he sat on her bed. "Well, you are right about that. He would be stupid to stoop so low when there are classier women out there."

His words hurt even worse than his slap. Her eyes watered and she flinched. Her lungs constricted and for a moment, she found it hard to breathe. She opened her mouth and sucked in deep breaths to quell her dizziness.

After a few inhales, she was able to see clearly again. She ignored his snide comment and sent silent thanks out that he seemed to have cooled down. But she wanted to get away from him. She turned and gripped the door handle.

"Where are you going?"

She glanced back. "I—I'm going to get you something to eat for lunch."

"No. Not yet. Bring the baby oil and come here." He pointed to space between his legs.

Her stomach lurched and she pulled in a fortifying breath. "Anayo, not now."

His expression hardened. "Do you really think this is the right time to refuse me?" He loosened his leather belt and lowered his zipper.

She swallowed hard and fought to maintain control of her emotions. He looked murderous and she had to keep him sweet. Moreover, she'd been the one who'd cheated on him on Friday. It didn't matter that he always used her this way. It was her penance.

She picked up the bottle of baby oil from her dressing table and settled on her knees before him. He pulled out his swollen penis. She didn't wait to be told, only wanting the whole ordeal to be over already. She poured the oil onto her hand and wrapped it around his manhood and started sliding it back and forth like he preferred. He groaned and she carried on. Soon, his groans got louder and he rocked his hips, thrusting upward. She tuned it out, taking short breaths to avoid his scent in her nose as she worked faster to bring him off. Soon, he was groaning and streaks of white cum coated her hand.

That's when she whirled around and ran out of the room into the bathroom. In agitated motions, she rubbed her hands in the sink, trying to scrub off his semen and scent from her skin as silent tears rolled down her cheeks.

At the beginning, Anayo had said this was his way of finding release since she wouldn't let him have full sex with her. She hadn't minded because it had meant he didn't go to other women for release and she'd kept her virginity. He could've asked worse of her. In her University days, she'd heard stories of girls who indulged in anal sex as a way of preserving their hymens.

A shudder passed through her. No. Thankfully, Anayo's depravity hadn't extended to that. He'd tried once to finger her, but she'd never come and he'd given up. Since then, he'd never bothered even trying to arouse her. It had become a ritual of her servicing him.

Before, she hadn't given it much thought. But after a weekend of having another man worship her body and give her the first ever climax, she now felt degraded being used by her boyfriend as a sex tool just for his gratification.

Tony Essien hadn't asked for anything in return after he'd given her an orgasm. He'd been content with just watching her come apart. Yet, her own boyfriend couldn't even be bothered with trying to satisfy her.

Was this what marriage between them would be like? Her giving and him taking? It wouldn't have mattered when she lived in ignorance, but now she knew she wasn't cold and asexual. She'd felt passion with Tony.

Now, she wanted more.

Wasn't it ironic that a man she hated cared more about her pleasure than one who claimed to love her?

CHAPTER SEVEN

"I'm home," Kechi said as she stepped into the living room space that housed two small, lilac fabric-covered sofas and a square coffee in the middle.

Rita sat at the small round four-seater dining table, laptop open and working. She looked up from the screen at her friend dressed in a pink fitted shirt, blue flared skirt, and blue platform shoes with pink side panels. One thing Kechi had in oodles—style.

"Welcome. How was your day?" she said.

"It wasn't too bad. I just wished my head of department wouldn't be such a pain." Kechi placed the handbag that matched her shoes on the table. "I wish I worked from home just like you. This new promotion is very good to allow you to work from home."

"I know. It's very good. As long as I meet the deadlines, I'm allowed to do most of the work from here."

"That's great."

"Also, I have to spend a lot of time shadowing the subject of one of the special features we're doing."

"Yes, you mentioned it. The feature on Nollywood movie industry. You are so lucky, getting to rub shoulders with the movers and shakers of the movie business. You better remember us when you are enjoying the glory."

Rita laughed. "As if that's ever going to happen."

"It will. Didn't you tell me you were with the likes of Tony Essien? He is from one of the richest families in Nigeria and he is so handsome. You'll get to audition for one of his movies. That's a big deal."

"But I'm so nervous about it. You know how much I love his movies. Now I have an actual chance of getting a role in one. It's a massive deal for me."

"You'll be just fine. You are a good actress. You just need to be noticed."

Rita screwed up her face and bit her lip.

"But what are you going to do about Anayo?" Kechi asked as if reading her unease. "He is going to flip if he finds out that you are auditioning for a role. After what he did to you on Sunday, I'm really concerned."

Rita shut her eyes and inhaled deeply as the trauma she'd endured rose in her mind. Even though she'd hidden the full extent of what had gone on, Kechi had questioned her in the kitchen as she'd been preparing lunch for Anayo. She had heard the shouting and had been concerned for her friend. Rita had to explain the misunderstanding. She had tried to hide the impact of the slap but her back had been sore from when she'd slammed backward into the door and she'd walked gingerly while she had been in the kitchen. Kechi had asked her what was wrong and she'd had to explain that she'd hit the door.

Her friend had accepted her explanation but she wasn't sure if Kechi totally believed her. Now, that concern manifested itself.

"What are you going to do if he finds out?"

"I told Anayo that I'd be shadowing Tony Essien for the next few weeks as he starts working on a new movie, so me going to Rebel Studios won't be a surprise to him. And I'm not even sure I'll get the role, so there really is no need to worry." *Yet.* She omitted the word.

"Okay. That could work. I've been wondering. Did he tell you how he knew you went up to Tony's room?"

"He didn't tell me, and I've been wondering the same thing."

"You know, it seems to me he is spying on you."

"I think so, too. How else would he know what I was doing? But it is so ridiculous because I have never cheated on him." Until last weekend.

"What really happened between you and Tony? I know something did. I know you too well. You came back a different girl. Talk to me."

Rita had been dying to share her experience with someone. But her guilt had held her back. For the first time in her life, she'd cheated. Okay, they hadn't gone all the way but it didn't diminish what she'd done and she'd been ashamed of herself.

But after Sunday... After what Anayo had done to her... The way he'd treated her. That guilt and shame had been replaced by resentment.

Now, she wanted to tell her friend at least some of what had happened.

"Tony kissed me."

"You are pulling my leg," Kechi said, wide-eyed with shock.

"No, I'm not."

"Tony Essien, bad boy biker movie producer. That same Tony Essien kissed you?"

"The very same one."

"Oh. My. God." Kechi plastered both hands to her cheeks before a huge grin split her face. "No wonder Anayo was 'hollering' on Sunday. He's got major competition. You scored mega, girl."

"Not really. It was a one-time event only."

"No way. You are going to be seeing more of him. I'm sure it could be more."

"No. He wanted to have sex with me. But backed out when he found out I was a virgin. Apparently, he and virgins don't mix."

"That's a shame. But you never know. He could change his mind."

"I doubt it. He was very adamant."

"Oh, well. Never mind. So tell me again about this kiss. What was it like?"

"Tony is a great kisser."

"So compared to Anayo, who is better?"

"Tony wins, hands down. That man knows how to use his mouth and tongue."

***

Rita still had Tony's oral skills on her mind as she made her way to the Rebel Studios venue for her auditions two days later. Due to the time of day, she'd wanted to arrive at the location in Victoria Island not feeling harassed of having other people's sweat on her, so she had taken a taxi. Expensive but worth it.

She stepped out of the cab in front of the two-storey building and paid the driver. At the gate, she showed the black card Tony had given her to the gateman. He let her in and pointed her in the direction of the door, explaining where she had to go.

She was half an hour earlier than her appointed time. But she wanted to show that she was immensely professional and serious about this gig.

The revving of a motorbike had her turning her head to see who had arrived. Two men sat on expensive-looking motorbikes. Heads obscured by black helmets and wearing black leather jackets and blue denims, the riders could've been anyone.

Surely, it wouldn't be actors auditioning for parts in the movie? A smirk curled the corner of her lips at the thought.

Gripping the handlebars with cool ease, the first rider had a powerful presence as he pulled up to a spot under the car port. The ground beneath her gold ballerina shoes vibrated before he killed the engine and she felt the tremors rumble up between her thighs.

"Oh." A soft moan escaped her lips and she closed her eyes involuntarily.

"Hello, Rita."

The familiar deep voice made her lift her lashes as her cheeks heated up. Tony Essien's compelling amber eyes met her gaze. Her heart nearly punched a hole through her chest.

Outfitted in a white t-shirt, blue denim, and black leather boots, he appeared so different from the man she had met last week and who had looked gorgeous in a black tie. Now, he had an edge of bad-boy biker as he held his helmet in one hand.

He was a man who would tempt a saint. She hadn't realised she had a thing for bad boys. But her resolution to avoid any intimacy with Tony stood on shaky grounds right now as she watched his lips curl into a very sexy grin. Those lips had given her the ultimate pleasure. And she wanted to experience that high feeling again.

"Hi, Tony." Her throat grew suddenly dry and she licked her lips as down below got wet.

Beside Tony stood the bodyguard he'd introduced as Freddie. The man nodded at her but didn't say anything before walking to the side of the building. She had to admit they both looked dark and dangerous.

"You are early for the auditions," he said as he took a black leather satchel from a compartment on the motorbike and hooked his helmet to the handle bar.

"I wanted to come early so I could familiarise myself with the venue and not get so nervous when I'm called in," she said, clutching her shoulder bag to her side.

"There's no need to be nervous."

He stepped up to her and she caught a whiff of the outdoors and his masculine scent. She had to stand rock-still to resist the urge to lean into him.

"I'll share a secret with you." He leaned in conspiratorially. "The first audition is a simple reading. Just one line. I'm sure you'll breeze through it."

He stroked her cheek with the back of his hand. Her skin tingled, electric sparks travelling through her body. She bit her lip to stifle the moan bubbling in her throat. His hand travelled down to her shoulder and he squeezed, massaging her tense muscles.

Her breathing evened out and her muscles relaxed beneath his touch. Her shaky anxiety dissipated. How did he do this? How could he get her to relax so easily?

"There. That's better," he said and she lifted her gaze to meet his.

"Thank you," she said after swallowing.

"You're welcome. You can go in through those doors." He pointed at a white door. "And I'll see you later."

"Are you coming in?" she asked with a frown. Wasn't she going to see him again?

"My entrance is down there." He pointed to the side of the building.

"Okay." She nodded and started walking to the door. As she reached the white panel, she heard his voice again.

"It's good to see you again, Rita."

She turned around and caught sight of him before he disappeared round the corner. "Same here," she muttered under her breath.

She walked into a reception lobby with rows of empty chairs. The café-au-lait walls had been covered with framed posters of Rebel Studio movies that she loved. A young, dark-skinned man at the desk greeted her with a friendly smile. He gave her a form to fill in and ushered her to a seat.

She completed the form that indicated her audition would be recorded and she released the recording for Rebel Studio's use, then she returned the form to the desk. The place started filling with prospective audition candidates. Rita smiled as she watched many of the men and women looking nervous. Being here early and Tony's magic fingers had already chased away her nervousness. Slowly, her smile faded as she realised she'd received special treatment from Tony.

Surely, he wouldn't be offering to ease the tension of other candidates. Yet, he'd done it freely for her. Why was the man so nice to her? At the party last week, he'd been brash and arrogant. Yet, he'd also been tender and generous. Such a ball of contradictions that confused the hell out of her.

How was she supposed to achieve her goals of taking him and his family down when she couldn't be sure how she felt about him?

"Rita Dike, please follow me."

She scrambled up from her seat, her legs wobbling as some of her nervousness returned. Glad that she wasn't wearing high heels, she followed the receptionist down a hall.

"You will meet the director and producer." He handed her a sheet of paper. "Good luck."

He opened a door and ushered her in. She found a large room with similar coloured walls as the front lobby. Tony and a man she recognised as movie director Joel Ali sat behind a long desk. Another man stood at the corner with a video camera equipment on a tripod stand.

"I'm Joel and this is Tony," the director said with a smile. "For this audition, we need you to read the line on the sheet of paper in your hand. You can start when you are ready."

Tony's expression spelled all business, neither a smile nor a frown.

She nodded and stared at the sheet of paper she held, reading the content. She closed her eyes and pictured the scene where the character would say the words. She practised them in her head a few times and then opened her eyes.

"I'm ready," she said.

Tony nodded to the camera man and said, "Let's hear it."

She sucked in a breath, puffed it out, and said the words with dramatisation.

"You can do this. The Martins don't know your background but you can adapt, blend in. I know you can pull this off. Trust me."

Her body trembled slightly and a sheen of perspiration settled on her skin despite the cooling air circulating from the air conditioner.

How had she done? Joel wore a smile but it was the same one that had been on his face since she'd arrived. Did that mean her audition pleased him? She couldn't tell. Tony's expression looked blank but his eyes glimmered.

"Thank you," Joel said. "You can wait at the reception area and we'll let you know soon."

She nodded, too nervous to speak as her anxiety became worse than when she'd arrived. She returned to the lobby but couldn't find space to sit, all the chairs being occupied.

"How did it go?" the receptionist asked.

"I don't know," she said honestly. "I was told to wait here."

"That's good. If you bummed, they would have sent you home straight away."

His words gave her hope as she waited. The other candidates were called in, too. Some stayed back. Others left.

After waiting two hours, they finally called her back into the audition room. A chair sat in front of the long desk, but the two men were not there.

"Please take a seat. They will be with you shortly."

She sat down and tried not to fiddle nervously as she waited, grateful that she'd used the ladies' while she'd been waiting to be called back.

A door to the far side of the room opened and Tony strode back in. He wore a smile this time and she relaxed at seeing him smiling.

"Well done for making it to the next stage of the auditions," he said as he sat down in the chair he'd previously occupied. "This stage involves getting to know you a little better. The crew and cast of each of my productions are like a team and we always make sure we pick people who will fit in with everyone else. So I'm going to ask you some questions."

"You mean like an interview?"

"Yes, an interview."

His lips tilted to one side in a panty-melting grin, making her toes curl up in her shoes.

"Okay. Is the director going to join us?" She sounded a little breathy, her body traitorously warm.

"No. This is a one-to-one interview. He has other candidates he is interviewing." He paused, his expression becoming inscrutable. "Would you rather have Joel interviewing you?"

She felt as if she'd upset him. "No. No. I was just asking. I'm sorry. I'm just a little nervous."

"Don't be. You did very well earlier so this should be a breeze for you."

His reassuring voice settled her anxiety and she nodded.

"So tell me about you," he continued.

"I'm a recent graduate of Mass Communications and finished my Youth Service a year ago. I'm the eldest of two girls. We are a close family. My younger sister is in her first year at Federal University of Technology in Owerri. My mother also lives there. I've had three small parts in movies." She recited the words she'd practiced for interviews.

"You grew up in Owerri?"

"Yes, I did."

"Interesting. I've never been there. What is the town like?" His eyes sparkled, showing genuine interest.

"It is a quiet, laid-back town compared to Lagos. Sometimes, I miss the tranquillity."

"I can understand that. Why did you come to Lagos?"

"I came to Lagos first to study. My best friend and I had always wanted to attend Unilag. Afterwards, it made sense to return here after our Youth Service. All the major movie productions are done out here except for a few in the east."

He nodded and scribbled something on his notepad.

"I know why you want to be part of my movie. Tell me why I should offer *you* a role."

She took a deep breath and plunged in a little excitedly. "I'm hardworking, punctual, and professional. I will always give you my best and I'm not afraid to do whatever it takes to get into the character. I will research the role and practice in my own time until I get it perfect. Whether you want a diva or a damsel, I'm your girl. I won't let you down."

Out of breath, she panted when she'd finished and studied his face.

His smile broadened and he nodded. "I believe you."

He scribbled on the notepad in front of him.

"Does that mean I have a part?" she asked, waiting with baited breath once the words shot out of her mouth.

"Yes, I think you will fit in with the rest of the gang. Joel and I need to decide exactly which of the roles will suit you best. We'll call you back in a few days for another reading, after which we'll offer you the chosen role."

"Oh, wow. That's fantastic. Thank you." She wanted to climb the table and give him a hug. But she quelled that desire. It amounted to inappropriate behaviour no matter what had happened between them previously.

"You are welcome." He stood up. "How are you getting back home?"

"I'm going to try and find a taxi," she said as she stood and picked up her bag.

"That's going to be difficult at this time of day. If you wait a few minutes, I'll drop you off."

"It's not a problem. I'm sure I can find a taxi. Don't bother yourself. I'm sure you have other things to do."

"It's not a bother. You are my last interviewee and I'd like to drop you."

She shouldn't look a gift horse in the mouth. "Okay. Thank you."

"Good. Just wait out in the reception area. I'll come and get you shortly," he said before walking out the door through which he'd come in.

CHAPTER EIGHT

"How did your interviews go?" Joel said as he strode into the office.

Tony looked up from the laptop he'd been about to shut down. Joel settled in one of the chairs the other side of the desk. Freddie sat in the other one, waiting for Tony.

"They went well. I have a few I'll be recommending for call-backs," he said as he leaned back into his leather armchair.

"Good. How did Miss Dike do?"

"She did quite well," he replied, remembering Rita's performance at the audition and the subsequent interview. "She is young, enthusiastic, willing to learn, and eager to please. I think she will fit in quite well with the rest of the cast and crew."

He'd been very impressed by her performance and attitude—that she'd arrived quite early, unlike so many other starlets who turned up late. Despite her shy demeanour outside in the car park, when she'd been in the audition suite, she'd performed the lines from memory as if actually acting it out rather than just reading it from the script. She really had great potential and he thanked his lucky stars that their paths had crossed even if it had started off on shaky grounds.

"That's good to know we're on the same page with her," Joel said with a broad smile. "I think she has great potential. Who else is on your call-back list?"

They worked through the rest of the shortlisted actors and actresses. His mind kept straying back to the one actress he couldn't wait to see again.

The little time they'd spent together in Abuja still played itself back in his nightly dreams, and every morning, he'd wake up wanting to re-enact that scene in real life. But he never broke his rules and Rita was out of bounds to him, not only because of her virgin state but also because they had to work together for the duration of this movie. And he refused to mix business with pleasure. His company was still in its infancy. He had so much at stake; most of all, the need to prove to himself and his family that he wasn't just a waste of space. That he could achieve something with his life.

After a lengthy discussion, they agreed the final list for call-backs.

"I'll get Dapo to call them tomorrow and let them know the day to come back," Joel said.

"Great. I'll leave that to you because I have to head off now."

"No problem." Joel glanced at his wrist watch. "I can meet you at Reams and we can discuss the rest of the production timetable."

"I'm not going to Reams, yet," he said nonchalantly. "I have to get to Ajah first. I said I would drop Miss Dike off."

"Miss Dike? I didn't know you too knew each other beforehand."

"Yes, I met her in Abuja last week and invited her to audition."

"Tony, you sly dog," Joel joked and gave him a knowing wink as he stood up. "Of course, I understand. Have fun and I'll catch you tomorrow."

"It's not like that." He suddenly felt the need to defend the girl. He was good friends with Joel and the man knew his sexual habits. But for some reason, he didn't want Rita tainted with the same brush as his other sex partners. "She's not like that."

He didn't want her to be like them, the reason why he'd sent her away that night instead of slaking his lust in her like he'd craved. Yet, seeing her again had awoken that lust once more. He looked at Freddie who just shrugged but didn't say a word.

Joel's grin only got wider. "You don't have to explain, man." He made a zipping motion across his mouth as he headed for the door. "Mum's the word. See you tomorrow."

Joel disappeared and shut the door behind him, and Tony turned his frustration onto Freddie. "You are no help at all."

"What do you want me to say?" The man just shrugged again. "That I think you are making a mistake by taking her home, if you don't want to end up in bed with her?"

"Look. I'm going to be working with her for however long it's going to take to produce this movie. So I need to start getting used to her presence."

"If you're not going to get involved with her, why take her home? You could've asked me to drop her off."

Tony had considered it for the briefest of moments. They'd both arrived on their motorbikes and Freddie taking Rita home would've meant she would be clinging onto Freddie's body all the way back to Ajah. A jealous rage had hardened his stomach at the image of Rita clinging on to Freddie and no way could he allow that to happen. Not as if Freddie would have taken advantage of her, or that Tony didn't trust him. After all, the man had saved his life before. Tony trusted him totally. But he couldn't allow Rita on the man's bike. No way.

"Dropping her off is not a big deal. I don't see why you are making a fuss about it." He scraped his chair back as he stood and unplugged his laptop.

Freddie lifted both palms in the air. "I'm not making a fuss, just reminding you of your own rules. You can do whatever you like."

"Yeah, I can." Tony shoved his laptop into his satchel and slung it over his shoulder before grabbing the spare helmet he usually left on the shelf in this office. He didn't head out through the side door as Freddie did. Instead, he went to the front reception area. He halted his steps as he rounded the corner and saw Rita. His heart stopped and then started thumping in his chest. She was laughing at whatever Dapo was showing her on his smart phone screen. The other man leaned towards her and he saw a certain familiarity in their poses.

His gut clamped, his muscles tightened, and he clenched his teeth. Dapo was flirting with Rita and she was lapping it up, laughing and joking with him like that. Why did he ever think she was innocent? She was a temptress. A cocktease. All that stuff about being a virgin must have been an act and he'd learned already she was a good actress.

He stomped across the foyer. "Are you ready to go?" he asked in an abrupt, tense voice.

"Yes." Rita's smile faded as she looked up, probably from the thunderous expression he wore.

Dapo stood and stuffed his phone into his pocket. "Remember to add me on Facebook."

"Of course, I will," she said and stood up. "Thank you for all your help and for keeping me company."

"You're welcome."

Tony's hand clenched around the helmet he held. Why he was getting wound up, he couldn't explain to himself. She wasn't involved with him and she had a boyfriend, anyway. She was someone else's headache, not his. So why the hell did he feel like tossing Dapo across the room? He stood rigidly as he held the door open and Rita walked outside. He followed her into the humid night air.

Being close to the sea meant the air hung briny and warm. He looked forward to the long ride on his bike as being on it tended to relax him like nothing else did.

"Is everything okay?" Rita asked tentatively as she looked up to him.

Lit by low street lamps, the light softened her features even more, making her almost ethereal.

His breath caught, warmth spread through his body, and blood rushed straight to his dick. The urge to pull her closer, touch and taste her again... It had been five days since he'd kissed her. He wanted to do it again now. *Take what you want.*

He shook his head, dismissing the thought. Instead, he fought the urge.

"Of course everything is fine." He practically growled the words and shoved the crash helmet at her. "Here, you're going to need this."

"Thank you," she said in a low tone, turning away from him before she put the helmet on.

He knew he was behaving like a bear with a sore head but he just couldn't seem to get a handle on his emotions around this girl.

He put his helmet on and straddled the bike. She got on behind him but didn't make body contact. He pressed the button and turned on the microphone built into his helmet.

"Come closer," he said.

She didn't respond.

He twisted his torso so he could see her and depressed the button on her helmet before speaking again.

"There's a microphone and speakers in your helmet. We use it to communicate while on the road."

"Okay," she said.

"I need you to sit closer to me and grab on tight. We'll be going fast and I don't want you falling off."

"Okay," she said again.

Her one-word replies were beginning to get on his nerves but he didn't say anything. He turned around and started the ignition. The bike kicked to life and vibrated beneath them. She made a soft gasp and grabbed onto his body tightly. He smiled even as his erection throbbed.

He kicked out the stand and rode the bike toward the gates. Freddie was already ahead. He'd given the man Rita's address when he'd mentioned he was going to drop her, so Freddie knew where they were headed. When they rode the bikes, Freddie always headed out first just to make sure there wasn't any danger. Then, most of the time, he would alternate between riding side-to-side or leading or trailing. They wore similar riding gear so it became almost impossible to distinguish between them from afar.

They took the side streets as a shortcut before heading for Ozumba Mbadiwe, the major road that would lead them toward the Lekki-Epe expressway and then towards Ajah. Even at this time of day, the place bustled and pedestrians and vehicles jostled for space. He knew the road very well since his motorcycle club did road trips down to the beaches towards Epe. They weren't some kind of gang, just a group of motorbike owners and enthusiasts that got together regularly for solidarity.

Focused on riding, his earlier unease melted away and he relaxed, actually enjoying the way Rita held on to him almost moulded onto his body. He loved her warmth and softness. He could get used to her touch. One thing she did for him, whenever she was close, he never thought about the past. She chased away his pain and replaced it with something different. The need to be with her.

It had to be because he hadn't had sex with her. Surely, if he did, all this would go away and he would be able to move on with his life.

"It's the next left."

Her voice came through soft and low on his headphones as they approached the next junction. They were already in Ajah and they'd left Victoria Island only thirty minutes previously. If they'd been in a car, it would've taken over an hour to get here at this time of day with the rush hour traffic.

He indicated so Freddie, now behind them, would know they would be turning left. He followed Rita's directions until they pulled up in front of a high-walled gated home just away from the light and stopped in the shadows. He didn't want to be recognised. Safer that way, especially in a neighbourhood he didn't know well. He killed the engine and hopped off before she could move. She pulled her helmet off and he hung it against the handlebar. Then he helped her off the bike. She wobbled on her feet and he pulled her to him to stop her from stumbling.

She felt so right in his arms as she stared up at him, her eyes glazed with desire.

"Thank you," she whispered in a husky voice.

Her pebbled nipples rubbed his chest. She was as turned on as he was.

He stifled a groan. "You got turned on by sitting on the bike." The words came out through a roughened voice.

She turned her face away, bit her bottom lip and shook her head.

He brushed his fingers through her hair, tidying it up as he slid his hand down to her nape and turned her head back so she stared at him once again.

"Don't ever pretend with me. Not about this. Otherwise, I will have to find out the truth myself."

Her eyes widened as she gasped.

"Yes, you know what I can do." He smiled at her, gentling his tone. "I will never lie to you about this. I want you. I've wanted you from the moment I set eyes on you. But I made both of us a promise that I wouldn't take you because I'm so wrong for you. Yet, that doesn't mean my craving for you has gone away."

He tugged her face up as he lowered his head and took her lips in a crushing kiss filled with his need for her. If he couldn't have her any other way, perhaps this was the only manner in which he could sate his craving. He drank from her mouth, at her lips, plundered and fucked her mouth. She moaned and before he knew what he was doing, he'd lifted her so she sat astride of him on the bike.

"Rita, I want you so much," he managed to say in a thick voice as they caught their breaths.

"I want you, too," she said in a breathy voice. "Take me."

"Don't say that." His words came out like a growl. "I'm an addict. If you offer it to me, I won't be able to resist you. Feel this." He took her hand and pressed the palm against his hard-as-rock bulge. Her heat seeped through the layer of denim fabric, scorching him. "Feel what you do to me, Baby."

"I...I don't want you to resist. Sitting on your bike turned me on, it's driving me crazy."

"I can help you with that, Baby. Do you want me to make you come?" he whispered against her ear as he slowly grazed his fingers against the crotch of her jeans.

She bucked against his hand. "Tony, we're outside."

"Don't worry about that. We are in the dark and I can make you come without taking your clothes off."

"Tony, I don't..."

"What is it, Baby? If you're not comfortable with doing it outdoors, we don't have to. We can go inside if you prefer. Talk to me."

"It's not that. I just wanted to know. How come you are so eager to make me come? In Abuja, you gave me a multiple orgasm but you didn't make me touch you or reciprocate. Now, again, you are offering me another orgasm when you've made it clear you won't take anything in return. I don't understand. I'm confused."

He tilted her head up. "There's nothing to be confused about. Giving you pleasure is fulfilling in its own right. Watching you come apart is a high I would love to experience again and again."

"Really?" She smiled. "Sometimes, I can't believe you are for real. Are men really this generous?"

"Baby, I know you haven't had sex, so it might come as a surprise to you."

"Anayo makes me touch his penis but he never touches me."

"What?" His nose flared as his knuckles cracked. "He makes you give him a hand job and he doesn't even finger you? What a sleazebag."

"To be honest, I didn't really question it until I met you. I always thought it was because he was saving me for our wedding night. But he's done some other things..." She trailed off and looked away.

Tony didn't like the sound of this. His whole body tensed with dread. "What else has he done?"

Her chest lifted as she took a deep breath as if gathering strength. "He hit me when he found out I went to your hotel room in Abuja."

He froze. "He did what? Hit you? Is he fucking crazy?" He lifted her off his body and paced up and down.

"Tony, please calm down."

"Rita, he had no right to hit you. Yes, you came up to my room. But it was my fault. I pushed you into it. If he wanted to hit someone, he should've come for me, not pick on a woman. If he was angry with you, he could have ended your relationship. But hitting you is out of order."

"It's okay."

"No. It's not okay."

Just then, a beam from headlights lit up the street as a red Toyota Celica pulled.

"Oh. My. God. It's Anayo," Rita said as she stepped away from Tony. "You have to go."

CHAPTER NINE

Tony's mouth slackened and he blinked at a rapid-fire rate. "You've got to be kidding me. This asshole hit you and you want me to leave you alone with him. Not going to happen."

Leaning back, he scrutinised Rita's face although she refused to meet his gaze. Despite the shadowed street, he made out her trembling lips. She was frightened. He could swear it. Shit. He reached for her shoulders.

She took another step backward and stepped into the beam of light from the car's headlamps.

"Tony, please don't make it worse for me."

Her voice sounded so small and tight.

His gut tightened and he wanted to haul her back into his arms. Wanted to shield her from anything that would hurt her.

Doesn't that include you, Tony? Aren't you going to hurt her? Who is going to protect her from you?

He shook off the niggling voice in his head. The car stopped beside the building, the other side of where Freddie had parked his motorbike. Tony's bodyguard was already at attention watching the car and the occupant and providing a barrier between whoever sat in there and Tony. This formed part of his job. But today, Tony wished he didn't have that barrier because he yearned to have a go at the new arrival himself. Give the man a dose of his own medicine.

Feet planted apart, all his muscles tensed as he waited. His hands balled into fists at his sides as his vein throbbed in his temple.

A dark-skinned man in a white shirt and dark trousers stepped out of the red car. Since he stood behind the beam of light, Tony couldn't see his facial features immediately.

"Rita. Is that you? What are you doing out here?" The newcomer stepped into the light and stared from Freddie to Rita to Tony, his expression and tone of voice harsh.

Older than the three of them, perhaps in his mid-thirties, the man stood large, not as tall as Tony or Freddie but wider and definitely bigger than Rita. She was really a tiny girl compared to the men surrounding her at the moment. Tony's fury rose at how anyone would want to take advantage of her vulnerability like her boyfriend had. Moreover, he was a man who should know better, not a boy.

"Yes, it's me. I'm just getting home. Welcome."

Her voice trembled a little and Tony noted she didn't make a move toward the man who had just arrived.

Good. He didn't think he could bear it if she'd walked into the man's embrace just moments after she'd been in his arms. As things stood, he didn't even want the man anywhere near her. *Shit.* This was so messed up already. And he wasn't even involved with her. Couldn't be involved with her. Still, here he found himself, dropping her off home and ready to fight monsters for her.

"Why are you outside with these men?"

The guy's harsh voice got louder and Tony took a step forward involuntarily. He so wanted to knock the living daylights out of the bastard.

"Ehm, this is Tony Essien. I told you I had an appointment with him today. It was late when we finished and he brought me home."

"Is that so?" The man eyed Tony and then Freddie.

"Yes, it is," Tony cut in. "I wanted to make sure she got home safely, something that her so-called boyfriend should be doing." He couldn't resist having a dig.

"Look Mr. Whatever-your-name-is, I don't need you to tell me how to treat my girlfriend." Anayo sneered at him. "We get on just fine without you. Rita, get inside the house. Now."

She gave him one last frightened look over her shoulder before rushing through the side pedestrian gate. Tony was glad she'd moved out of earshot and he strode up to her boyfriend and stood in front of him, blocking his entrance.

"You should treat women a lot better, mister," he said as he towered over the man, making himself appear much bigger. His fists itched to connect with the face of the fellow in front on him. In therapy, he'd been taught techniques to control his temper. Right now, he struggled to apply any of them. "You should be honoured that a beautiful girl like her gave you her time."

"What are you talking about? Get out of my way," Anayo replied in a condescending tone.

Bam. Tony's fist connected with flesh and bones on the man's chin. Anayo cried out and fell with a dull thump onto the bonnet of the car. Tony shook out his right hand. It hurt like hell but seeing the cowering asshole of a man made the pain worthwhile.

"I know you've been using her as your sex slave, taking advantage of her because she's young and innocent," Tony said in a low menacing tone as Freddie stood next to him, keeping watch in case someone turned up.

The man's eyes widened and he clutched his jaw. "She's my girlfriend and what we do in bed in my business. You have no right to interfere."

"That may be so, but I also know you hit her because of me," Tony continued, ignoring his complaint. "Here's the thing. Yes, she came up to my room in Abuja, so if you want to pick a fight, pick me. Name your place and your time and I'll be there. If you want to do it now, I'm also ready."

He had learned boxing skills from his older brother, Felix, and their chief of security, Kola, had taught him some mixed martial arts techniques. So although Anayo packed a lot more weight than he did, as long as he had room to manoeuvre and didn't get cornered into a tight spot, he could take the man anytime.

It seemed that Anayo had no inkling to fight another man and only picked on women. He cringed back, covering his face as he stuttered, "I...I..."

Tony leaned into his space, crowding him. "If you ever hit Rita again, I'll break your bones. I'll put you in a fucking wheelchair for the rest of your miserable life. You'll drink your food through a fucking tube. Do I make myself clear?"

The man's head bobbed up and down rapidly as he snivelled.

Tony stepped back, allowing the man to stagger forward. Freddie hooked his arm around Anayo as if to help him up but punched the man in the gut.

Anayo grunted and doubled over.

"You dey craze, abi wetin dey worry you? How you take go beat babe? Abi you no get sister or mama sef?"

Freddie held the man up by the scruff of his shirt with his left hand, the right balled into a fist. Anayo pleaded for mercy. Tony could sense his bodyguard's restrained fury. When he grew angry, the Warri boy in Freddie came to the fore. Nothing pissed the man off more than violence against women, his own family history being a case in point. He was ready to go all gangsta on Anayo's ass.

"Boss, make I arrange this man, now. Make I sort am."

"I might just let you do that—"

"Please, don't. I will do whatever you say," Anayo pleaded in a whiny voice.

"Oh, good." Tony nodded. "First, you go in there and apologise to Rita for the way you've been treating her. I mean you'll get on your knees and grovel. Then you'll tell her you are no good for her and that you are ending your relationship with her. I want you to come back here and get into your car. You'll leave and never come back here."

"Ehm—"

"This is not up for negotiation." Tony slashed his hand through the air. "You either do as I say or I'll have Freddie pound you into the dirt and dump your body and your car into the Lagoon, right now. I'm rich enough to get away with it. Don't fucking dare me."

"Okay. Okay. I'll do it. I'll do what you said."

"In case you think we are bluffing, my friend here has something to focus your mind."

Freddie lifted his jacket and revealed the hand gun strapped onto the back of his trousers.

Anayo swallowed and stumbled back away from him. "I think it is better if I just leave."

"No. You will go in there and do as I said. We'll be waiting right here for you. If you don't come out in five minutes, you can kiss goodbye to your fucking life."

Freddie pointed two fingers in the shape of a gun at the man's head.

"I understand." Anayo stumbled toward the gate and knocked. He was let in seconds later.

Tony paced outside the building for a few seconds, taking deep breaths until he'd worked some of his temper out. When he'd calmed down, he leaned against his bike and crossed his arms over his chest as he waited. He hoped Anayo didn't test his resolve. The way he felt, murder wasn't far from his mind.

****

Rita paced up and down her living room as panic flooded her system with adrenaline. Anayo was going to kill her. The expression on his face when he'd come up outside the house and seen her with Tony had been murderous. She'd been surprised to see him turn up at her house. Usually, he would call her before showing up. But the past week, he'd been acting strangely. Like the way he'd popped in on Sunday, and then tonight. Was he having her followed? There was just something creepy about having him show up at odd times.

She'd been glad when he'd commanded her to go inside and had been quick to make her escape indoors. But now, she was here she felt very shaky and vulnerable. Kechi wasn't home yet. She didn't have anyone as buffer to stop

Anayo from causing any real harm to her. She could still feel the slap he'd given her on Sunday.

She remembered Tony's outrage when she'd told him what Anayo had done. He'd looked furious when she'd asked him to go. Perhaps she had been really rash by sending him away. Now she wished Tony was here and she didn't have to face Anayo alone.

She twisted her hands together before rummaging in her bag for her phone. She dialled Kechi's number to find out where her friend could be. Hopefully, she was almost home.

Kechi's phone rang a few times before she picked it up.

"Are you almost home?"

"Almost, but I'm stuck in traffic down by Lekki Phase 1. Why?"

"Anayo is here and I'm worried about what he's going to do."

"Not again. What happened this time?"

"The audition ran late and Tony volunteered to bring me home. We were chatting outside the gates when Anayo turned up and saw us."

"Oh, no. Did you know Anayo was coming over tonight?"

"No, I didn't. I was shocked to see him and now I'm in so much trouble. He looked very angry."

"Oh, God—"

Loud knocking on the front door made Rita jump. She shivered as sweat dripped down her face and made her hand clammy. "He's at the door. What am I going to do?"

"Stay calm, Rita. Where is Tony?"

"I left him outside the gates. I told him to go. I wish I hadn't. I don't want to be alone with Anayo."

"I don't blame you. Call Tony. He'll come back if you ask him. I'll be there as soon as I can."

"Okay. I'll call him."

Before she could scroll through and find Tony's number, the knocking got louder.

"Rita, it's me," Anayo said through the door. "I need to apologise for my behaviour. Can you let me in?"

"I'm coming," she replied and walked to the door to open it just a crack. "I'm sorry, Anayo. I'm really tired right now and I'm not feeling well. Can we talk another time?"

She knew she was being a coward but she couldn't face him alone today.

He glanced behind him as if expecting someone to be there. "It's okay."

To her huge surprise, he lowered onto his knees.

Her mouth dropped open. "What are you doing?"

"I want to apologise for the way I have been treating you and for hitting you. I—I'm sorry."

She was so shocked to see him apologising for the first time, all she could say was, "Okay..." in a wary tone. Was it just a ruse so she could relax and he would hit her or do worse?

He stood up and glanced back again. "I also wanted to say that it's over between us." He leaned closer and sneered at her. She noticed a gash in his swollen bottom lip. "I don't want anything to do with a slut like you."

Rita flinched at the menace on his face as he bared his teeth at her before stomping away.

Her body shook as she shut the door and slid down to the floor. Her legs couldn't take her weight any longer. She was still on the floor when her phone rang.

"Hello?" Her voice wobbled as a lump clogged her throat.

"Rita, are you okay?"

"Tony?" She swallowed as relief flooded her body.

"Yes, I'm outside your gates. Tell the gateman to let me in."

"You came back?"

"Let me in and I'll explain."

"Okay. I'm coming." She suddenly couldn't wait to see him. Knowing Tony was at the gates, she didn't even bother to check if Anayo had actually left before opening her front door and heading toward the side gate.

She instructed the gateman to let the visitor in. As soon as the wrought iron pulled back, Tony strode in and she'd never been happier to see anyone. She ran into his arms and he hugged her tight as if knowing what she needed at that moment. They stood there for a few seconds while she allowed his strength and warmth to seep into her clammy skin.

He pulled back and lifted her chin. Tears blocked her from seeing his face clearly.

"Are you okay? Did he hit you again?"

"No. He didn't. I'm just so relieved he is gone and you are here. I was scared about being alone with him because my flatmate is not home yet. I thought he was going to do something bad. But he didn't. He broke up with me, instead." She was talking in such a rush as adrenaline flowed in her veins.

Tony visibly tensed. "Let's get you indoors and then we can talk."

She led the way but held onto his hand, not wanting to break contact. Inside her living room, he allowed her to plop down first before sitting next to her.

"You know, I was going to call you to come back when I realised my friend wasn't home. But Anayo started knocking on the door. So why did you come back?"

"I didn't come back." He rubbed the nape of his neck. "I never left. I just couldn't bear to leave you alone with him. I wanted to be sure you were okay. So I talked to him."

"You talked to him? You stayed? Thank you so much. I'm glad you did. But what did you say to him? He apologised and then told me it was over. I have to say I'm so relieved about it. He saved me the hassle of breaking up with him."

"You mean you are not upset about breaking up with him? I thought he was the man you wanted to marry."

"No. I'm not upset about that. I was going to break up with him, anyway. It was what he said to me that upset me. He—" She choked. "He called me a slut." Tears ran down her face.

"Oh, Buttons. I'm sorry he upset you. But if he comes near you again, I'm going to kill him." Tony folded her in his arms again, his scent and thoughtfulness comforting her.

Rita grimaced. "Thank you for trying to cheer me up, but those are strong words."

"They are, and I mean every one of them. I won't let him hurt you again. And if he tries, he'll end up being food for the birds."

She pulled back, shocked by the vehemence in his voice. Now that she thought about it, Anayo had bruises on his face. "Are you serious?"

"I am."

He brushed back hair from her face, her skin tingling from his touch.

"Why?"

This was the man she should hate. A man who'd benefited from her father's demise, her family's grief. He shouldn't care about what happened to her. And yet, here was comforting her, threatening to kill her ex. For her. She needed to understand him. "Why would you risk getting into trouble and going to prison for me?"

"Good question." He stood and walked over to her window and stared outside, then he turned around and shoved his hands into his jeans' front pockets. For the first time since she'd met him, he looked confused. "I really don't know the answer to that except that since I met you, I haven't been able to stop thinking about you. When I sleep, I dream about you. When I'm awake, thoughts of you plague my day. I've tried to push it all aside but seeing you again today has stirred those feelings again."

Was it possible he felt the same way she did? Warmth bloomed in her chest and she tried to suppress the smile making her lips curl.

"The thing is, I'm not good at relationships. I don't date the way other people do. I'm very screwed up and there are things about me that will send you running away if you found out. I really am no good for you."

Perhaps he wasn't. Mr. Petersen had said some bad things about his family. But hearing Tony disparage himself after coming to her rescue tonight didn't quite match up to that image.

"Let me be the judge of that. I'm obviously no good at relationships, either. But I have been thinking about you since Friday, too. And..." She trailed off when he came closer.

"You are so sweet and beautiful. I'm going to ruin you." He drew her up so their bodies merged. He leaned his head against hers and sighed. "And I honestly don't want to hurt you."

But you have already. Your family hurt mine.

She closed her eyes, knowing she should step away from him and end this thing brewing between them. It wouldn't end well. For him or her. She had a job to do. She had to think of her father, her sister, and her mother. She couldn't bring back her father but she could give her sister a future, and completing this assignment would help her achieve it.

But how could she spy on a man who said and did the kind of things Tony did for her? Any hate she'd felt for him had already melted away, being transformed into something that could destroy her.

"Will you come over to my place tonight?" he asked, his voice deep and gentle, so unlike the crass tone he'd used on her in Abuja. "I don't want you staying here especially with your flatmate not being home."

He was inviting her to his house. She would have the opportunity to do what she was being paid for—spy on him. Her stomach roiled and nausea rose in her throat. She untangled herself from him and stepped away.

"I don't think that's a good idea, Tony. Moreover, Kechi will be home soon. So I won't be alone for long."

Warm hands settled on her shoulders and gently turned her to face him. His amber eyes held concern and tenderness. Her heart and her body melted. How could she resist him when he looked at her like that?

"I know this seems drastic but I know I'm not going to be able to sleep tonight if I don't know what's happening with you. That you are safe. I couldn't bear it if anything happened to you."

His eyes darkened with torment and her heart went out to him. Something bad must have happened to him.

"Tony..."

He closed his eyes and sucked in a deep breath. "A girl I was involved with died. I blame myself for it because I couldn't help her."

She sucked in a breath. From the grief in his voice, he must have loved the girl. "I'm so sorry," she said.

"I couldn't bear it if something happened to you, Rita. Please, come and stay at my place, at least for tonight. I promise you I won't do anything you don't want me to do."

She opened her mouth to refuse him and closed it, swallowing instead. She'd never been in such a quandary. Not when she'd taken the assignment to spy on the Essiens. Not when she'd agreed to offer up her virginity to trap Tony. Now, she had the chance to visit his home. To find out more information about him. Yet, she couldn't seem to bring herself to do it. Not after what he'd just done for her. Not when he was being so nice to her.

Didn't he know he was inviting trouble into his life by inviting her into his home? She couldn't go there without accomplishing the task set to her. Yet, could she really turn him down and miss this opportunity? Could she give up on her goal when she was a step closer to achieving them? One little show of kindness from Tony didn't cancel out his family's atrocities, did it? No. Her father was still dead and her family still worse off for it.

"Okay," she said at last, although her response lacked any enthusiasm. "I'll stay at yours tonight. Let me grab a few things I'm going to need."

"Great. Thank you." His shoulders slumped as he sighed in relief.

CHAPTER TEN

As she packed a small overnight bag to take with her, Rita called Kechi and gave her a brief rundown of what had happened and that she would be spending the night at Tony's. Kechi got excited and wished her the best, telling her not to worry—it was probably best.

After the phone call, she returned to the living room with her bag to find Tony just finishing a phone call.

"Are you ready to go?" he asked as he took her bag.

"Yes." She bit her lower lip and led the way outside. After locking up the door, they both walked to the gates.

"Is Freddie still waiting outside?" She felt bad for the man having to stand there all the while they'd been indoors, but she guessed it must be part of his job as bodyguard.

"Yes. He preferred to wait. I rarely go anywhere without him these days," Tony replied offhandedly.

"Surely, it is weird having to go everywhere with a bodyguard. Don't you miss your privacy?" She couldn't imagine having someone follow her around everywhere.

"It's the price I have to pay for my actions," he said when they stood outside.

As expected, Freddie was there waiting for them. "Is she okay?"

"Yes," Tony said.

"I'm okay. Thank you," Rita added. She was grateful both men had inconvenienced themselves to help her out.

"Don't mention it," Freddie said.

Tony handed her the spare helmet but she didn't put it on immediately. "You said losing your privacy was the price you had to pay for your actions. What did you mean by that?"

He looked down at her, his body rigid. "I told you there are some things about me you are better off not knowing. This is one of them."

His tone had returned to being as harsh as it had been the night in Abuja. She caught a glimpse of that Tony again. The dark and dangerous one that made her mad at him and still want him to do whatever he wanted with her.

"But I want to know, Tony. I want to know everything there is to know about you." Not just because she was supposed to spy on him. But because she genuinely wanted to know who he was. He seemed like such a ball of contradictions, he confused her. She shrugged. "I've learnt a few new things about myself in the past week. One of them was that I don't like being used."

"Good for you," he said in a harsh tone and then he puffed out a breath and said in a gentler voice. "What else have you learned this week?"

She smiled shyly. "I also learned that I have a thing for bad boy bikers."

"You do?" He grinned at her.

"Yep. I've got it bad, too."

He chuckled.

"This is why I need to know who you really are before we both get tangled up."

"Buttons, in case you didn't know this already, we *are* tangled up, whether we like it or not." He brushed his knuckles against her cheek and her skin tingled. "My past is not up for discussion tonight. I never discuss it with other people."

That hit her like a punch in the stomach. She needed to remember that she was just a girl to him. She knew about his reputation. He never kept anyone close except his bodyguard, apparently.

She nodded. "Fine."

She slid her helmet on and watched as he put his own on before getting onto the bike. Her pulse rate spike as she climbed on, too, and wrapped her arms around his body. The scent of the leather combined with rippling hard muscles beneath and his body heat made her cling on tighter. She really did have a thing for this bad boy biker.

The ride back toward the Island and Ikoyi proved uneventful, the approach to his house even quieter as they rode along a sedate, tree-lined street and stopped in front of a gated mansion. When the gates opened, they didn't go down the windy driveway and instead, they rode down a separate lane leading down the side of the house, past a huge lawn and garden, to another smaller house on two levels.

He killed the engine and took his helmet off. Rita removed hers, too. But he didn't get up immediately. His shoulders rose and fell a few times before he straightened and got off the bike.

"Welcome to my home." He helped her off the bike.

"Thank you. The place is massive."

"I don't live in the main house. My parents are over there. I live here." He took her hand and led her into the duplex. Freddie had already unlocked the door and gone in.

She found it sparsely decorated in black and white tones, with an accent wall in black and the rest in white. Not exactly what she'd been expecting to see in his house but now that she'd seen it, she realised it represented Tony so well, his personality being so contrasting. One minute he was dark and dangerous; the next, sweet and tender.

"You have a lovely home" she said.

"Thank you. I'm glad you like it. Sit down."

She settled into one of the black leather sofas.

"I'm going to ask the housekeeper to cook something for you. Usually, I don't eat at home in the evenings so she doesn't cook dinner."

"You don't eat at home?" she asked, incredulous.

"I co-own a restaurant with my brothers and I'm the manager, so I'm usually there most evenings. I eat there."

"Oh. So you are supposed to be there right now and I spoiled your plans. I'm sorry."

"No need to be, Buttons. I would rather be here with you. Moreover, I'm the boss so I can do whatever I like. Relax. I'll be right back."

He disappeared down the hallway and Rita took his advice and relaxed into the seat. Her phone rang. She dug in her bag.

It wasn't her normal phone, though, but the one given to her by her boss. Her heart thudded in her chest and she glanced over her shoulder to make sure Tony wasn't coming back yet before answering it.

"Hello?" she said in a tentative voice.

"Miss Dike, you were supposed to call me after your auditions at Rebel Studios today," Mr. Petersen said without preamble.

"I'm sorry, sir. I haven't had the chance."

"No problem. I'll let you off this time. So tell me, did you manage to impress Tony Essien? Has he invited you back?"

"Yes, sir. He was happy with my audition and I've been invited to come back next week."

"Oh, good. On a personal note, is there any indication if he wants to carry on with you from where you left off last week? You know this is very important. You have to get him to really like you on a personal level. Otherwise, this won't work. And your poor father's death would have been in vain."

Rita's spine stiffened, her anger rising. No way would she let her father down. "I understand that, sir. And I'm currently in Tony's house. He invited me over for the night."

"Wonderful. Very wonderful. You are better than I thought. Now, you have a good opportunity to find out a lot of things. You will have to find time away from him to search his house."

"What? I can't do that."

"Yes, you can. You've already come this far. And Tony is not the kind of man who invites a girl to his house more than once, so this could be your only opportunity. I have an idea. I'm going to make sure he goes out of the house. While he is out, you need to search through his things and use the camera on the phone I gave you to take pictures of his house. Of everything you can see."

"Sir, I'm not sure I can do all that."

"Remember your father, Miss Dike. You will be letting him down if you don't do this."

She sucked in a deep breath. "How are you going to get Tony out of here?"

"Don't worry about that. Just remember as soon as he leaves, do as I say. I'll call you tomorrow and tell you where to meet me." He hung up.

Oh, God. What have I gotten myself into? How am I going to do this? She clutched her head to her hand, leaning her elbows on her knees as her stomach churned.

A warm hand touched her left shoulder and she jumped. Tony stood next to the sofa, his face screwed up in a frown. Had he heard her talking on the phone? Her heart thudded.

"Are you okay?" he asked.

"Yes. You scared me."

"I'm sorry." He came around and squatted before her, clasping her head in his palms. "I know tonight has been tough for you. But I'm going to do everything I can to make the rest of the evening go smoothly. Dinner is being prepared as we speak. So we can relax and do whatever you like."

Oh, no. He was being so nice to her. Why couldn't he go back to being an arrogant ass so that she wouldn't feel so guilty about what she was going to do to him? And how was Mr. Petersen going to get him to leave the house, anyway?

"Ehm, I don't mind doing whatever you want to do."

"How about I show you round the house and where you will be sleeping tonight?"

Her cheeks heated as she remembered Petersen's instructions. His showing her around would make it easy to find everything later when she needed.

"Okay." She stood and followed him.

The ground floor had been set up in an open-plan living room with the sitting area at one end and the dining area at the other. The space down here looked large enough to fit the two-bedroom BQ she shared with Kechi. There was a downstairs cloakroom and then he showed her the kitchen, introduced the woman cooking as Florence. Apparently, she wasn't the normal housekeeper. That one had gone home. Florence worked in the main house but had been called in to prepare dinner since Tony's housekeeper wasn't here. The kitchen seemed bigger and nicer than hers, too.

Then he took her upstairs. Freddie nodded at them from where he sat on a low sofa in a room with a pool table and large TV on the wall, a game console attached to it. On the TV screen, Freddie was shooting aliens in whatever game he was playing. Tony called it the games room.

He pointed to a door at the end of the hall. "That one is Freddie's room."

"You live with him?"

"I told you there's hardly anywhere I go without him."

She wondered what the story was between those two.

"This is the main bathroom, although technically it's Freddie's since I have a bathroom suite in my room," he said when he opened another door.

The black and white theme continued in here, with white units and tiled with a black mosaic border breaking up all the bright whiteness.

"And for the main event. Ta da." He opened the door at the far end of the hallway. "This is my room." He stood aside for her to step in.

Her jaw dropped. After all the whiteness of the walls in the hallway and bathroom, this, she wasn't expecting.

The walls sported a charcoal colour that shimmered as if it had millions of micro stars embedded in it. Very light grey and tall drawers stood along one wall, while floor-to-ceiling glass windows occupied the middle wall. But what got her attention was the massive bed at the other end of the room. The frames were metal, the design of the head and foot panels quite intricate and breathtaking. Black sheets covered the bed and pillows.

The bed appeared so imposing but also so sensual. She pictured herself spread out on it with Tony looming over her. Her core pulsed and her nipples tightened.

"Do you like it?" His warmth caressed her back as he stood behind her but didn't touch her.

"Yes," she said breathlessly. "I've never known black to be so sexy. It makes me want to..." she trailed off, embarrassed by her naughty thoughts.

"It makes you want to have sex?" His hands settled on her shoulders.

"Yes," she answered truthfully and stared as her feet in her gold ballet-style shoes. "I know I shouldn't think it. I mean, you've made it quite clear you don't want me like that and I'm not your type of woman. Maybe Anayo is right. I am a slut."

"What?" He swivelled her around so fast, her head spun. "How can you believe what that asshole said?"

The muscles on his neck bulged and his eyes hardened. She'd never seen him that furious before.

"Look, Tony. Just like I don't know much about you, you don't know much about me, either. Before I met you, there were some things I'd never done. For one, I'd never kissed anyone outdoors before. Yes, it was dark tonight. But we were making out on your bike and I was ready to let you make me come. That was pretty slutty."

"Stop saying that word," he shouted. "There's nothing wrong with wanting to explore your sexual side. You are only twenty-four, for goodness's sake. Live a little."

"Yeah, it's easy for you to say when your father is the richest man in Africa and you live in a mansion where people cater for all your needs and you don't have any worries—"

His phone rang out, interrupting her rant. He yanked the cell from his pocket. "What?" he barked in an annoyed tone as he stepped out of the room and pulled the door shut behind him.

Rita paced the room, her energy level now spiked from her argument with Tony. How had things deteriorated so quickly between them? One minute, she was imagining him between her legs, and the next, they were having a shouting match. Although the sexual energy between them had remained high.

The squeak of the door handle had her turning around. Tony opened it and stepped in.

"I have to go to the restaurant. They need me there," he said in a curt voice.

The way he stood with all his muscles tense, she knew he was still angry. Whether with her or himself, she wasn't sure.

"Oh, do you want me to come with you?" she asked.

"No. It's not necessary," he answered in a clipped tone. "Just stay here. Florence will let you know when dinner is ready."

"Okay." She nodded, a little disappointed that he didn't want her with him. Maybe she should apologise to him for the harsh words she'd said about his wealth. Not his fault what kind of family he was born into.

He turned and walked down the hall, his shoulders stiff. At the top of the stairs, he stopped for a moment and she hoped he would look back at her. Something to give her the sign that she meant more to him, and she would call him back and apologise.

He just stood there for a few seconds and then descended the stairs without looking back.

Tears clogged her eyes as she massaged her aching chest.

CHAPTER ELEVEN

All the way to Reams, Tony fumed, his anger boiling. The normally calming effect of riding his bike didn't manifest since he found himself in the car with Freddie. On the nights when he knew he would be late at the restaurant, he preferred to take the car. That way, Freddie could drive on the way back if Tony felt too exhausted.

Anyway, driving didn't have a calming effect on his strung-out mood. Perhaps because it was a short trip, taking about ten minutes. Or perhaps it was just this sudden obsession he had for Rita and his need to obliterate anything that made her consider herself less than she was.

Great that Anayo would no longer feature in her life. He'd waited outside her building for the man to come out. When he had, Tony had repeated his threat and warned him never to come close to Rita again

Now, he wanted to get hold of Anayo once more and wring the man's neck for the things he'd said to Rita. What kind of number had he played on a girl like her? Obvious she must be very impressionable for her to fall for the wiles of a dubious man such as him. The guy had eroded her self-esteem so much, she would think herself a slut just because Tony had kissed her outside her building.

What a fucking mess.

Now even though he knew he shouldn't get involved with her, he couldn't just wash his hands of her. He needed to find a way of making her believe in herself and have a healthy image of her sexuality. Otherwise, the next man that came along could mistreat her again.

But how was he supposed to help her if she kept fighting him? That dig about his father's wealth had hurt. Surprisingly. He'd never heard anyone disparage his family like that before. If people did, they'd never said anything to him directly.

He wasn't naive enough not to be aware that people envied his family. But they usually kept their prejudices to themselves.

But with Rita, her vitriolic words had been filled with negative energy. Almost as if she hated him for being rich.

Okay, he would admit he hadn't done anything amazing with his wealth. In fact, he had misused some of that fortune in the past.

But his family supported many charitable foundations generously and his mother had recently set up a charitable fund to help out cancer patients and their families.

All that didn't matter to Rita. He was just a stuck-up rich kid as far as she was concerned.

The phone call from the staff at his restaurant had come at a good time. He'd needed to step away from Rita to allow both of them time to cool down.

Yet, as he set foot into the busy restaurant, he couldn't shake the depressive feeling that settled on his shoulders. He gave perfunctory nods to people he recognised but didn't stop to chat with anyone until he reached his office.

The head waiter knocked on the frame of his open door.

"Yes, come in, Jim. What happened?" Tony asked as he leaned on his desk.

"One of the waiters accidentally spilled a drink on Mr. Petersen and the man demanded your presence."

Shit. What was the waiter thinking? Mr. Petersen was one of their regulars, easily spending a huge chunk on food and drinks here every week. He practically used this place as his personal diner.

"Where is Mr. Petersen?"

"I took him to the private lounge as we don't have a booking this evening, and we've tried to clean him up as much as possible. He is currently being offered drinks on the house."

"Good. Get me the waiter."

"Okay, sir." Jim stepped outside and, after a couple of minutes, came back with a young waiter who'd only started working here a few months ago.

"I'm so sorry, Mr. Essien," the boy said as he prostrated on the floor.

"Stand up and tell me what happened," Tony said.

The boy straightened but kept his gaze fixed to the ground. "Mr. Petersen ordered a cocktail, which I thought was strange since he usually drinks wine with his meal. Anyway, when I brought his drink back, I tripped over his legs. I swear, sir, it was as if he'd stretched out his leg on purpose, as if he wanted me to trip over them."

"Are you stupid? How can Mr. Petersen do that on purpose? Meaning he wanted you to spill the drink on him? You must be out of your mind. I have the good mind of sending you home right now."

"No, sir. I'm sorry, sir. Please don't sack me."

"Do you know that Mr. Petersen is one of our regulars? That if he stops coming here, I will have to fire you."

"Yes, I know, sir." The boy hung his head.

"Right. From now on, you better be on your best behaviour. If I hear any more complaints about you, I will let you go on the spot. Do I make myself clear?"

"Yes, sir. I will be the best waiter here."

"Good. Get out of my office."

"Yes, sir. Thank you, sir." The boy scrambled out the door.

"I'm going to see Mr. Petersen. Keep an eye on that boy and make sure there are no more accidents," Tony said to the head waiter.

"Yes, sir." The man stepped out.

Tony took a deep breath and headed out to see Mr. Petersen.

"Ah, Tony, there you are," the man said as soon as Tony stepped into the cordoned off private lounge. Mr. Petersen sat on a low sofa with a glass of wine in hand and a bottle of South African Cabernet Sauvignon on the table.

"Kris, I heard what happened. Are you okay?" he asked when he stopped at the table.

"Of course, I'm okay. The boy was just clumsy, that's all. No harm done." Petersen waved his hand in a dismissive gesture.

"I'm sorry about that. Of course, we'll pay for whatever the damage is to your clothes." There didn't seem to be any damage to the man's clothes, from what he could see, and he wondered where the spill had happened.

"Don't worry about it. It was just a splash of drink. Nothing the drycleaner can't take care of. Sit down. Have a drink with me."

Tony nodded and sat down in one of the chairs opposite the man. "Okay." He raised his hand to get the attention of the bartender. "Get me another glass."

"Yes, sir" the bartender said and came around with a wine glass.

Petersen poured the drink. When Tony lifted his glass, they both clicked rims and said cheers. Tony took a sip and put his glass down. With the mood he was in tonight, drinking alcohol sat on a list of bad ideas. He would need a lot more than one glass to drown out his mood.

"So, has Miss Dike been to her audition yet?"

Petersen's question shocked Tony. He leaned back and wanted to ask the man how he knew about the audition before he remembered that Kris had been with Rita in Abuja.

"Yes, she came in to the studio today. She is quite good and she definitely has a role in the movie," he said as he scratched his chin.

"That's good. I knew she was very talented. I'm sure she won't disappoint you."

"I'm hoping not." He took another sip. "How do you know Rita, anyway? How come you brought her to the event?"

"Oh, I was just doing a favour to another friend who wanted me to help introduce her to some movie producers and directors. You know how it is."

"Okay. So you didn't know her before Friday."

"Oh, I'd seen her a few times beforehand."

"You mean at one of your parties."

Petersen laughed out loud. "No. Not at my parties. She is a little too young for me. I thought she would be more suited to you."

Tony breathed a sigh of relief that Rita hadn't attended one of Kris's orgies. "I hardly have a squeaky clean image, Kris."

"I know that. But you are young and so is she. She could learn a thing or two from you."

"Perhaps." Tony didn't want to discuss his suitability for Rita so he changed the subject. "Did you see the game this week?"

Football proved a safer topic, something they discussed quite regularly. As they chatted, some other friends turned up, including Bukky whom he hadn't seen since they'd returned to Lagos from Abuja on Saturday.

Drinks and conversation flowed all around him. Tony's mind remained on the woman he'd left behind in his house.

Hours later, he strode into his place. The lights were off downstairs and he turned them on as he went looking for Rita. When he didn't find her on that level, he went upstairs, trying to be as quiet as he could as he assumed she was asleep.

He would just take a shower, grab a change of clothes, and bunk down on one of the sofas. He pushed his bedroom door open and his whole body stilled. Warm air greeted his skin, the AC in the room seemingly switched off. One of the side table lamps emitted grey diffused light illuminating Rita who lay on her side, one arm tucked under the pillow that held her head. Asleep, she looked so small and delicate on his massive bed. What got his attention was the t-shirt she wore—his t-shirt. It covered most of her body, except the stretch of her slender legs and the curves of chocolate skin over her thighs.

His stood there, making no move to go farther into the room, and his heart thudded in his chest, sending a rush of blood south and hardening his dick. He licked his lips, his fingers clenched by his sides, although he itched to mould and caress and explore all of her body.

The addict in him craved her and he wasn't sure that if he took a step inside the room, he'd be able to walk past her without going straight to where she laid. The sound of Freddie's door opening and closing spurred him to move. He stepped into his room, shut the door, and leaned against it, head back and eyes closed as he inhaled deeply. Her essence scented the air.

"You are back."

He opened his eyes to find Rita staring at him with a sleepy gaze.

"Yes," he said. "You are wearing my t-shirt." The only thing he could think of to say when all he wanted to do was climb into the bed and lie down beside her.

"Oh. Yes. I forgot to bring a nightie. I—I went through your things. I'm sorry," she said, turning away and swallowing repetitively.

"You don't have to feel bad," he reassured her as he took a step closer. "I like you in my t-shirt."

"Okay. Thank you."

He stopped at the foot of the bed, realising he'd moved towards her instead of to the bathroom as he'd originally planned. "You should go back to sleep. I'm going to take a shower and grab a few things. I didn't mean to disturb you."

"It's okay." She sat up against the pillows. "I'd only just drifted off to sleep before you came home."

"What were you doing?"

She turned her gaze away again. "I had dinner and watched some movies on the TV. Then I chatted with Kechi for a little while."

"How is she?"

"She's fine. She got home, eventually."

"Oh, good." He didn't want to leave her but if he didn't go now, he wouldn't be leaving. "Well, try and sleep. I'll see you later."

He strode into the bathroom, turned on the faucet in the shower enclosure, and stripped off his clothes. Warm water cascaded down from the shower head as he stepped beneath the spray. He let out a sigh as he stood there for a few seconds before reaching for the shower gel. What he wouldn't give to have Rita in here with him. He lathered his body and rinsed it off as a picture of her in the cubicle with him rose in his mind.

His erection swelled, throbbed, and he poured more shower gel onto his hand and palmed his heavy dick. Letting out a groan, he closed his eyes and worked his hand from the root to the tip of his cock. Slowly and loosely at first, imagining he was gently working his way into Rita's pussy. He squeezed his ball and his legs shook as he let out another groan, then he leaned a hand against the tiles to hold himself up as he lost himself to the pleasure of his actions. He imagined she was calling out his name as he filled her with his cock. Soon, he was squeezing tighter and working the slide up and down faster, rocking his hips with his motion. She would gasp out in ecstasy as he rammed into her. At that thought, his balls tightened and hot pleasure streaked through him as his cum erupted from his cock and dripped from the tiles onto the floor.

A small noise had him looking up. He noticed the bathroom door lay ajar. Had he forgotten to shut the door? Had Rita heard him? As per his habit, he rarely shut his bathroom door when he was in here because this was his room, after all. But he'd forgotten he had a guest staying in his bed, one he couldn't touch. He rinsed off his body and the evidence of his orgasm and shut off the water. Then he stepped out and grabbed a towel, drying his body quickly. He then wrapped it around his waist, something he usually didn't do as he always walked around his room naked until he dressed.

Rita was lying in bed. Her body under the thin sheet looked tense and he knew she wasn't asleep. She'd heard him and perhaps had watched from the open door. He could swear it from the rapid rise and fall of her chest.

"So, did you like watching?" he asked in a casual tone.

She didn't say anything although her body stiffened.

"Bad move." He strode across the room and yanked the sheet away from her body. She yelped and turned her head to look at him, eyes wide with shock. "I told you once never to pretend with me. Turn around."

Shoulders stiff, she rolled onto her back immediately, clutching her arms against her midriff. He smiled at her eager response. Nipples like bullet tips poked through the t-shirt. He would bet she was dripping wet for him.

"Take your knickers off and show me your pussy."

"Tony, I...I can't," she stuttered. The pulse at the base of her neck jumped and her throat rippled as she swallowed.

"Sure you can, baby. I want to see for myself if you got turned on watching me since you didn't answer my question."

"I'm sorry. I don't know what made me do it," she said, shamefaced.

"Baby, I'm not angry with you for watching me masturbate. I think it's hot that you did." He swept his gaze from her head to her toes and back to the hem of the t-shirt. "Just take your knickers off. Otherwise, I'm going to do it myself and who knows where that will lead."

She sucked a sharp breath and he grinned. Slowly, she reached and pulled her undies down, lifting her legs to get them off. She clutched the scrap of cotton in her hand and pulled the t-shirt down to cover her thighs.

"No, baby. Lift the t-shirt."

She did, tugging it gently and slowly exposing her hips. With her legs clasped together, all he could see was the V at the junction of her thighs.

"Spread your legs, let me see you."

Her thighs fell apart, revealing a brown and pink pussy with a neatly trimmed bush of dark hair glistening with her juices.

He groaned. "You look edible and beautiful. I want to taste you, eat you. Tell me you'll let me eat you."

He stared up at her face as he restrained himself from climbing onto that bed and taking her. With any other girl, he knew exactly where he stood. If they were on his bed spread out like confectionery, then it would be clear what they wanted from him.

With Rita, the lines were always so blurred. So he always needed her word even when her body gave him a clear message.

"Yes," she said in a low voice that sounded more like a whisper.

He didn't need to be told again. He dropped his towel and climbed onto the bed, settling between her spread thighs. The way he craved her infused no finesse into his actions as he lifted her legs onto his shoulders and buried his face into her pussy. He lapped, nipped, licked, and sucked like a man who had been starved. And he had been. Since last Friday night in Abuja, he hadn't been able to stand another woman's touch.

Tonight, one of his friends with benefits had even suggested a quickie in his office. His anger and frustration had pushed him to agree. But after she'd palmed his bulge through his trousers and he'd pulled her in, his hard-on had deflated. The woman hadn't smelled like Rita or felt like her.

He was ruined. *Ruined.* By this little scruff of a girl. And he couldn't have her.

Except like this. So he carried on his ministrations as her moans got louder and she writhed beneath him. Oh, he loved the sounds she made and the way her body responded to him in passion.

It turned his dick back into stone and he'd had an orgasm only minutes before. Soon, he was wringing out climax over climax out of her and he didn't let up.

"Please, Tony. I—I feel as if I'm going to die." Her words came out between pants of breath.

"Just one more, baby." He sucked hard on her clit and she keened, her body trembling as she arched off the bed in climactic pleasure.

He rose then and captured her lips with his, letting her taste herself as he thrust into her mouth with his tongue. He became possessed, his body feverish. He needed to be buried inside her. To feel the rush of orgasm again.

He broke off the kiss and pressed his lips close to her ear. "I need you. Let me come between your legs. I promise I won't enter you."

As if he suffered withdrawal symptoms, his entire body ached and shook from his need. He held his hot and hard erection in his palm as he leaned on one elbow to her side.

She reached down and covered his hand with hers. "Let me do it for you."

"No." His growl sounded harsh. "I'm not going to let you service me like you did your ex."

"But I want to."

"No." He moved away. He knew he was being silly comparing the two situations. After all, he'd let women blow him before. But it had always been mutually consenting situations. And this time, he felt as if letting Rita do it would be like taking advantage of her again. Even if she said she wanted to. No matter how desperate he was to feel her skin to skin, he wouldn't use her that way.

"Don't go, please."

Her soft plea tugged at his heartstrings and he turned back to face her.

"It's okay." He folded her into his arm, spooning her with her back to his chest, his still rock-hard dick lodged between the soft cheeks of her ass.

He slid his palm under the t-shirt and played with her breasts, flicking from one to the other. Soon, she started moaning and grinding her butt against his erection. He slid his cock between her thighs, her juices forming the lubrication to aid his movement back and forth, the heat from her pussy warming his blood. He was close but not inside her. This would have to do. Otherwise, he would die if he didn't feel her flesh against his feverish skin.

"Hold your legs tight together, baby." She did. "Yes, just like that. Let me feel you all around my cock, gripping me like a glove."

He started rocking his hips with hers as he pressed his other fingers against her pussy, working her clit and labia. Soon, they were both rocking together in rhythm. She moaned and he groaned as his pleasure climbed. She felt so good. He knew he was near so he rubbed her clit harder, determined to get another orgasm out of her before he came. With a cry, her body trembled around him and he lost all control, the movement of his hips going wild. With a massive grunt, he detonated as hot cum sprang from his dick and his entire body shook for seconds on end.

Out of breath and out of energy, he clung onto her body, glad that he was already lying on his side. He'd never had an orgasm quite like this before. And he hadn't even been inside her.

What would it be like when he fucked her for real? It would blow his mind, for sure.

CHAPTER TWELVE

Rita couldn't fully explain how she felt in that moment, wrapped in Tony's strong arms, their bodies slick with sweat and slowly cooling. Her body hummed with a euphoric buzz.

"That was..."

"Incredible."

"Yes. I'd never believed I could feel this way. I mean, you were fantastic in Abuja. But afterwards, I thought it had been a fluke. A one-off. But here we are and this time, it exceeded my expectations. Thank you."

"You don't have to thank me, baby." He pressed his lips to her shoulder in an open-mouthed kiss. "You deserve to be pleasured again and again. I love being the one to give it to you."

"I feel so selfish. You give me so much delight and I don't give you anything back."

"Baby, you just blew my mind like no one ever did. Everything about you gives me pleasure."

"Are you sure?" She frowned. She hadn't actually done anything except lie here and writhe and moan uncontrollably. He'd done all the work.

"Yes, I am. Now just lie back and let me clean you up." He swung his legs over the end of the bed and padded away to the bathroom.

There he goes again. Treating her like she was some princess and he her servant. Was he for real, or was she dreaming all this? She sighed, relaxing back into the pillows. He returned with a damp face towel and wiped her clean of his cum. He tossed it aside and joined her in bed, spooning her again.

"Sleep, Buttons," he whispered in her ear.

His words had the desired effect as her eyes drooped and she succumbed to exhaustion.

Rita woke hours later. The sun streaked in through the parting of dark curtains. She stretched out before the unfamiliarity of the room had her sitting up to assess her surroundings. Then she remembered all that had happened the previous day. She was in Tony's house. In his bed. They'd had sex last night. Well, not quite. He hadn't penetrated her. She was still a virgin. And it had been amazing. More than she'd ever fantasised about.

What would it feel like to have him inside her? As much as she wanted to find out, she was afraid to do the actual deed. After the loving and generous way he'd treated her last night, she didn't want it to end. And Tony Essien wasn't a man who kept a woman for long. Once he actually got inside her, the probability grew high that he would toss her aside. At least, this way, she would still hold on to something after this all ended. Even if she'd already lost her naïveté.

Logic told her she had to get up, get dressed, and get out of his house before he actually kicked her out. She didn't want to face that humiliation after everything that had happened to her. Getting over Anayo was one thing. But turning into the clingy girl for Tony would never work.

Her heart sinking, she rolled to the side and walked into the bathroom. After brushing her teeth, she managed to figure out how to use the fancy shower faucet that actually produced warm water. Her shower at home only had one setting—cold. Nigeria lay close enough to the equator to be hot most of the year. Having hot water out of a tap didn't matter so much especially for someone less affluent like her, who couldn't afford to pay for the luxury.

Since the water came from an outdoor tank, it usually felt warmish as it absorbed heat directly from the sun. However, on some cold Harmattan—the West African equivalent to winter—mornings when she needed warm water to wash, she used a bucket, mixing cold tap water with hot water from a kettle.

So she stood under the luxury of a warm shower and enjoyed the cascade of water on her skin. The image of water running down Tony's body last night as he stood in this cubicle and masturbated played in her head. She'd been taught in church that it was a taboo and a sin. She'd never masturbated. Never touched her body sexually. What would it feel like to do it? As she massaged shower gel over her body, she lingered over her mound. Tingles and warmth spread out from that point.

Cheeks burning, she withdrew her hand and rinsed off her body. She'd done many forbidden things in the past few weeks; she didn't need to add masturbation to the list. Moreover, Tony seemed to know her sexual points a lot better than she did. And with him there was a higher purpose for her sinful actions although she didn't want to think about them right now.

He hadn't been afraid or ashamed of his actions as he'd stood under the steam of the shower last night. Instead, his expression had been rapt with bliss as streaks of white cream had painted the tiles with his ecstasy.

Her knees loosened, trembled, the memory of Tony's exquisite virility assaulted her mind. Her core throbbed, her breath shortening. She wanted him, back between her thighs, touching and tasting her.

Shaking her head to clear the haze of lust, she stumbled out of the shower cubicle. What was wrong with her? Craving him this way hadn't been part of her plan. She needed to get a grip. She needed to get out of here. Away from Tony.

Snatching a towel from the shiny chrome rail, she dried her body and rummaged through her bag to find the spare clothes she'd brought. She took out the top and jeans, and when she finished dressing, she picked up her overnight bag and headed to the living room. She stopped when she found Tony at the dining table with a laptop open.

"Good morning, Buttons. Where are you going?" He stood up and strode across to her.

"'Morning, Tony. I thought I'd head home," she said in a casual tone, although it nearly killed her to push the words out.

He pulled her into his arms and it felt good to be there again. He smelled nice and felt even better. She wanted to stay in his arms forever.

Girl, you need to get a grip. Tony doesn't do forever.

"Not yet. Kudirat is making breakfast. Then we are going to spend the day together and get to know each other a little more."

"Don't worry yourself. I can have breakfast when I get home." Her stomach rumbled as if in protest to her words. But the idea that he did this with his other many female companions made her mouth taste bitter. She didn't want to be just another notch.

"It's not a worry. I've never had a girl stay for breakfast before. I'd love you to be the first."

A smile broadened her face and she looked up at him. He had such a boyish grin on his face, she wanted to lean in and kiss him. "When you put it like that, then I'd love to have breakfast. Thank you."

"You are welcome." He took her hand and led her to the table.

Surprisingly, he pulled out a chair next to where he'd been sitting and made sure she had settled down before he retook his.

"Do you have things you need to do today?" he asked as he caressed the back of her hand.

She enjoyed the tingles that ran down from her hand to the rest of her body. "Nothing urgent that can't wait."

"Good, because I'd love to do what we did last night a few more times today."

Her whole body seemed to catch fire and heat flooded her from her toes to the roots of her hair.

"Would you like a repeat, Buttons?" He swiped his thumb across her lips.

"Yes," she breathed out.

"Great. I can't seem to get enough of you."

He leaned across and kissed her. First, just a gentle brush of his lips, almost as if he didn't touch her. Wanting more, she leaned into him and he captured her nape and devoured her mouth. She melted against him, wishing he'd carry her back to bed and eat her for breakfast. She'd turned into a wanton woman overnight.

A cough made them break apart and embarrassment flooded Rita's cheeks. A woman stood by the table.

"Aunty Kudirat, this is my friend, Rita."

Tony didn't take his eyes off Rita as he lifted her hand and pressed a kiss to her knuckles. She tugged her hand but he didn't release her. She'd never known anyone willing to display affection as openly as Tony did.

"This is my housekeeper, Buttons," he said in a low voice close to Rita's ear.

"Good morning, *ma*." Rita got up from the chair and curtsied. The woman was much older, probably middle-aged, and she'd been taught to respect her elders.

"Good morning, Rita. It's nice to meet you." Kudirat laid out the dishes of food from the silver tray she carried. "Enjoy your breakfast," she said before walking out of the dining area.

"Wow. This is a lot of food." Rita stared at the spread of scrambled eggs, grilled sausages, fried plantains, and toasted bread.

"Well, have you heard the expression, 'eat breakfast like a king'?" he asked with a huge grin

"Yes," she couldn't help replying with a huge grin on her face, too. His smile was so infectious. It made her happy seeing him happy.

"Well, I live by it." He grinned. "Moreover, Freddie will be joining us for breakfast."

The table certainly held enough food to feed two strapping young men like kings. Curious and fascinated by his relationship with his bodyguard, she asked, "Do you always eat breakfast with him?"

"Most of the time." His broad shoulders lifted and fell in a casual shrug. "We live together. So it makes sense to eat together."

"I guess." She didn't know of any employers who ate with their employees. This was Nigeria, after all, where most rich people tended to trample on the poor. So the kind of relationship Tony had with Freddie went against the grain. "You guys must have a very close relationship, similar to the kind I have with Kechi."

He nodded and his face became inscrutable. "We are close. I trust him with things I don't trust other people with."

He reached across to the cafetière and poured black coffee into the porcelain cup in front of him. "Would you like coffee?"

"Yes, please. In which case, Freddie is probably your best friend," she announced as if she'd made a great discovery.

He paused for a while as if in thought. "True. I would consider Freddie to be my best friend. He is a lot more than a bodyguard to me."

"That's good to know."

Freddie chose that moment to join them. They exchanged greetings and settled to eat their meal. The food was very delicious and she made a mental note to thank the housekeeper. The three of them chatted idly about current affairs and local matters. She enjoyed the easy conversations with both of them. Freddie, who usually didn't talk much outside, seemed to have a lot to say with Tony. They both looked relaxed and made jokes as they talked, sometimes in pidgin English. She realised the two of them were very close indeed as they chatted more like brothers than anything else.

After breakfast, she excused herself and went upstairs to call her friend. Kechi was at work so they didn't chat long. They agreed to catch up later that evening. As she ended her call, she heard footsteps and turned around.

Tony had come upstairs and strode into the room. The door slammed after he kicked it, his expression so intense. His heat warmed her back as he proceeded to nuzzle her neck. Slowly, he stripped her of her clothes while kissing every area of skin he exposed and caressing her body from neck to thighs. By the time she was naked, she was trembling for release. All she needed was his thumb to her clit and she was shouting her climax. He carried her over to the bed, stretched them out side to side, and worked both their bodies to completion.

She drifted off to a light sleep only to be awoken by the sound of a phone ringing. She tried to ignore it but it kept ringing.

"You should pick it up. It might be important." Tony's voice rumbled deep as his palm rubbed up and down her bare arm.

"You are right." She scrambled off the bed and picked the phone from the floor where she'd dropped it. But it was not the one ringing so she dug into her bag for the second one. "Hello," she said, raising a hand to Tony as she walked into the bathroom and shut the door.

"Miss Dike, is this a good time to talk?" Mr. Petersen asked from the other end.

"Not really, sir. I'm still at Tony's house." Her voice sounded a little shaky. If Petersen kept calling her while she was in Tony's house, she would likely be found out. And she felt bad enough as it was.

"Okay. I'll make this quick. I'll text you the address where you will meet me at three pm today. Bring everything we discussed yesterday."

"Sir—" She couldn't reject his command as he'd already dropped the call.

Frustrated, she growled. She didn't want to go out to meet Petersen. But what else could she do? Bad enough that he'd made her go through Tony's things yesterday. She'd felt so guilty riffling thought his personal items. She hadn't found anything of importance. No documents or incriminating items. And she certainly didn't want to have to do it again.

She would have to tell Mr. Petersen to find another way to bring down the Essiens. From what she knew of Tony so far, he wasn't as bad as he first appeared. He was extremely kind and generous and he made her feel good about herself. Something she hadn't felt in a long time. And it didn't seem as if he was involved in his father's businesses, anyway.

A knock sounded on the door, and then Tony said, "Is everything okay in there?"

"Yes," she called out. "I'll be out in a minute."

She washed her hands and flushed the toilet, pretending as if she'd been using it. Then she opened the door and stepped out. "I'm going to have to go out this afternoon, after all."

"Oh. Is there something I can do?"

"No. You've done plenty for me. Just something I need to take care of myself."

He pulled her into his arms and tilted her head up so she became mesmerised by his amber eyes.

"You know that you can tell me anything, don't you?"

He looked so concerned and her guilt ramped up for deceiving him. She glanced towards the window. They'd only know each other for less than one week and she was already feeling so terrible. He'd helped her and continued to behave as if he cared about her. How could she carry on deceiving him?

"Of course. But you don't really have to fuss over me. I'll be all right." She tried to sound dismissive and hoped he would buy it. "My ex is not going to come back, and you have other things to do with your time—"

"No. I don't," he cut in, holding her attention once more. "Nothing is more important than you."

They both sucked in their breaths. Rita stared at him wide-eyed. He looked as surprised at his own words. "What are you saying, Tony?"

He held her chin up, his gaze not wavering. "I'm saying that I'm serious about you. This past week, I haven't been able to think of anything else but you. I can't get you out of my mind. I want us to be an item, exclusive. Monogamous."

Her whole body froze, her breath stalled and her mouth slackened. Had she heard correctly? "By exclusive, you mean you want to date just me? You won't be having sex with a different girl every other day like normal?"

"Yes, Buttons. I want only you." The expression on his face looked so intense and sincere, she had to believe him. "And you are not allowed to have any other lover for however long we are together."

Blood rushed in her ears and giddiness overtook her. She resisted the urge to squeal. Did he really care about her that much? Would he give up all his women?

"But Tony, you said it yourself. You need sex. And I'm not really giving it to you at the moment."

"I know that, and I'm happy to wait until you are ready." His voice remained steady and low-pitched, his determination apparent.

He would wait for her. Warmth spread through her body and she couldn't help the smile of amazement curling her lips. "What if I want to wait until my wedding night? You may never get it."

"I'm willing to wait as long as I get to be with you every day. I don't think I can bear not seeing you. I don't want this to be a one-off." His palms stroked her sides, and tingles ran through her. "Do you understand?"

She took a deep breath and puffed it out. "I do. Okay. We should date and see where we end up. But I have one condition."

"Name it."

Her cheeks warmed up and she squirmed uncomfortably. She might not be street wise, however she knew enough about human behaviour to know that people were fallible. Her father had been despite the obvious love he had for his family. "If you have sex with someone else, you will tell me."

He frowned. "Why do you think I'll have sex with someone else?"

"You told me you are an addict. I presume you meant a sex addict. Addicts need to have a fix regularly. If they don't get it, they go looking for it and will do anything to have it. Am I right?"

He sighed, flicked his gaze away and back at her. "Yes. You are right."

"Then the probability of you cheating on me is very high. Promise me you'll tell me if you do. I would rather know."

His chest rose and fell as he sighed. "I promise you I'll tell you *if* I'm unfaithful."

"Thank you." She rested her head on his chest, needing to gather her strength to go out and deal with her boss. "I have to get dressed and get to my house."

"Okay. While you are getting dressed, I'm going to arrange for a driver and a car for you to use."

She leaned back and looked up at him. "A car? A driver? Really, there's no need. I can find transportation. It's the middle of the day."

He rubbed his knuckles against her cheek and she leaned into his touch. "In case you haven't noticed, you just became the girlfriend to the son of the richest man in Africa. A chauffeured car is par for the course." He winked at her as he teased her.

"You are kidding me. Seriously, I'm not dating you for your car."

He brushed his lips against hers. "I know you are not. You're dating me for my hot body."

His lips curled into sexy grin, his cheek dipping with a dimple.

She couldn't help laughing. "Be serious."

"I am. The car is part of the perks of dating me and I'm giving it to you freely. No strings attached."

"Okay. Thank you." She stood on tiptoes to kiss his lips and he took over, kissing her passionately.

"You better get dressed quickly before I maul you," he said with a crooked grin when he broke off the kiss.

Body heated, she smiled as she picked up her discarded clothes and put them back on. Tony disappeared into the closet. When he came out, he had a slip of paper in his hand, which he handed to her.

She stared at the paper and her heart stopped. "What is this for?"

"Pay it into your account. It's a gift from me."

"Five hundred thousand Naira? That's way too much. I can't take it." She pushed the cheque back toward him but he didn't take it.

"Think of it as an advance payment from Rebel Studios."

"But I haven't signed a contract yet. I might not get the role."

"Trust me, you'll get it. No question about it."

"It's okay. Keep the cheque. You can pay me when the project actually starts."

His shoulders drooped and he sighed heavily before taking the cheque back. "Okay."

CHAPTER THIRTEEN

Rita rubbed her hands with agitation all the way to the location where she was supposed to meet Mr. Petersen. It had been difficult leaving Tony. The way he'd held onto her so tenderly this morning, the little kisses and caresses he'd given her, had made her want to stay cuddled up to him for the rest of the day. She'd wanted to forget the rest of the world. To forget her deal with her boss and the tragedy that had befallen her family. Being with Tony made her want to get lost in him.

Still, she couldn't.

Despite his declaration this morning, the truth remained. Her father had died. The Essien family was partly responsible. Their business decisions had led to her father's job loss, his slide into total despair, and his subsequent stoke and death.

Their actions bred consequences. They couldn't live untouched by the result of their deeds.

She'd been determined to be the one to drive the bulldozer that would crumble their ivory tower and send their world crashing just as hers had crashed.

However, she hadn't reckoned on Tony being the one to cripple her. Her Achilles heel. His words, his actions—his entire behaviour—since she'd met him had been contradictory to what she'd expected from him. He'd shown her a side to him that no other person seemed to know.

A man selfless and capable of caring about others without asking for anything in return. She'd witnessed the way he treated his staff. He'd referred to his housekeeper as "Aunty Kudirat," showing great warmth and respect for the woman. He displayed fondness for his bodyguard. The way Tony treated Freddie, they could've been brothers.

Then there was the way he'd behaved towards her. From his professional attitude when they were at Rebel Studios, to how he came to her defence with Anayo and helped in getting rid of her ex. When they were in bed together, he gave himself freely, making sure she had satisfaction over and over again before taking his. He wouldn't let her do anything that he considered degrading.

Now, he wanted them to date. To become boyfriend and girlfriend. He would drop everyone else. And who was she? A girl out of nowhere. He cared about her that much.

What am I going to do about him?

She sighed as she stepped out of the car. They had stopped in front of a gated house on a quiet street in Victoria Island. She knocked on the metal barrier. A uniformed man opened it.

"My name is Rita Dike and I'm here to see Mr. Petersen," she said when he greeted her.

"Ah, yes. *Oga* Kris is expecting you." The man pulled the gate in. "Go straight through and knock on the front door."

She stepped into the compound. "Thank you."

A walk down the short drive to the portico led her to the huge house, similar to other residences in the area. She pressed the bell on the white door. After a few seconds, another man opened it.

"I'm Rita," she said tentatively.

"Come in," he said and led the way down a hallway. "Have a seat in here. I'll tell Kris you are here."

"Thanks." She walked into the sitting room and sat on one of the red sofas.

Rita stared at the space around her. Expensive paintings accented in red frames hung on the white walls. African masks and sculptures either stood on white tables or on the cream carpeted floor. The room looked bright but tastefully done, matching Mr. Petersen's flamboyant personality.

"Welcome to my home, Miss Dike."

She looked up as Petersen walked in dressed in a casual red shirt and black trousers.

"You found the place alright, then?"

"Yes, I did. Thank you." Well, she hadn't had to do anything. Just told Tony's driver the address and he drove her straight here.

"Did you bring the things as we discussed?" He settled on the sofa opposite hers.

"Sir, I'm not sure exactly what you wanted me to bring." She squirmed uncomfortably in her seat. "I didn't find anything of importance in his house."

He cocked his head and lifted one eyebrow. "You searched the whole house and found nothing? No birth certificate? No contracts?"

She shifted in her seat again and tugged the collar of her t-shirt. "I searched the living room, the bathrooms, and Tony's bedroom. I didn't search the bodyguard's room or the kitchen."

"Hmmm." He blinked rapidly and ran his hand through his hair. "You must have missed something. Was there a safe?"

"A safe?" She hadn't thought about that. Surprised at not finding anything of value, she'd assumed he kept his paperwork in the office and any cash he had would be in his satchel, which he'd had with him that night.

"Yes, a safe. If you couldn't find drawers with documents, then they will be in a safe. The safe is usually behind a wall. Were there any paintings or pictures on the wall? Especially in his bedroom. It could be behind one."

"No. Surprisingly, he doesn't have any hanging paintings on the walls."

"Then it could be in the floor. You have to look for a break in the carpet or look under the rugs."

"Sir, what would be the point of looking for a safe? I won't be able to open it if I find it."

"Don't worry about that. Just find the safe first and let me know where it is."

"Why do we need the safe? I don't think I can keep spying on Tony. I felt so bad snooping around his house. I don't want to do it again." She'd agonised over it already. Spying on Tony made her feel ill.

Petersen's gaze hardened, as did his voice. "What do you think investigative journalism is about? It's about digging out the story. Sometimes, it involves doing the things we don't enjoy but we have to think of the end result. The big story and making bad people pay for their crimes. Have you forgotten your father already, Miss Dike? Did he die for nothing?"

She avoided his unforgiving gaze and swallowed. "No. Of course I haven't forgotten my father. It's just that I think Tony has nothing to do with his father's business. It's unfair of me to blame him for it. To keep doing this to him. If he finds out, he'll never forgive me."

"So you spend one night with Tony Essien, he turns your head and you fall for him. Tony is an Essien. Who do you think spends the money his father's companies make? Who do you think benefits from Chief Essien ripping off poor people? His children. And you want to let them off. Just because Tony Essien had sex with you?"

Her cheeks heated up with embarrassment. "This isn't just about sex. Tony actually cares about me. He wants to get serious with me. He asked to date me."

"Really? Tony Essien, who can't keep his hands off women, wants to date you. Don't tell me you were stupid enough to believe him."

Balling her hands, she refused to back down. Tony could've had sex with her and moved on. He didn't have to tell her he'd wait since she'd already offered her body in Abuja.

"Sir, I'm not stupid. He was genuine. He promised he wouldn't have sex with any other woman." She bristled that the man would call her stupid. She knew about Tony's reputation so she was getting involved with him with her eyes open.

"Oh, he did, didn't he, now? Did he also tell you that he had sex with another woman last night?"

Blood drained from her head and her eyes lost their focus, becoming blurry. "No, sir. That can't be true. Tony was with me last night."

"Before he was with you, he was at Reams, his bar and restaurant not far from here."

"Yes, I know he went there because he had a phone call from the staff at the restaurant."

"I was there. I arranged it. He came and hung out with me and some friends. He had sex with one of the girls in his office."

Rita gasped. Did Tony do that? Have sex with somebody else and then come home to her? But he'd promised her this morning he would tell her if he ever cheated.

"No. I don't believe you, sir. Tony wouldn't lie to me."

"I thought you'd say that so here's something I prepared earlier." He leaned over and picked up a remote control from the centre table. "You know smart phones are great devices. This was recorded last night in Tony's office."

The TV screen flicked on.

A woman was recording herself on what was obviously her mobile phone. She then place the gadget on a surface and moved back, leaning against the desk at the end of the office with her legs crossed over. Not long after that, Tony came into view.

"Lisa, what are you doing in my office?" he said in a bored voice.

"Waiting for you, big boy." She uncrossed her legs, making her short skirt ride up her thighs and giving Tony a show of what lay between them.

"No panties, hmmm. Looking to get fucked, are you?" Tony said in an amused tone as he stood between the girl's legs.

"Yes. I want you to fuck me. Right here. Right now." Lisa reached down and grabbed Tony's crotch.

Rita's head swam, her eyes misting with tears, but it was Tony's next words that sent her over the edge.

"Are you ready for me?"

Bile rose in her throat. "I'm going to be sick. Where is your bathroom?" she asked as she stood in a rush to get away from the TV and the image of Tony and the girl that had now imprinted in her mind.

"Down the hall. First door on the right," Petersen said.

She ran out of the room and found the bathroom just in time to retch into the toilet bowl and empty out most of what she'd eaten this morning. She knelt on the floor trying to catch her breath. When she had some energy back, she grabbed the counter's edge and pulled up to stand in front of the mirror above the sink.

The girl in the mirror looked ready to bawl her eyes out. What good would that do? Yes, her heart was breaking. She had fallen for Tony and had been ready to give up on this mission for him. She'd thought that perhaps if he truly loved her, she could learn to forgive his family for their crimes against hers.

But not now. Not until she achieved her aim. If Tony only wanted to use her, then she would use him, too. She couldn't feel guilty any longer.

After rinsing out her mouth, she tilted her chin up with determination and returned to the sitting room. Thankfully, Mr. Petersen had switched off the TV and she didn't have to look at those two on the screen anymore.

"Are you feeling okay?" her boss asked.

"Yes. I'm fine. What are the next steps?"

"Are you sure you want to carry on with this assignment?"

"Yes. I want to do this. I can't let Tony or the Essiens get the better of me."

"Good. The Essiens have a family get-together every Sunday. Since you and Tony are now an item, there's a possibility he'll take you to meet his family."

"I don't think that will happen. We've only known each other a few days."

"Tony doesn't play by the normal rules, as you can gather. But even if he doesn't invite you, you should persuade him to take you. I need you in his parents' house."

"But how am I going to persuade him?" At the moment, she didn't want any kind of contact with Tony.

"According to you, he was all but declaring his love to you this morning. I'm sure you are smart enough to find a way to wrap him around your finger."

Just great. Now she was supposed to play at being some kind of seductress as well as a spy.

"Yes, sir. I'll get it done."

"Good. It's time for you to meet someone," Petersen said, his hands steeped together. "Andy, you can come in now."

A door she hadn't noticed before opened behind her and the man who had let her into the house stepped in. He sat down on one of the chairs to her right.

"Miss Dike, this is Andy, and you are going to take him to the Essiens' house on Sunday and introduce him as your cousin."

"What? Why would I want to do that?"

"Andy has a job to do for me in the Essiens' house and you are his way in."

"What exactly is he going to so there?"

"You are better off not knowing. Just do your job and he will do his."

"Look, sir. If you are going to kill a member of the Essien family or something like that, I need to know. I like to know what I'm getting involved in, especially if it's murder." She shuddered at the thought.

"Do you think I've come all this way just to have them killed?" Petersen spat the words out with vehemence and she flinched. "I've had various opportunities over the years for that. But I haven't taken them up because this is bigger than just murder. This is about revenge. And I'm going to get it. Do you understand me?"

"Yes, sir. I understand. But I'm not going to go further with this deal until I know exactly what Andy is going to do on Sunday. Otherwise, this ends here and I walk out." She'd gotten tired of people taking advantage of her.

"You understand that if you walk out, you lose your job. Everything." Petersen scowled.

"And if I walk out, you lose your chance of getting back at the Essiens," she retorted. "Are you willing to take that risk?" She understood his need for revenge but she needed to know the full picture.

"Fine," Mr. Petersen said. "I'll tell you. Andy is going to plant listening devices in their house. Happy now?"

"Yes, sir." She nodded. She hadn't been expecting that but it made sense to her. She would like to be a fly on the wall in that house and this was a good alternative.

"Now, I'll let Andy give you his cover story and you can tell him some details about you so there are no slip ups in case you are asked questions about each other, which I expect will happen."

"Okay," she said, turning her attention to the man on her right. She listened as Andy gave her his cover story and other tidbits. He asked some questions which she answered. By the time she left Petersen's house, she had enough information to get through Sunday.

Outside the gate, Tony's car and driver were where she'd left them. As she got into the vehicle, she heard the driver talking on his phone. "She is here, *ma*." Then he turned to face her. "Madam wants to talk to you."

"Sorry. Who?"

"Tony's mother."

Her heart jumped and her skin flushed. What did the woman want from her? How did the woman know her? "Okay," she said and reached for the man's phone, which he passed over.

"Good evening," she said when she put the phone to her ear.

"Is this Tony's new girlfriend?"

"Yes, *ma*."

"I need to talk to you. Meet me at your house. I'm heading over there now."

How did the woman know where she lived? "Madam, I live out in Ajah."

"Yes, I know that. You didn't think I'd know everything about the girl my son is involved with?" The woman laughed haughtily. "Don't keep me waiting. Give the phone back to the driver."

"Yes, madam." Rita gulped down apprehension as she passed the phone back.

"Okay, *ma*," was all the man said on the phone before starting the ignition and diving out and back down the road.

Rita's stomach knotted tight with dread. Her life had just gotten more complicated.

CHAPTER FOURTEEN

Tony parked his bike in the space reserved for him in the Apex Towers' parking lot. He didn't work in the building, but he had an office and parking space reserved for him. His father hoped that one day, he would join the rest of his brothers and work in one of the Apex Holdings divisions.

But Tony had no inclination to do that. He was going to carve his own niche, make his own name. Even if it killed him.

"I'm going to catch up with Kola," Freddie said as they strode through the revolving doors. "I'll meet you on this level when you are done."

"No problem. I'll text you when I'm finished. I won't be long."

Tony took the lift to the penultimate floor. His father had an office on the top level. But he hadn't come to see his father. In fact, he hoped he didn't bump into the old man. He wasn't ready for an earful.

At the secretary's desk, he smiled at the young girl. "Is it okay to go in?"

"Yes, Mr. Essien. He is expecting you."

Tony pushed the door back. His brother sat behind the glass desk and looked up when he stepped in.

"Tony, it's good to see you." Mark came around the desk and hugged him. "How are you?"

"I'm good, bro. How are you doing?" he asked when they broke apart.

"I'm doing great, thank you. Have a seat."

Tony sat in the black leather seat in front of the desk. "What about Faith? I didn't see both of you last Sunday. Mum said Faith wasn't doing too good."

"She's fine. She's just having a tough time with the pregnancy. I wanted her to have a rest last Sunday. But she's better now and we should be there this weekend."

"Oh, that's good to know." He knew how much his brother loved his wife. Mark was very protective of Faith and always put her first, before anybody else. Even family events. "You'll be there to meet my date?"

Mark's face widened in a big smile. "You are bringing a girl over to meet the family? I didn't know you were seeing someone."

"I wasn't. I met her last weekend."

"Last weekend? And you want her to meet Mum already? Are you sure?"

Tony nodded. "With Faith, when did you know she was the one you wanted to spend the rest of your life with?"

Mark scratched his chin. "I think I knew the first day I saw her at a conference in South Africa. I looked at her from where I stood at the podium delivering a speech and my heart stopped and I knew I had to get to know her."

"It's the same thing with Rita. I saw her walk into the ballroom at the movie premiere after-party and I knew I had to have her. But that feeling has since morphed into something else I can't explain. All I know is that I have to keep her in my life."

"Wow. You are serious about a girl. I never thought I'd see the day." Mark laughed.

"Rita is a special girl," Tony said with emotion in his voice.

"I can see that. You've gone all dreamy-eyed."

Tony's face heated up and he coughed. "Anyway, she's the reason I came to see you."

"You need me to talk to Mum? To smooth the path?"

"No. I'll do that myself." He shifted in his chair. He didn't usually do this but his hands were tied. "I came to ask for an increase in my monthly allowance."

Mark frowned and leaned back into his chair. "Why? What do you need the extra budget for?"

"Things are tight at the moment. All my money and savings, I've put aside for the upcoming movie project I'm working on. This has left me with little room to play. And I need to pay to lease a car for Rita and pay for a chauffeur. I borrowed one of Mum's cars today. But I want to make arrangements for a regular car for her."

"How much exactly do you need and for how long?"

Tony told him.

"Okay. You know this exceeds the buffer amount set up for you. I'm going to have to tell Dad that your monthly budget is going to be increased."

Tony sighed. "Can we keep this between you and me, please? I really don't want Mum and Dad making a fuss and I promise you this is just for Rita. Nothing else."

"I know. But this protocol was set up for a reason. I'm loath to break it."

"I understand." Tony's heart weighed heavy. He didn't want to put his brother in a tight spot. But his parents getting involved would only spoil things for him and Rita.

"Look. Tell you what," Mark said after a few minutes of silence. "I'm going to pay for the car and driver myself. That way, it doesn't show up on your expenditure."

"You'll do this for me?"

"Of course. You are my brother. Just promise me you will keep your nose clean."

"It's been clean for the past five years and I'm not about to go back there."

"It's good to know. Send me the details of the specific car you want and I'll get it sorted for you."

"Thank you so much. I owe you big time," Tony said. He stayed a few more minutes to chat with his brother before heading downstairs to meet with Freddie.

***

On the drive back to Rita's house, she felt overwhelmed by everything going on. For one, she knew that getting involved with Petersen had been a bad idea. No matter what he'd said about investigative journalists, it seemed she wasn't cut out to sneak behind people's backs and digging out dirt on them.

Petersen had also proved he couldn't be trusted. She knew he was still hiding things from her, and he would not hesitate to destroy her if he felt she represented a threat to him.

And her life had grown even more complicated now. She'd lost her heart to Tony and fallen in love with him. She'd known as soon as she'd seen the video of him and Lisa. Perhaps it wasn't a big deal to him. He'd never tried to hide his nature. But she couldn't help the way her heart hurt.

She covered her face with her hands and groaned. How had she gotten so entangled? All she'd wanted to do was highlight the injustice done to her father. Now, she'd become mixed up in something even bigger than her, trying to find her feet in an environment that changed every second, so she decided to sway with the wind at the moment. Until she confronted her feelings for Tony and dealt with them, which she hadn't done, she didn't know if she was coming or going.

When Tony found out, he would hate her. But she had to tell him and walk away. She couldn't allow Petersen to hurt him or his family.

Rita arrived home to find a BMW X6 SUV parked in the landlord's driveway. Her landlord's wife came out to meet her.

"Rita, you're back. You have a guest waiting for you in my living room," the woman said.

"I do?" she asked, taken aback.

"Mrs. Essien is waiting for you. She's been here for about ten minutes."

"Oh my God. Why is she in your house?"

"She came looking for you but I couldn't allow her to sit outside in the car and invited her in. It's not every day that a woman of her calibre turns up in my house."

"Thank you for entertaining her. Is it okay to go in and see her?"

"Of course. She is in the living room."

Rita walked inside the house. She'd been in here a few times so she knew her way around. An elegantly dressed woman dripping in jewellery sat on one of the sofas.

"Good evening. I'm Rita." She stood nervously by one of the seats.

The woman glanced up from the newspaper she was reading and looked her over from head to toes. "So you are Rita. Have a seat." She waved at one of the chairs.

"Thank you." Rita sat at the edge of one of the sofas.

"So tell me, what are you doing with my son?"

Rita coughed. "I don't understand your question, madam."

"I mean, what do you want from Tony?"

"Ehm, we are just dating, in a relationship."

"But you spent the day in Mr. Petersen's house. Are you having an affair with him?"

"No! No way. Mr. Petersen is just someone I know through a mutual friend and he is helping me out. He introduced me to Tony at a party last week. How do you know I was at his house?"

"I know Mr. Petersen, so when the driver told me the address you went to, I knew straight away."

"I promise you, my relationship with Mr. Petersen is purely professional."

"I believe you. But tell me why were you searching Tony's house last night?"

"I—I. How..." Rita swallowed hard as her stomach knotted. She'd been seen. How did the woman know? She'd been very discreet and she'd thought there'd been no one in the house. Florence hadn't come out of the kitchen. At least, she hadn't seen her.

"You are wondering how I know. You thought you could walk into his house and snoop about without anyone knowing?"

"I'm sorry. I didn't mean—"

"Save your excuses for someone who cares. What I want to know is why you were searching my son's property. What were you looking for? Were you itching to steal some money? I know for sure you didn't find any. Tony is not allowed any cash in the house."

"What, no! I'm not a thief."

"Yes, that's what they all say. You are not the first girl to go looking through his things expecting to find dollars tucked away somewhere. I can tell you now, you are wasting your time, girl."

"I'm telling you, I'm not interested in his money."

"Liar. I saw you searching everywhere. His room. The bathrooms. The living room. I saw it all."

"What?" Was the woman in the house all that time? Following her around unseen. Something was not right. "How did you see me?"

"Everything you did was recorded on a video camera."

"Oh my God!" She covered her mouth with her hand as she wished the ground would open up and swallow her. "Does Tony know? Did he see me?"

She pictured the disappointment on his face at seeing images of her going through his things and her whole body heated up. She wanted to be sick for the second time today.

"No. Tony doesn't know yet. And we're not going to tell him."

Rita breathed a sigh of relief and then something hit her. If there were cameras in his house, shouldn't he know about the images streaming from them? Unless, of course, he didn't know there were cameras.

"Tony doesn't know about the cameras, does he?"

The woman's eyes widened but she didn't say anything.

"What kind of sick person are you? How can you have cameras in your son's house? In his bedroom, watching all he does? That is just sickening."

"You don't know anything about my family or Tony. As sickening as it might seem to you, the cameras are there to keep him safe. To keep him alive. I nearly lost him once. I won't go through the nightmare of feeling helpless again." The woman's face contorted in pain.

Rita was so stunned by the woman's words, she didn't say anything.

"Look. I understand you are young and want to get the most out of the situation, so I'm going to make you a deal. Stay away from Tony and I'll give you one million Naira."

"I said I don't want your money."

"Five million, then."

That was a lot of money. More than her annual income. "You are not listening to me."

"Twenty million and you can have the check right now." The woman pulled a cheque book out of her bag and started scribbling on it.

Gobsmacked, Rita's mouth fell open and a gasp escaped her. This woman meant business. The money was huge. More than Petersen was paying her for this deal, including the pay rise he'd promised her if she pulled it off. Twenty million would set her and her family up, pay her sister's bills, and help her mother's flailing business.

"Here, take it," Mrs. Essien said.

Rita took the cheque and stared at the number of zeros. She'd never dreamt she could see that amount of digits with her name at the top of a cheque. It felt good to hold it in her hands.

She sighed. She couldn't keep it, no matter how much she needed the money.

"Mrs. Essien, I understand that you want to protect your son. But he is a grown man capable of making his own choices. If Tony wants to break up with me, I will happily walk away. I suggest you talk to your son and tell him of your displeasure. Thank you for the offer, though."

She dropped the cheque on the table and walked out of the room without looking back.

CHAPTER FIFTEEN

Tony dialled Rita's number for the third time that evening as he paced his office at Rebel Studios. After his meeting with Mark, he'd come here to do some work and finalise production plans with Joel.

He'd tried her phone on the occasions he'd had a break but she hadn't picked up. He assumed she'd still been busy. But he'd just spoken the driver he'd assigned to her this morning and the man had confirmed he'd dropped Rita off at her house in Ajah and that she'd dismissed him for the day.

So by now, he'd grown really worried, imagining that her ex had come back. He would have to go out there if she didn't pick up the phone this time.

"Hi, Tony," Rita finally answered.

He exhaled in relief. "Oh, thank God. I was beginning to worry. Are you okay?"

"I'm fine. I'm at home," she said casually.

"Didn't you see my missed calls? I've been trying to reach you," he said, a little worked up at her blasé response.

"I saw them but I was in the middle of something," she replied.

He didn't like her tone at all. It sounded withdrawn, and a knot tightened in the pit of his stomach. "What's wrong, baby? Don't tell me you are fine because that would be a lie."

"Look, Tony. This thing between us needs to end. It's not a good idea for us to see each other."

"Says who?" he snapped.

"Says your mother."

"What's my mother got to do with this?"

He heard her resigned sigh.

"Your mother came to my house this evening to warn me off you. She offered me twenty million Naira to stay away from you."

His head swam and his knees buckled. He gripped the desk and leaned his weight into it.

"She did what?" he said in a low, hoarse voice.

And he prayed to the God in Heaven that the woman he'd fallen in love with hadn't swapped him for money. Okay, perhaps he didn't have twenty million Naira right now to give to her. But he would've given her a whole lot more in the long run.

He was afraid to ask the question. Dreaded the answer he would get. But he still asked. "Did you take her money?"

"Of course I didn't take her money, even though I was tempted. That kind of dough could do a lot for my family."

"Thank God." He swivelled and sat on the desk. "So why are you breaking up with me?"

"Things are so complicated with you. I'm in way over my head and I don't think I will survive this encounter with you. I'd rather walk away now and keep my head," she said in a low tone that broke his heart.

"You will survive, baby. I'll make sure of it. Just wait there for me. I'm coming over to your house."

"No, Tony. It's not a good idea."

"Rita, I'm not letting you go. And I think after everything that has happened between us, I deserve a chance to explain, don't you think?"

She sighed. "Yes, you deserve a chance."

"So I'll see you soon," he said as he hopped off the table to grab his satchel.

"Okay. See you soon."

"What happened?" Freddie asked him as soon as he slid the phone into his satchel.

"Mum paid Rita a visit and told her to back off. She offered her twenty million."

Freddie whistled. "Mama is not playing this time."

"Tell me about it. I hope I can convince Rita not to break up with me."

"You are really serious about this girl, huh? Even after what you saw on the video feed."

"Like a heart attack." He nodded. Kola had shown him the images of Rita searching his house. "She's hiding things from me. But I don't care. If she loves me, I think we can work it all out."

"It's not going to be easy, especially if Mama is already on the war path. But you know I have your back."

"Thanks, man. I'm going to need all the help I can get."

He was grateful to have Freddie's support. He'd tried living life on his own terms once and had nearly destroyed his existence in the process. Part of maturity implied understanding your weaknesses and accepting help when you needed it. He'd learned that the hard way.

On the ride out to Ajah, he must have broken so many international as well as local speed limits. But the need to see Rita and explain his mother's actions drove him. His mother had been out of order to confront Rita like that, but he understood the woman and her actions hadn't come as too much of a surprise. She had a habit of intervening on matters that concerned him.

Freddie kept pace with him. When they got off the expressway to ride down the local street leading to Rita's house, Tony had to slow down considerably to navigate the troughs and ridges on the road.

It seemed the gate man had been informed of their impending arrival since he opened the gates for them. They rode in and parked their bikes in front of Rita's house. She opened the door for them and he scooped her into his arms, giving her a tight hug. He felt so good to be holding her again considering he hadn't seen her since before lunch.

Rita introduced her housemate as Kechi and they exchanged pleasantries before he said to Rita, "Where can we talk privately?""

"We can talk in my room," she said with a frown. Her body had tensed and he wanted to soothe her worry.

"Lead the way." He didn't let go of her hand as she took him down the hallway. Freddie stayed behind in the sitting room with Kechi.

Once inside her room, she tugged at her hand. "Tony, can you let go, please? I can't think when you are holding onto me."

He grinned but released her hand, then sat on the bed. "This is a nice, bouncy bed. Wanna ride my cock on it?" He wiggled her eyebrows at her.

"Tony! Is that all you can think about?" Her face cracked into a smile.

"Well, it had the desired effect. It got you smiling again."

"Oh, you! I'm trying to be angry with you," she huffed out.

He attempted to be serious and put his hand on his chest. "I'm sorry for whatever it is that has upset you. If this is about my mother, I'll deal with her. Don't worry about it."

"But I'm worried. She offered to buy me off. That is a big deal. And it wasn't just that."

He reached for her and tugged her so she sat down beside him. He couldn't bear to have too much space between them. "What else happened?"

She sucked in breath as if shoring up her strength. "She told me she has cameras everywhere in your house. Everywhere including your bedroom."

Tony let go of her hands and scrubbed his face. Then he dropped his hands and looked up at her.

"You don't look very surprised, Tony," she said, scrutinising his face and looking more upset.

He sighed. "I'm not surprised because I know about the cameras."

"But...but your mum was behaving as if you didn't know about them," she blurted out.

He heaved an even bigger sigh. His life was weird and complicated and he really didn't want to scare Rita away. "She doesn't know that I know."

"You let her film you?" She shuddered and shifted back on the bed, putting space between them.

He kept his gaze averted, afraid of seeing disgust in her eyes.

"It's not like that. She doesn't actually see the images. They are recorded by the security team and only Kola Banks, the head of security, has access to them. They are deleted pretty much straight away unless there is something in the images that needs attention. My mum just gets told."

"You mum says she saw me..." She trailed off.

"What did you do? Tell me."

"I know you are not going to forgive me for this." She twisted her hands together as her gaze darted away and she bit her lip.

"There is nothing you could've done that would be worse than what I've done in the past." He placed his hand on hers, trying to reassure her and give her the chance to tell him the truth. He already knew. He just wanted her to say it.

"This is bad, Tony."

Her brown eyes misted and his heart clamped tight.

"Trust me. Just say it. I'll forgive you."

She exhaled and said the words out in a rush. "I searched your things."

"You mean when you were looking for a T-shirt to wear?" He pushed, testing her. Wanting to find out if she would take the easy way out he was offering.

"No, before that. I riffled through your drawers, searched your cupboards, even under the bed."

He closed his eyes and inhaled a deep breath, glad that she'd come clean.

"You see. It wasn't so bad saying it." He opened his eyes and met her gaze. She seemed surprised by his words. "I forgive you. Next time, if you need anything from me, just ask me. I know things must be tough for you, especially being out of work, but we're working on getting your contract sorted out at Rebel Studios in a few days so you can have some money coming in. So just ask me, okay."

"Thank you for forgiving me but you still don't understand. I was—"

"It doesn't matter to me." He tugged her close again and pressed his lips against her forehead. "Let's leave all our transgressions in the past and focus on a future together. As long as we promise to always be true to each other, the past doesn't matter."

"Tony, you make it sound so easy but there are things about me you need to know."

"Just as there are things about me that you should know. And I'm going to tell you everything. I promise. I just need to sort out a few things first. Please trust me."

He leaned back to find tears running down her face.

"Baby, what's the matter? Please talk to me." He brushed his lips against her cheeks, kissing her salty tears.

"Today has been a tough day, Tony."

"I know. But it will get better." *I promise,* he wanted to add but he wasn't sure when things would get better.

With a tight jaw, she looked up at his face and met his gaze. He saw steely determination in her eyes. "I need to know what you did last night."

Had she forgotten already? He'd be happy to remind her.

"I came home and found you in my bed and we rocked each other's worlds," he said in a husky voice as he remembered how she'd rocked his world. He wanted to do it all again tonight.

"I meant before that. What did you do at Reams?" Her voice thrummed low but the steel in her eyes said she wasn't just thinking of the two of them in bed.

His face puckered in a frown. "I told you this already this morning. I dealt with an issue with a staff, hung out with some friends, and then came home."

Looking annoyed, she tugged out of his embrace and stood up again. "That wasn't all you did. You had sex with a girl named Lisa!"

"Lisa? How did you know?" He couldn't hide his shock.

"The same way there are cameras in your house, there are cameras in your office at work."

His narrowed his gaze and stood from the bed. Something was wrong. She wasn't telling him the truth.

"That's a lie. I dismantled the camera in the office and Freddie does a regular sweep for any listening devices in there. Tell me the truth, Rita. How do you know about Lisa?" His voice had hardened as he knew this wasn't a doing of his security team. Something else must be at play here.

"Lisa recorded the two of you. I went to see Mr. Petersen this afternoon and he showed me the video."

The bitch! She'd recorded him. What was she playing at? His temper flared. Usually, he didn't care about being recorded even if it ended up going viral on the Internet. Rita had been shown the video and it had upset her. That, he didn't like, one bit.

"You actually saw Lisa and I having sex?" He raised his eyebrow, wondering how that was possible.

"Not exactly. I didn't watch the full thing. I felt too sick after the girl touched your crotch and I ran into the bathroom to be sick. When I came out, Mr. Petersen had turned the video off."

Tony stomped to one end of the small room away for Rita and swivelled. "I don't know what game Petersen is playing and I advise you to stop seeing him."

"Really? That is all you have to say when you've been caught having sex with another woman?" She placed both hands on her hips, glaring at him.

He strode back to where she stood and demolished her personal space. She backed up until her shoulders hit the wall and she had nowhere to run.

"Okay. Here's the thing. Technically, whatever happened between Lisa and I happened before you and I became an item." He gripped her chin and held her face up so she could see his face and know he was telling the truth. "And secondly, I didn't have sex with Lisa. She offered herself, palmed me, but I didn't go through with it because I was thinking about you all the time and I couldn't get it up with her. If you'd watched the rest of the video, you would've seen that."

"Are you serious?" She frowned but didn't look away. "Are you saying you didn't go through with it?"

"I swear on my life I did not have sex with Lisa last night. Do you believe me?" He kept his tone serious and hoped she believed him. If not, he didn't know what he would do except find Lisa and make her tell Rita the truth.

She nodded and gave him a small smile. "I do. I believe you."

He could have passed out with the relief that flooded his body. "Thank you."

He lowered his head and crushed her lips with his.

CHAPTER SIXTEEN

"You belong to me," Tony growled when he lifted his head briefly to emphasise his claim. On her body. On her heart.

The kiss he'd given her had been a mix of pent-up frustration for her making him wait this long to feel her skin against his and the passion of finally having her in his arms. After their phone call earlier, he'd gone through all kinds of scenarios in his mind where she said she wanted out. None of them had ended well.

So this was a huge relief.

She slid her hands up his arms and shoulders and linked them around the back of his neck.

He groaned. Exactly what he wanted. Her giving herself over to him totally. On second thoughts, perhaps not tonight. He wanted her to understand all of him before she gave all of herself.

She wanted wedding bells and he wanted to give her all she wanted. But a huge barrier stood in his way. His parents. And the contract he'd signed with them that forbade him from having any serious entanglements for ten years. Five years had run its course. He still had another five to go.

So no matter how much he wanted to marry Rita today and make her his wife, he couldn't do it without risking everything he'd worked so hard to build in the past five years.

"We belong together," he said in an out of breath voice as he looked down at her. "Don't you think so, baby?"

"Tony, I..."

"I was telling my brother, Mark, about you earlier today and something he said made me realise that you were mine right from that night in Abuja."

She stood against the door, her head tilted back, her neck exposed to him. The urge to suck on her delicate skin rose and he lowered his head and sucked on the spot where her neck met her shoulder.

"Ohhh." She moaned, canting her hips and pressing her soft belly against his already hardening dick.

"I love hearing you moan," he said as he repeated the sucking action on her neck and her soft voice filled the room. "It makes my cock turn to granite."

He palmed her ass, digging his fingers down the crack until he felt the heat from her pussy. With the other hand, he covered her breast and squeezed. He rubbed against her core, pressing in until he felt the hard button of her clit. She swayed, her crotch rubbing onto his hand.

"Tell me you belong to me, baby." He rubbed her clit harder and she rocked wildly. "Tell me and I'll give you whatever you want." He stopped his action, waiting for her to respond.

She opened her eyes and stared up at him as she licked her lips. "I'm in love with you, Tony. I've been ever since that night in Abuja."

His entire body stilled at her declaration. He'd been hoping for it. But hearing it now came as a very welcome surprise. He brushed her hair back from her face and bent his knees so they were both at eye-level. "Oh, baby. I love you, too."

"Tony, you don't have to say it back if you don't feel the same way. I just needed to get it off my chest, no matter what happens from now on." She closed her eyes tight and her voice choked. "God knows I shouldn't love you, but I do."

He brushed his lips against her forehead. "Baby, open your eyes."

She did and he was greeted by irises as warm and beautiful as hot chocolate.

"You really don't know how much you mean to me, do you? This is no longer just about fucking you for a day or a few weeks. I'm talking forever, baby."

"Forever? Tony, are you out of your mind? Last week, you were sleeping with a different girl every other day."

"Last week, I hadn't met you. You are the girl I've been waiting for—beautiful in body and spirit. Pure and passionate. I never knew what I wanted in a woman until you walked into that ballroom."

A lovely smile curled her lips. "You say the sweetest words. Sometimes, I can't believe you are the same man who swears and curses half the time."

He chuckled. "Oh, the bad boy hasn't gone away, Buttons. Think of me as having a dual personality. I can be a gentleman when you need me to be one, and a bad boy when I need to be one."

"I like the bad boy Tony. I remember the way you grabbed hold of me and the rough way you handled me in Abuja. It was part scary. But I was so turned on, I thought I was going to explode."

His grin widened. "You like it when I'm rough with you?"

She smiled shyly and turned away. "Yes. I mean, I like it when you're gentle, too, like last night. I guess I love both the gentle man in you and the bad boy."

Hearing her affirmative words proved uplifting to his troubled soul as he'd wondered if he would have to tone down some of his rough sex play. She was naive about most sexual acts and introducing them to her would be torture for him if he had to be gentle all the time. But he would always make sure she had pleasure. "I'm so glad you love everything I do to you. Let's head back to my place. I really want to get you naked soon."

She bit her lower lip and lowered her gaze. "Tony, I can't go to yours."

"Why? What's wrong?" He frowned.

"What about the cameras? People are going to see everything we do."

Her voice held huskiness. He couldn't tell if she was just worried or turned on. He'd known women who loved being watched. And last night, Rita had enjoyed watching him masturbate. She'd dripped her wetness all over his sheets even before he'd touched her. His erection throbbed in his trousers. He couldn't wait to get her wet all over again.

"Not people. Just one person. Kola. And as I said, he only looks at the images to check that nothing out of the ordinary is going on."

"Even so, how do you function knowing that somebody watches all your movements, everything you do? I'm not sure I can cope with that."

He shrugged. He'd lived with the cameras for five years. He didn't even notice them anymore. "I got used to it a long time ago. To be honest, I forget the cameras are there until I get alerted of something someone has done in my house." He gave her a pointed look.

Her breath hitched and her eyes widened. "You saw me searching your house?"

He nodded. "Yes. I saw the video today when I went to Apex Towers. Kola showed it to me."

"Oh, God." She blinked rapidly as if close to tears and covered her mouth with her hand. "Why didn't you say anything?"

He rubbed his palm up and down her arm, seeking to soothe her agitation. "I wanted you to tell me yourself. I needed you to tell me. I want you to know that you can tell me anything, no matter how bad it seems. Do you understand? Anything." He tilted her chin up, fixing her with an intense gaze.

"Okay." She nodded and her lips trembled. "I'm really sorry about going through your things. I won't do it again."

"I know, Buttons. It's forgiven." He leaned down and brushed his lips against hers tenderly. "So you don't mind the cameras?"

Her throat rippled as she swallowed. "I'm going to have to work my brain around it. But not tonight. Just give me a few days to work up the courage to go back to your house, please."

"Okay. If you don't want to go to mine, I'm going to have to stay here tonight."

"Here?" She looked around, bewildered and confused, as if seeing her room for the first time. "My house is not as nice as yours. Don't you want to sleep in your own bed?"

"It doesn't matter to me." He massaged her arms again. "I need to be with you. Don't think about sending me away because I won't go. If you don't want me on the bed, I will sleep on the floor. Moreover, I've lived in a hut with nothing to sleep on but a bed made from bamboo poles and covered with a raffia mat. So your room is luxurious in comparison."

"Hang on. You, the son of the richest man in Africa, has slept in a hut." She snickered. "I can't believe that."

He gave her a rueful smile and shadows of his dark past played in his mind. Sleeping comfortably had been the least of his worries in those weeks and months. There had been times when getting through the day had been sheer hell as he'd battled with his desperation and obsession. That he'd survived must've been sheer miracle. Some higher being had wanted him to live. For what purpose, he'd wondered for so long. Now, he thought he had an inkling. This woman standing before him and the chance to feel true love.

"Very few people will believe it, too. It was at the lowest time of my life. I lived for three months in a village up in the mountains on the Nigeria-Cameroon border. I had no personal belongings but some clothes in a small rucksack."

"Seriously? Hang on. Was that during your Youth Service deployment? Surely, your father could have wrangled a posting in Lagos or somewhere cushy."

Yes, she was right. Most rich parents could afford to pay to have their kids posted to less remote areas for the Nigerian Youth Service Corps programme that every graduate had to undertake before getting a job in Nigeria.

But this wasn't about that.

"It wasn't during my Youth Service. Can we not talk about this right now?"

"No, Tony. You have to tell me what all this was about. You expect me to accept the cameras in your house but you won't tell me why. You live with your bodyguard and he goes everywhere with you. You expect me to believe you lived in a remote village but you won't explain the reasons. I can't take it anymore. If you won't explain, you might as well go home."

She crossed her arms over her chest, lifting her breasts in the process. But it was the fury in her eyes that got him agitated.

He stepped away from her, needing the space to gather the courage to tell her something that would shatter the relationship they were trying to build. His body trembled and his heart pounded, heat flushing his body and sweat beading his forehead.

"I was forced to go and live in the village," he said with his back turned to Rita. "My parents set it up to save my life. They needed to isolate me from the destructive life I'd been living."

He turned around to face her, his whole body rigid as he swallowed the bile that had risen in his throat.

Rita stared at him, her face contorted with worry. "Why would they do such a thing?"

He sucked in a deep breath and said the words that would destroy her love for him.

"I was a drug head. A cocaine addict."

CHAPTER SEVENTEEN

Rita's mouth fell open and a gasp escaped her lips. Drugs? Tony? No. She shook her head.

"You took drugs?" Her accusing voice rose high, almost to a shriek.

He nodded, and the rest of his body shook visibly. He jammed his hands under his armpits and bunched his shoulders in a stooped posture. Fear and desperation seemed to make his eyes flame.

Disappointment curdled her stomach. Her knees buckled and she swayed. He rushed towards her, hand extended. She flinched back and grabbed the door handle, turning away from him. "Don't touch me."

"Baby."

The plea in his voice made her want to look up at his face. But her mind traipsed all over the place. She couldn't bear to look at him right now. "I need to get out of here."

She yanked the door open and stumbled down the hallway and past Kechi and Freddie in the sitting room. Her chest felt so tight, it hurt painfully. She doubled over, grabbing her midriff. She had to suck in deep breaths to quell her rising nausea.

What had she gotten herself into? Wasn't it bad enough that she had to deal with a near psychotic Petersen and an overprotective Mrs. Essien? Now Tony had revealed he was a drug addict.

I'm in love with a drug addict whose father's business decisions caused the death of my father. How screwed up could her life get?

She heard the door open and Kechi's voice reached her.

"What's going on? Are you okay?"

She stood up and faced her friend who looked worried. "Just give me a few minutes. I'll tell you about it later. Please."

"If you are sure." Kechi hesitated.

"Yes." Rita nodded.

She waited for Kechi to shut the door behind her after she went back inside before pacing back and forth in her small back yard lit up by the security light, her rubber slippers slapping against the concrete floor in an agitated march.

All the pacing didn't seem to help. The awful sensation curdling her belly remained. She felt devastated. Difficult to explain this feeling considering she'd only known Tony for a few days. Not as if she'd actually seen him doing drugs. But she couldn't shake the disappointment she felt.

She loved Tony, even when he was being domineering and controlling during sex. She'd been scared at first that he would treat her the way Anayo had. But when she'd realised he wasn't going to hurt her and had given her ultimate pleasure, the fear had dissipated.

Despite the rough way he'd handled her, there'd always been a rawness and honesty about his actions. He'd been showing her who he truly was right from the beginning and allowing her to make the choice if she wanted to be with him or not.

This had made her fall in love with him although it had only been a few days. She'd wondered how they would ever have a future together due to her involvement with Petersen's plans.

Now this? What am I going to do?

A shiver ran down her spine and she hugged her body. She'd never been so conflicted. A cool breeze whipped the leaves and branches of the mango tree beside her and she leaned against it. Lightning flashed in the distance and thunder cracked.

The suddenly stormy weather added to her anxiety and sadness. The weather matched the storm that seemed to have hit her relationship.

The scared and vulnerable part of her wanted to send Tony away and never have anything to do with him. After the recent tragedies in her family, could she really afford to get involved with someone who was so obviously damaged? What if he started using drugs again? How was she going to cope with the fallout? It would crush her and drag her into hell, especially if she invested more of her heart with him. Wasn't it better to cut her loses and walk away now?

Still, another part of her—the part that loved him and couldn't bear to be without him—wanted to stay and have a relationship with Tony. She wanted to learn more about him and find out how deep their feelings for each other really ran. If his declarations to her tonight were true, then there could be a way of getting past this. He had to promise her that he'd given up on the reckless life he'd lived before. At least, there was the reassurance that his parents and siblings monitored his goings and comings and would not hesitate to do what proved necessary to save him from himself.

She hated feeling so conflicted and at a loss but she had to go back inside and face him again. They would have to talk and she would take it from there as she couldn't make a decision with her mind all over the place.

Returning inside the house, she wondered where Kechi and Freddie were until she found them in the hallway outside the door to her room.

Her heart pounded at the worried look on Freddie's face.

"What's wrong?" she asked.

"It's Tony," Freddie said. "He locked the door and won't let me go in to talk to him. I'm worried about him. He is not allowed to lock himself away."

Chills ran down Rita's spine and her heart rate slowed. She knocked on the door. "Tony, it's me, Rita. Please let me in so we can talk."

There was no response so she knocked again. "Tony—"

The key clanged in the lock and the door pulled back.

"Man—"

"Freddie," Tony cut him off. His head was bowed and his gaze fixed at some point on the floor. "Let me talk to Rita and then I'll be out."

"Okay." Freddie stepped aside so Rita could walk into her room.

Tony shut the door and but didn't lock it. He turned his back to Rita and walked to the other end of the room.

"Are you okay?" she asked, worried about his demeanour. He appeared damaged and defeated.

"Have you decided what you want to do about us? Do you want me to leave?"

His voice came out so low, she had to strain to hear it. But she didn't miss the despondent emotions making it hoarse.

"No," she said, hating the depressing slump of his shoulders and the angle of his head but not knowing exactly how to help him. "I don't want you to leave."

His head bobbed up and down before he lifted his right hand and swiped it over his face. Was he crying? She couldn't hear any sobs or see his body racking.

"Tony, please look at me." She couldn't hide the desperation that had seeped into her bones.

He wiped his face again and turned around in two steps. When he lifted his head, she saw his bloodshot eyes before he looked down to the side. Her heart twisted, ached. Tears welled up in her eyes to see him so broken and vulnerable.

"I'm ashamed of myself, of the things I did in the past," he said in a low, raw voice. "I was a stupid boy who thought he could do whatever he wanted. I hung out with the wrong crowd and got sucked into doing a line of coke every now and again at parties. But after a while, I wanted the high to last more than a weekend so it became a daily habit."

Tipping his head back, he sucked in a long breath and closed his eyes before he swallowed and continued. "I was hurting and wanted to lash out at my parents for the unfair demands they made on me. Looking back now, it doesn't excuse my behaviour. The short of it is that I screwed up my life. And now, I'm going to lose the only thing that makes me feel good about myself in a long time."

A tear rolled down from her eyes. Where was the dark and dangerous bad boy she loved? He seemed buried under a lot of anguish. She couldn't allow him to lose hope and wallow in despair. She tilted her chin up haughtily and hardened her voice even though it killed her to do it. "Are you just going to give up? Aren't you even going to fight for me? To convince me that we belong together?" she demanded.

He opened his eyes and met her gaze but his amber eyes seemed devoid of hope. "I don't deserve you."

"I'll be the judge of that, don't you think?" she retorted.

"Rita—"

"No. *You* listen to me, Tony. Getting involved with you was asking for trouble. I knew that from the first moment I saw you, but I still did. There was something about you I couldn't resist. In all the time we've been together, you've shown me love, more than any other man in my life has shown me. So you did some bad things in the past. Yes, they were bad, I can't deny that. But you've changed and I'm glad I met you. I won't swap you for anyone else. Do you hear me? I. Love. You, Tony Essien."

At the end of her speech, her body shook like a leaf in the wind. But it was Tony's response that had tears clouding her vision.

He fell on his knees before her and wrapped his arms around her waist, clinging on like she had become his lifeline.

"I really don't deserve you," he said in a deep voice choked with emotions.

She held his head to her chest as tears fell down her face.

I'm the one who doesn't deserve you.

CHAPTER EIGHTEEN

He was getting a second chance with Rita.

Tony's body sagged against her, his hands grabbing onto the back of her cotton top. He opened his dry mouth but couldn't seem to find the right words to express his relief and gratitude that she hadn't kicked him out after his revelation. That she was giving their relationship a new beginning.

He'd shed silent tears when he'd thought he'd lost her for good. Then his knees had buckled after her vehement speech declaring her love for him. He had hoped for her love. But that she would remain steadfast after he revealed his past sins had exceeded his expectations of her. After all, why would she want to move from a boyfriend who'd been abusing her to one who'd been a drug addict?

Still, here she was, holding his head against her chest, giving him much needed comfort and strength as her warmth seeped into his previously cold body. They stayed that way for a few minutes until his composure returned.

Leaning back, he held onto her sides and looked up at her tear-streaked face. God, he adored this girl. He swallowed the lump in his throat. "Thank you for giving me another chance."

"I know you think I'm perfect, Tony. But I'm not. I might be a virgin but I'm not Mary. We all need our sins forgiven. Including me."

Was she saying she'd done bad things, too? Nothing she could've done would exceed his transgressions. He stood up and pulled her into his arms. "Whatever you've done, I forgive you."

She tugged back, looking up at him with a wary expression. "Don't you even want to hear what it is?"

"I'll listen when you are ready to tell me. But don't feel the need to confess to me right now. Just know that I will forgive you, whatever it is." He pressed his lips against her forehead. "I have to go and talk to Freddie. He is worried about me and I need to reassure him that I haven't had a hit of any substances."

"Of course you haven't taken anything. You've been in my room all this while."

His heart warmed at her vehement defence of him. But she needed to learn a few things about addictions. They never went away. Not totally. No magic pill to cure it. It was a daily struggle and reaffirmation to not go back down that slippery slope. All it would take was one sniff.

"Buttons, you need to understand that while cocaine was my drug of choice, it isn't the only thing that can give me a high."

"Oh?" She screwed up her face. "What else?"

He nodded in the direction of her small dressing table. "An example is the bottle of hairspray over there. When my parents blocked my access to cash and I couldn't get hold of any coke, I started sniffing whatever substance I could get hold off. Hairspray was one. No hairsprays are allowed in my house and my mother stopped buying them."

"Oh my God!" she gasped, staring wide-eyed from him to the table. He could see the fear in her brown eyes. "You haven't, have you? Tell me you didn't sniff the hairspray, Tony."

"No, I didn't." He closed his eyes momentarily, remembering the despair that had threatened to pull him under. "I was tempted. When you walked out and I thought it was the end for both of us, I didn't know if I could cope. For a moment, I wanted something to block out the pain. Then I thought about how disgusted you would be if you came in and found me spaced out. I knew I couldn't do that to you or myself."

"Oh, thank God," she exclaimed. "I'm going to throw the can away."

"No. You don't have to," he said. "Leave it. It's a reminder of the weak and horrible person I once was, and a warning for all the things I could lose if I go back there again."

"Are you sure?" She frowned.

"Yes, I am. I'm stronger than the person I was then, and having you in my life gives me even more determination never to go back down that road. I haven't taken any substances in five years. I don't intend to start now."

She grabbed hold of him and hugged him hard. He realised then her body was trembling uncontrollably. She'd been really afraid that he'd sniffed her hairspray. He held her tight.

"Promise me you will never take any drugs, substances, whatever, ever again," she demanded, gripping his t-shirt.

"I promise." Not an easy promise to make, though, and he had to be honest with her. "You have to know that with addiction, the risk of slipping back is always there, and it increases with certain triggers."

"What triggers?" She looked up at him, worry lines wrinkling her brows.

"When I started doing drugs, I was feeling inadequate. Being the last child in a family of over-achieving brothers, I found it difficult to find my place. Felix was a star athlete. By the time he turned eighteen, he'd won trophies upon trophies and he was our dad's favourite. Mark was a whiz kid. By the time he reached eighteen, he'd made his first million dollars."

He sucked in a breath and shook off the gloom hanging over him.

"They both knew their places and thrived knowing they would be working in the finance business. I, on the other hand, didn't want any of that. I didn't know what I wanted for me except that I didn't want anything to do with the family businesses. When my parents pushed, I just pushed back. My father didn't let up. By the time I was eighteen, I was using drugs almost every weekend."

"Oh, Tony." She squeezed him so tight.

"I was so angry and upset all the time. I hated feeling inadequate and less than my brothers. Taking the drugs was a way of escaping all that." He sighed.

"I didn't know things were tough for you growing up. I assumed you had a very cushy life."

"I had all the good things money could buy but I never really felt good about myself."

"I'm so sorry you felt that way," she breathed against his skin.

"It's okay, Buttons. It wasn't your fault. I wasn't telling you so you could feel sorry for me. I just wanted you to understand what my triggers were. I don't do so well when I feel inadequate, especially when it comes to do with my family."

"Okay, I think I understand." She leaned back to look up to his face. "So you feeling upset isn't going to make you want to do drugs, but if being upset is about being compared to your family, then that could trigger a craving for drugs?"

"Yes." His breath hitched, surprised that she'd understood him so quickly. He'd thought he would have to explain a little more and wait for it to sink into her mind.

"Good to know." She gave him a small smile. "For one scary moment, I thought every time we had an argument, you would go looking for some drugs."

"What? Give up fabulous make-up sex for one lousy hit? I don't think so. Having sex with you gives me a high that no drug has ever done. And I know it's only going to get better."

"Trust you to bring sex into it." She giggled.

The sound of her laughter came as close to any high he'd ever had. "Haven't you ever heard of make-up sex? Ask any of your friends with boyfriends. They'll tell you."

He chuckled as he rubbed his hands up and down her sides, grazing the soft under-flesh of her breasts through her top.

"You are so bad," she said in a husky voice.

"And you love me this way." He leaned down and gave her a quick kiss. Not wanting to get lost in her yet, he didn't linger. He still needed to speak to Freddie.

"I do," she said when they broke up.

"Let me talk to Freddie before I forget where I am and show you how great make-up sex can be." He winked at her and she lowered her eyes shyly. He chuckled again. He so loved her innocence.

After breaking apart, they walked out together, holding hands. Freddie stood from the sofa when they strolled into the sitting room. Kechi sat at the edge of her chair.

"Is everything okay?" Freddie asked as he shoved his hands into his front pockets of his jeans.

Tony detected the double meaning of his question. He squeezed Rita's hand. "Yes. I told her everything. We are fine now."

"Okay." Freddie nodded. "Are you ready to go home?"

"Not yet," he said. "I'm going to stay here tonight. Rita isn't comfortable with the cameras at home, and I'm going to ask for them to be taken down."

"No," she interjected. "I didn't understand why they were there in the first place. Now that I do, I want them to stay up."

"Are you sure?"He turned to face her and leaned down to whisper in her ear. "They'll be on when I'm fucking you."

Her breath hitched and he knew that if she'd had porcelain skin, it would be beetroot-coloured right now. He grinned at her.

She swallowed, her eyes aflame with lust. "Yes. I want them there."

His dick throbbed to life. He could have an exhibitionist as well as a voyeur on his hands.

"That's settled, then. But we're still staying here tonight." He was exhausted. He didn't want to get on a motorbike after he'd been through the emotional wringer.

"Great," Rita said and nodded to her friend. "You two stay right here while Kechi and I sort out dinner."

She gave him a brief peck on the cheek and disappeared through the kitchen door with her friend.

Tony slumped onto the sofa and stretched his legs out. His body felt as if he'd just run a marathon.

"Do your checks, Freddie." Tony extended his arm so that his bodyguard could verify his heart rate.

Freddie didn't move from his spot. "I don't need to. I know you are not high. You said everything was okay."

"I know what I said." He met Freddie's gaze. "But you have to do your job. I locked myself in a room with access to substances. You need to check me over for your report. I don't want you to get into trouble, and I don't want you to lie for me."

"It's not a lie." Freddie stood his ground.

Tony appreciated the man's loyalty. But he'd signed a contract that specified certain dos and don'ts. If the man didn't check him over now, then he'd put himself at risk of speculation and his mother would insist he see their doctor and do a blood test.

"Just do it. It will save everyone a headache later."

Tony sat still as Freddie took his pulse and timed it on his watch. He checked the dilation of his pupils and muscle control by squeezing his arms.

"How many fingers am I holding?"

"Three."

"Your vision is not impaired," Freddie said when he sat back on the sofa. "Your pulse rate, pupil dilation, and muscle control are all fine. Like I said, you are not high on any stimulants or inhalants."

"Thank you," Tony said as he tipped his head back on the sofa and closed his eyes.

This was his life. It had been a hard slug the past five years keeping to the agreement he'd made with his parents

and the necessary protocol. But with Rita in his life, he
knew he couldn't slip up now. A wrong step and he would
lose everything.

CHAPTER NINETEEN

The next morning, Tony uncoiled himself from around Rita's warm body and padded out of the bedroom barefooted to use the toilet. For the first time in a long time, he'd slept in his boxer-brief.

And sex hadn't been the number one thing on his mind when he'd gone to bed with a woman. He'd been happy to just hold her in his arms and listen to the light noises she made as she slept off.

It seemed she'd been as tired as he when they'd finally left Freddie on the sofa with the pillow and blanket Kechi had provided. Rita's housemate had gone off to bed only a few minutes before them.

Perhaps this was a sign of the depth of his feelings for Rita. This ability to luxuriate in her company without seeking sexual satisfaction. Something he hadn't done with any other woman. If they were in his bed, they had better be ready for a night of sex.

He returned from the bathroom and caught Rita as she stirred in sleep and turned over. She wore a cotton night shirt. Right now, it clung to her curves and his morning wood reawakened.

Just as he wanted to chuck his shorts and get back into bed, a phone started buzzing. He glanced in the direction of the sound. Two phones sat side by side on the dressing table. Both Rita's. He'd wondered why she kept two phones but had only given him the details for one. He'd been meaning to ask her but events had run away from him.

The phone kept ringing and he glanced over at where she still lay curled in up the sheets. She was sleeping peacefully, and not wanting to wake her after the long night they'd had, he picked up the phone and gathered his jeans up. Then he stepped outside her room, closing the door behind him. He hoped to dismiss the caller and tell them to call back later.

"Hello," he said, his voice gruff from his half-awake mind as he pictured getting back into bed with Rita's warm body. He yanked his jeans on with the phone tucked between his ear and shoulder.

"Hi, I'm trying to contact Rita," a young male voice spoke hesitantly. "Did I dial the wrong number?"

Tensing up, a twinge of jealousy made Tony's clench his teeth. It wasn't the voice of her ex, Anayo. Something about this male caller didn't quite seem right.

"No, you didn't. This is Rita's phone," he said a little abruptly as he strode into the living room. Freddie, who always woke early, sat stretched on the sofa, tapping on the screen on his phone. Tony nodded at him and held up a hand to tell him to stay put before pushing the door open and stepping outside.

It was early dawn, the sky light blue. The floor beneath his bare feet felt damp from last night's rain, and a fresh breeze whipped the air. He curled his toes into the concrete. Being barefooted reminded him of his time up in the mountains. It made him feel alive.

Birds chirped. A creaky door opened somewhere. Someone greeted another not too far away. Perhaps members of the landlord's family.

"I'd like to speak to her," the man said on the phone, drawing his attention once more.

Tony tuned out the sound of people waking up all around him. "She is unavailable right now. If you tell me what the call is about, I'll pass on the message."

The line went quiet for a few heartbeats and he thought the man would hang up.

"This is Andy, her cousin, and I'm coming over to her house tomorrow. I wanted to find out what time she wanted me there."

"Oh, you are her cousin, you said?" Tony frowned, still unsure about the guy. For one brief moment, he thought it was someone who was interested in Rita amorously. After all, Rita had implied that she'd done something bad. Was this guy the reason?

Then again, Tony didn't know any of her family members. She'd told him about her mother and sister in Owerri. She could very well have relatives in Lagos.

"Yes," Andy replied, his tone more confident. "We haven't seen each other in a long time. You know how it is, trying to survive in Lagos. I'm looking forward to catching up with her tomorrow."

"Okay. It'll be good to meet a member of her family," Tony said as he leaned against the mango tree. He genuinely wanted to meet members of Rita's family and to make their relationship official. "I'm her boyfriend, Tony."

"Is that so?" He heard slight amusement in the man's voice. "But the last time I spoke to her, she said she was dating some guy named Anayo."

If Andy knew about Anayo, then he would be genuine. "Yes, she was. We only met recently"

"Oh, good. I'd like to meet you, then. Will you be there tomorrow?"

"I will try and make myself available." He had the family get-together tomorrow and he wanted Rita to be there so he could introduce her to the rest of the clan and let his parents know he was serious about her. Maybe her cousin could come along, too.

"How are you related to Rita?" Tony asked as he kicked a stone.

"We are cousins on her mother's side and I always visit their house when I'm in Owerri," Andy said in a cheerful tone. "I visited Lily at FUTO the last time I was there."

Sounded like the man knew Rita's family well, too. Rita had told him her sister's name was Lily and that she studied at FUTO. And he already knew she'd grown up in Owerri from her resume during the interview for the Rebel Studios upcoming movie.

"That's great," he said, feeling a lot more relaxed about the man than when he'd first spoken. "I'll let her know you called and hopefully, we'll see you on Sunday."

"Nice talking to you, Tony."

"Same here."

He ended the call and was about to head back into the house when the door opened and Freddie stepped out.

"How are you feeling this morning?" Freddie asked as he lowered his body onto the concrete veranda.

Tony met his gaze briefly and nodded before leaning against the opposite wall. Chatting with Freddie had become one his coping mechanisms. One of the problems he had that had led him into the addictive lifestyle was his inability to express himself or talk to other members of his family. Felix and Mark had always been close. And when Tony came along, he'd felt like the third wheel encroaching on an already developed brotherhood. The age gap between him and his brothers hadn't helped. They'd always treated him like a kid brother.

So he'd never felt he could talk to them, especially when he was having so many arguments with his parents. He'd tried talking to his friends but they'd only led him astray. So after he'd detoxed and been undergoing addiction therapy, his therapist had suggested he found someone close to his age who genuinely cared about him and who could become his confidant. Someone who would listen to him without accusations or ulterior motive.

He'd already had a good relationship with Freddie by then. The man had found him when he'd nearly overdosed. Had been with him throughout his hellish detox. Had seen him at his lowest point and held him together. It made sense that he would be the one Tony chose as his confidant. He didn't think he would've made it this far without Freddie.

Tony heaved a sigh. So much had happened in the past two days. From meeting Rita again outside Rebel Studios when she'd arrived for her audition to bringing her home and getting rid of her bully of a boyfriend. To telling Mark about her yesterday, only to find out later that his mother had been to see her and warn her off. Then, of course, the night had culminated in his confession of his addiction. Things could've gone so wrong.

"I feel quite good. Great, in fact, considering everything." He puffed out air. "There was a moment last night when things were looking very dicey. But I'm so glad for Rita."

Warmth spread through him when he remembered the way she'd held on so tightly to him after declaring her love for him. He couldn't have wished for anyone better.

"She is really something." Freddie nodded. "Any other girl would've thrown you out."

"Don't I know it? You know, I'm going to spend the rest of my life showing her what she means to me." Tony pushed off the wall as he suddenly made a realisation. "I'm going to ask her to marry me this weekend."

"Marry ke?" Freddie grabbed a pole and straightened but tilted his head to the side to study Tony. "Are you serious? Do you feel that strongly about her?"

"Man, you don't know the half of it. Rita is it for me. I swear to you, I have never felt this way for anyone before."

"Not even for Tamara?" Freddie asked, eyebrows raised in a disbelieving fashion.

Tony sobered when he remembered his ex-girlfriend. "Not even her."

"Really?" Freddie still didn't sound convinced.

But Tony understood he was only trying to be the voice of reason especially when Tony was being impulsive.

"You were married to Tamara. As I recall, you eloped to Vegas to get married because they two of you were in love."

Shame and regret washed over him and he lowered his head and kicked the leaves on the floor around with his feet. He'd done some really stupid things and marrying obsessive Tamara had been one of them. She'd dragged him down into hell. Together, their relationship had been destructive for both of them. Addiction had taken her life and nearly his, eventually.

"I was high half the time in those days. My decisions were not rational."

Commandeering a private jet and instructing the pilot and crew to fly him and his bride over to Las Vegas so they could get married without telling their parents had never been a rational decision. His father had since ordered their private jets to be sold off. All because of what he'd done. Now, he couldn't use a private jet without leasing one and he certainly couldn't afford one. Not on his restricted allowance.

He scrubbed his face and pushed off the wall. "With Rita, it's different. I'm sober and rational. I love her, and she loves me. There's no doubt about that and I want to marry her and show everyone that the best girl in the world belongs to me. The only way to do that is to put a ring on her finger."

"But you know you can't actually marry her. At least, not for another five years. Not with the contract and everything. You can't put your recovery at risk now." Freddie waved his hand in the air. The voice of reason again.

Tony sighed his frustration. His parents had made him swear he wouldn't get deeply involved with another woman, afraid he would end up in the same destructive cycle he'd had with Tamara.

"I know. I guess it will have to be a very long engagement." He lifted his shoulders in a blasé shrug but couldn't shake the tight knot in his stomach.

"Tony, your parents will flip if they find out. I think you should wait, give them time to get used to you being with Rita. Maybe in a year or so, you can get engaged."

"Look." He lowered his voice. "I'm not going to announce it to the world yet. This is just between you and me and Rita, of course. I will explain to her why we can't announce it yet."

"Hmmm. What about the ring? That's going to grab attention," Freddie said as he scratched his chin.

"Yes." His euphoria deflated. He obviously hadn't thought this through yet as the idea had only just occurred to him. Then another idea came to him. "I'm going to take her to Beya."

"What?"

"I'm going to show her where I did my detox and how tough things were back then. I want her to know that I've been to hell and back. I think showing her will help both of us. It'll make her really understand. Don't you think so?"

"I think you have a good point." Freddie nodded. "Seeing how life was for you will make her more aware of the risks. So that she doesn't do anything to put you at risk."

Something in Freddie's voice made Tony look up. "Do you think she'll do that? Put me at risk?"

Freddie's opinion mattered to Tony. The man had always been a good judge of character.

"At the moment, I'm trying to keep an open mind." Freddie wore a pensive expression. "She was caught searching the house and she hasn't really said why. We assume it's because of money. But then, she spent yesterday with Petersen. That man is bad news and you know it."

Tony nodded. "I know Petersen has had some run-ins with Mark and Felix, but that had to do with the Apex businesses, of which he is a shareholder. I don't have anything to do with Apex so I don't have any reason to be worried about him."

Freddie shifted from one leg to the other. "But he is the one who introduced you to Rita. And then, he ends up showing her a video of you and Lisa. I'd say the man is going to stir trouble for you and Rita."

"I already told Rita to stop interacting with him," Tony replied immediately.

"And what did she say about that?"

He scratched the stubble on his jaw. "She didn't actually say anything about it. She was berating me about Lisa at the time."

"I think you need to be careful about Petersen and persuade her to stay away from him," Freddie said and placed one foot on the step. "What do you want done about Lisa?"

"I think she'd be wise to keep away from me at the moment. I don't want to see her; otherwise, I will lose my temper. And that's never a good thing." He opened the door. "I'm going back inside. I'll catch you later."

He headed inside to find Rita and grab some personal time before he had to go home and face his parents.

CHAPTER TWENTY

Rita uncurled and stretched her arms out. She opened her eyes expecting to find Tony beside her. Instead, she met an empty space.

How long had she been sleeping? She glimpsed the peek of daylight through the shield of curtains.

Had Tony left already? Her heart thudded and she sat up abruptly. His t-shirt and jacked hung over the chair at the corner, his shoes underneath. He couldn't have gone far with only his jeans on.

After everything that had happened yesterday, she felt quite refreshed with a night of sleep made even better for the way he'd held her until she'd slept off. Now, she missed his presence and wanted to find him.

She swung her leg over the side of the bed as the door pushed open. Tony walked in, a grin splitting his face. Her heart leapt at seeing him bare-chested, tight muscles rippling as he closed the door.

"'Morning, Buttons." In two strides, he stood before her and pulled her into his arms. She murmured her greeting as he nuzzled her neck. "Did you sleep well?"

"Yes," she replied in a breathy voice. His lips on her neck were sending tingles all over her body and these were causing devastation between her thighs. She slid her palms up from his hard abs to his chest, feeling the undulating ridges of his muscles.

"How about you?" she managed to ask when her brain kicked in for a few seconds. "Did you sleep well?"

It couldn't have been an easy night for him, sleeping in a different bed that wasn't that big or comfortable. They'd slept in each other's arms for most of the night. She was sure he'd wanted room to stretch out and not overheat, since there'd been a power-cut overnight and she couldn't use the fan in her room. In his house, the generator kicked in with a power cut, so he didn't have to go through a hot night. Thankfully, the rain last night had cooled the air, making sleep bearable.

"I did." His breath feathered her sensitive cheek. "Having you in my arms made it all the better."

Soft lips descended on her mouth. Pulse racing, she gasped, opening up to him. He didn't hesitate, his tongue diving in, tangling with hers. Heat flooded her body, her insides going mushy. Lust and passion flared in her veins. She lost the ability to think and just acted. Grabbing his shoulders, she climbed his sturdy legs. He grabbed her bottom with his palms, his fingers digging in the soft skin.

She felt the hardening of his erection between her legs and he sat down on the bed, pulling her down on top of him. He angled her head, deepening the kiss, and she moaned out loud.

He broke away. "Baby, I want you," he said before pressing his lips against her bare shoulder where he'd pushed her shirt to expose her skin.

His hands slid up from her waist, lifting the night shirt she had on. His palms were hot on her skin, leaving a trail of electricity.

"Lift your arms for me."

She did, her heart pounding. He pulled the shirt over her head and tossed it aside, leaving her just in her panties. Last night, he'd let her sleep but she'd known he'd worn his erection all night long. And it was still evident this morning. His touch drifted up her belly and he squeezed her breasts.

"You have such sweet, plump tits," he said in a husky voice before his warm mouth covered her right nipple.

"Ohhh," she moaned and arched her body, tilting her head back, wanting more of his decadent lips, more of what he was doing to her.

How was it that when she was with Tony, she lost all her inhibitions and wanted him to do whatever he pleased with her? She'd never been that way with anyone. And her resolution to keep her virginity until her wedding night had disappeared. He moved his mouth to the other nipple, sending more electric currents to her core. She ground her hips against him, feeling the bulge of his manhood and wanting him inside her. What would he feel like? She wanted to find out.

"Tony..." she trailed off as her brain seemed to short circuit.

"Baby, I want to make you feel so good." His hand covered her mound.

She sucked in a breath and blurted out the question. "Will you make love to me? You know, for real?"

He lifted his head and stared at her, his gaze so amber and intense, she got lost in it.

"More than I've ever craved anything else, I want to be inside you. Have wanted to be since the first day I saw you." He closed his eyes as if fighting for control. When he opened them, his gaze had softened. "You said you wanted to wait for your wedding night and I respect that. I respect you. So we're going to wait, even though it's probably going to kill me before then."

"It's probably going to kill me, too," she whispered. The way she felt right now, that could well be true.

He grinned so naughtily. "I plan to make it good for both of us until we get married."

Huh? Did she hear that right? She tilted her head to the side and stared at his face. "Did you just say we're getting married?"

He grinned sheepishly. "You love me and I love you. We want to spend the rest of our lives together. So why not make it official?"

She frowned. "Tony, this isn't exactly how I expected a proposal."

"I'm sorry." He lifted her and sat her on the bed and then he knelt in front of her. "I know this isn't exactly glamorous and luxurious. Honestly, I'm not a flowers or roses guy. But if you want flowers, I will buy you as many as I can handle. I was planning to wait a while before I buy the engagement ring. But this afternoon, we can go to a jewellery shop and have a look at what kind of rings you might like."

Her heart thumped loudly in her chest. She so wanted to be married to him. But getting engaged without telling him the truth wasn't a good idea.

"Tony, I don't care about flowers or jewellery. I just care that you love me." She grabbed her night shirt from the floor and pulled it over her head before standing up to walk away.

"You know I love you, baby." He turned, watching her walk away.

"I know, and I love you, too."

"So what's wrong?"

The bed squeaked. She turned around and found him sitting on it.

"You need to hold off on your proposal until you know the truth about me." Despite the warm room, a chill ran down her spine and her body trembled. "I'm afraid of what it will do to us when I tell you."

"I told you already I will forgive you." He pushed on the bed as if to stand up and she raised her palms.

"Please, sit down. I need some space to think clearly. I don't do so well when you are close."

He nodded and stayed put. "Just tell me, Buttons. It can't be that bad."

"It is." She sucked in a breath, closed her eyes, counted to five, and expelled the air in her lungs. "Meeting you at the post-premiere party in Abuja wasn't just a random event."

She opened her eyes. He just stared at her.

"Meaning?"

"Meaning Petersen and I planned it. He brought me to the party purely so that we could meet."

Lines appeared between his brows. "Why?"

Her stomach twisted with self-disgust and she averted her gaze. "So that I could get involved with you and get close to your family. He wants private information about your family. He says he wants to take you guys down."

Tony lowered his head onto his hands.

The knot in her stomach tightened. She knew she'd hurt him with her words and she was afraid to carry on. He lifted his head and his expression hardened.

"Petersen has had a vendetta against my family for a long time. That is old news. But why would *you* do this to me? To my family?"

The quiet way he said the words didn't match up to the anger that blazed in his eyes. Bile made her mouth bitter and she swallowed hard trying not to be sick all over the bedroom carpet.

"I..." She couldn't seem to form the words as her head pounded and her vision blurred.

"You can't talk now?" Tony stood, his whole body coiled tight with tension, his hands balled at his sides. "How much is he paying you to ruin my life?"

His words cut through her like a knife and she swayed on her feet and leaned onto the wall.

"Tell me, for fuck's sake! My mother offered you twenty million and you rejected it. So it has to be more!"

Despite her self-disgust, the tone of his voice irritated her. "This isn't about money. I didn't do it for the money."

"Yeah, like I'd believe that." Contempt dripped from his words. "You are obviously just like every other girl out there. A little flash of money and you sell your soul."

"In which case, you don't know anything about me," she snapped with her spine stiffened and chin tilted up in defiance.

"Apparently not," he retorted.

He had a point, and shame made her body heat up as she spluttered the words. "I wanted revenge on you and your family!"

He flinched, rocking on his feet as if she'd delivered a physical blow to his body. His mouth opened as he blinked several times. "What revenge? I had never met you before last week!"

"No. But your family's business decisions caused the death of my father. He lost everything during the recent Pensions' scandal. His job. His pension. His life. He'd worked for the company most of his life only to end up with nothing, leaving us with nothing."

Depression weighed down her shoulders as she remembered everything her family had been through and the hatred she'd felt for the Essiens. She closed her eyes and sucked in a deep breath to shore up her strength. "I wanted someone to pay for what my family lost. When I found out Apex Financials oversaw the defunct pension scheme that lost all the money, I wanted your family to pay. That's why I agreed to Petersen's plan."

He nodded as if it all made sense to him. "I must have looked like a real idiot to you, following you around like a puppy, falling in love with you." He waved his hands in the air. "All the time, you've been laughing behind my back with Petersen."

"No. I never laughed at you," she insisted, knowing she had to convince him that her feelings had changed. "I fell in love with you and I realised I couldn't go through with the plan."

"And you expect me to believe that?" He glared at her.

"Of course. I'm confessing everything to you, aren't I?" She stiffened when all she wanted to do was go back into his arms and carry on from where they'd left off. She needed his forgiveness badly.

"After I've already confessed my drug addiction to you. I've given you enough ammunition to bring my family down."

"And I swear I won't tell anyone else your secret, least of all Petersen. I promise you." She took a step to him, her hands raised in a plea. Her body trembled still. If he rejected her now, she didn't know what she'd do.

"I want to believe you." He sounded wary. "I really do."

Her heart rose from where it had lodged in her stomach. Hope flared. "Please do. I love you too much to hurt you like that."

"What about your need for revenge? Has that gone away?" He still sounded unsure.

She exhaled, suddenly realising she'd been holding her breath. "The need isn't as strong as it was before. Moreover, since I got to know you a bit more, I've come to realise you are not as stuck-up as you are portrayed in the media."

"Even my mother who was trying to buy you off?" He quirked an eyebrow. Was he amused?

"Your mother was only trying to protect you. I can understand that."

He heaved out a breath, as if accepting her words. "Promise me this is the end of your involvement with Petersen, and I'll forgive you and we can start afresh."

"I promise you. I will call him and let him know I don't want any part of his plan," she said and glanced at the table where she'd left her phones. Only her old phone sat there. "Let me find my phone and I'll call him right now."

She glanced around the room and spotted her bag. Maybe it was in there.

"Is this what you're looking for?" Tony pulled her phone out of his back pocket.

"Erm, yes." She frowned as she took the cell from him. "Why did you have it?"

"It rang this morning while you were asleep. I didn't want to wake you so I answered it."

Her cheeks heated up as her heart nearly thumped through her chest. Did he speak to Petersen?

"Who was it?" Afraid to ask, her voice trembled.

"Your cousin."

That couldn't be right. None of her relatives had this number. "My cousin? Did he say his name?"

"Yes, Andy. He said he was coming over tomorrow and wanted to confirm the time."

Oh, no! He'd spoken to Andy. She had to come clean about him, too.

"Tony, Andy is not my cousin. He works for Petersen. I was supposed to introduce him to you as my cousin so that he would be invited to your house. He's supposed to plant a listening device somewhere in there. I'm sorry."

"What? You agreed to this. To invade my family's privacy?"

"I didn't know how I managed to agree to it. Petersen was very persuasive." She had to admit it was foolish of her to agree to it.

Tony shook his head and reached for his t-shirt hanging over the chair. "I can't believe you agreed to let a stranger pose as your cousin. He could have gone into my house and killed a member of my family. Is that how much you wanted revenge? Would you be happy if my father was killed?"

"No. Of course not. Petersen promised me it was just to plant a listening device."

"And you believed him. How naive can you be?"

She flinched at his hurtful words but she deserved it. She'd swallowed Petersen's words hook, line, and sinker.

"I'm sorry. I was stupid." She knelt beside him where he sat, putting his socks and boots on. "Please forgive me." She reached for his knees.

"Look." He sighed. "I forgive you. But I have to get home. I need to talk to my parents. Plus I need the space to really think."

"Okay," she said in a sad voice and turned away, head bowed as her eyes watered.

He placed his fingers under her chin and tilted her head until she was looking at him through blurry vision. Tears dropped from her eyes.

"I'm glad you told me before any serious harm was done. I really appreciate it," he said in a calm voice.

"Thank you," she whispered.

"I need the phone." He opened his palm and she dropped the phone back into his hand. "If my parents' lives are in danger, they need to know and prepare for it. We're going to need any evidence on the phone. Don't call Petersen yet. I'll let you know what to do later. Okay?"

"Okay."

"Good." He brushed his lips over her forehead before standing and pulling her up. "I've got to go."

She felt so cold and hugged her body. "We are not breaking up, are we? You *are* going to call me."

He turned around when he got to the door. "I've never lied to you before and I won't start now. We are not breaking up and I *will* call you."

He opened the door and stepped out. She grabbed her robe and followed him. Kechi was already up and dressed, chatting with Freddie who seemed ready to go, too.

"We are off now, Kechi. Thank you for your hospitality," Tony said as he headed for the door.

"You're welcome. But I'm coming with you," Kechi said with a smile. "Freddie said he would drop me at the shop. I need to get some things."

"Cool," Tony said.

Rita watched Freddie and Kechi climb onto his bike. Tony walked to his bike, stood for a few heartbeats, before walking back to where Rita stood on the veranda. He sealed their lips together. Passion flared within her, and when he pulled back, she didn't want to let go afraid it was the last time she would see him.

"I love you," he said before walking back to his bike.

Speechless, she took moments to catch her breath and watched them as they rode to the gates.

"I love you, too," she finally said before they disappeared from sight.

Moments after the roaring of the bikes had faded, she turned and walked back into her house. She ran to her room and picked up her laptop which she took to the table in the living room. She would delete the article she'd been writing about Tony and his family. There was no way she was going to pass on the information to Petersen to get it published. She couldn't do that to Tony or his family.

She was just opening the folder with the file in it when she heard a knock at the door. Thinking it would be a member of her landlord's family, she walked over to the door and opened it.

Andy stood on the threshold and her heart dropped.

CHAPTER TWENTY-ONE

"Andy, what are you doing here?" Rita asked when she finally got past her shock at seeing him at her doorstep. They had arranged to meet up tomorrow. Now that she'd told Tony about him and Petersen's plan, the arrangement had gone out of the window.

"I came to see you," Andy replied in a cheerful voice. A smile curled his lips in a charming way. "Can I come in?"

She relaxed a little. "Ehm. Okay." She shifted away from the door, giving him space to walk by.

He stepped in and looked around as he stood in the middle of her living room. "You have a nice home," he said, hands shoved in his back pockets in a relaxed pose.

"Thank you," she said, still standing by the open front door. She wasn't going to make the mistake of shutting herself inside the house with Andy. Although he was being totally friendly at the moment, he still worked for Petersen and he was way bigger than her, tall and broad. Beneath the red t-shirt, his arms bulged with muscles. He could easily overpower her. At least this way, she could escape if he got threatening.

"How can I help you?" she asked, wanting to move things along so he could leave her house as soon as possible.

"May I sit down first?" he asked, still smiling.

She wanted to tell him no. But she didn't want to rouse suspicion since Tony had told her not to call Petersen yet. Maybe the Essiens would plan a way of catching Petersen out. She couldn't spoil their plans—the least she could do in the circumstances.

"Sure. Have a sit." She waved at the sofa.

He lowered his body onto one of the chairs and looked up at her. "Are you going to sit down?"

"No. I'm fine." She brushed him off and crossed her arms over her chest.

"You look very tense standing there." He looked at her curiously. "Is everything okay?"

Damn! She really needed to get herself together. She couldn't give anything away. "I'm fine. I'm just still surprised at seeing you here. We're not supposed to meet up until tomorrow."

"That's why I came," he said, waving his hand. "I wanted to make sure everything was still okay. I called this morning and Tony Essien picked up the phone. But I think I managed to convince him."

That phone call had nearly ruined her life. If she hadn't told Tony already about Petersen, he would've been thinking she had a cousin visiting. "Yes, Tony told me he spoke to you. You really did convince him. He thinks you are my cousin."

"That's very good." Andy's smile widened. "I was a little worried he would become suspicious."

Rita pulled her lips into a wide smile, digging into her acting skills. She needed to reassure him everything was still okay. She hoped it worked. "Oh, you don't have to be worried. He bought your story. Totally. I think tomorrow should be a breeze."

"Great." He coughed like he had something stuck in his throat. "Can I get a drink, please?"

"Are you okay? Do you need some water?" She stepped forward.

"Yes, water will be fine." He coughed hard a few more times.

"Okay."

She walked round the sofa and into the kitchen. Pulling a bottle of water from the fridge and a glass from the cupboard, she returned to the living room to find he still sat where she'd left him. She placed the bottle and cup on the table before pouring water into the glass. He took it and drank.

"Thank you," he said. "Is it okay for me to use your bathroom?"

"Yes. It's down the hallway. Second door on the right." She pointed in the direction.

He stood up and disappeared into the hallway. She took the opportunity to return to her laptop and delete the file. Her laptop screen was the way she'd left it. Strange. It usually went to sleep mode when she left it for a few minutes, especially if it was just the batteries on. She accessed on the file with the article she'd been writing and clicked the delete button. She also went to her trash folder and emptied it.

She puffed out a deep breath, glad she didn't have to worry about Petersen getting hold of the file or Tony discovering it. The only thing she had to worry about now was how to get rid of Petersen. With the help of the Essiens, she hopefully wouldn't have to do it alone.

She closed her laptop as Andy returned.

"Thank you. I'm going now. I'll see you tomorrow. Right?" he said as he headed for the door.

"Sure. I'll see you tomorrow."

"Good." He turned around when he got outside her door. "Kris will be pleased that you are still on board. Nothing pisses him off more than being double-crossed."

Her heart thudded. Did he suspect something? She swallowed. "I wouldn't dare double cross him," she lied.

One thing was certain, she would lose her job at Zen Media, for sure. She couldn't go back to working there, anyway. Not knowing what she knew about Petersen.

"I'll see you tomorrow, Rita." Andy nodded and walked towards the gate.

She shut the door and leaned against it, puffing out a huge breath of relief.

***

Tony pulled on a fresh t-shirt after his shower. All through the ride home, his mind had been turning over Rita's words.

"*Meeting you at the post-premiere party in Abuja wasn't just a random event.*"

He remembered seeing her walking into the ballroom, dressed in shimmering crimson silk and 'fuck me' heels. He'd been so rapt in wanting her that he'd missed all the obvious signs that something had been amiss. The mixed signals she was giving off at the time. Kris's eagerness to pass her over to him. Rita following him up to his room even though she was a virgin.

Fuck! She'd been willing to let him fuck her just to trap him. What a fool he'd been. All this time, he'd been so keen on preserving her virginity until they got wed. Meanwhile, she'd been willing to give it up in exchange for getting information out of him. Somehow, that annoyed him the most.

Not wanting the thought to eat away at him, he'd focused on informing key people about what he'd found out. He'd arrived home and called Kola, the Essien chief of security, telling him briefly what Rita had revealed about Petersen. Kola had then said he would convene an emergency meeting at Tony's parents' this morning which would involve the three Essien brothers, their parents, and Kola.

Tony had met his father briefly before going to take a shower and get dressed. He'd avoided telling his mother directly as she would've been the most distraught. His father would know how to break the news best.

He put his boots on and headed out to the living room. He loved walking barefoot in his house but he knew he'd have to head over to his parents' house soon, so wearing shoes proved practical.

Freddie sat at the dining table and Kudirat had laid out the food on the wide surface. Tony sat down. Pushing his meal around with his fork, he didn't have an appetite for anything. He remembered sitting at this table yesterday, chatting and laughing with Rita and Freddie. She'd seemed so genuine. Yet, she'd been in his house to spy on him and his family.

He dropped his fork and it clattered onto the china plate.

Freddie looked up at him. "You have to eat."

"I'm not hungry." He pushed his still-full plate aside.

"Your mum is going to be worried if you don't eat."

"That's the least of my worries right now."

"I understand," Freddie said. "It's a lot to take in about a girl you thought was innocent. She fooled me, too. But this is going to be sorted out. I know it."

Tony shuddered. He couldn't shake the feeling it was too late. "I bared my soul to her."

"And she promised you she wouldn't tell anyone."

"Do you really believe her?" Tony asked.

"Don't you?" Freddie replied.

"I want to believe her. I really do. But the fact that she's played me so well really irks. She is such a great actress, you know. If she hadn't confessed this morning, I would never have known until it was too late. How do I know she still isn't just acting? This is doing my head in."

He pushed his chair back abruptly and stood, striding over to the window overlooking the courtyard and the pool. He'd had it installed when this house was refitted for him.

The weird thing was that he wanted to pick up the phone and call Rita. He wanted to go to her house and get her out. He wanted to spend the day with her like he'd originally planned, window shopping for engagement rings and making love to her after she accepted his proposal.

But she hadn't accepted his proposal. Instead, she'd shattered his amorous mood by baring her secrets.

"Look, she told you already." Freddie stood beside him. "This means we can be ready for whatever Petersen has planned."

Tony's phone buzzed and he pulled it out of his back pocket. Kola's name flashed on the screen. He swiped the screen and answered it. "Hi, Kola."

"Everyone is here," the head of security said. "We're in your father's den. See you shortly."

His father's den was used as the family meeting room and in case of an emergency, it turned into the war room. If anyone ever wanted to find out what went on in the Essien household, they simply had to be a fly on that wall. If Petersen was planning to bug a room in their house, then that's where all secrets that couldn't be discussed anywhere else were mentioned and talked about.

"I've got to go," he said when he shoved his phone back in his pocket. "I'll let you know how it goes. I just know Mum's going to hit the ceiling."

He sighed as he headed for the door.

"You will get through this," Freddie reassured.

He nodded before stepping outside. He really hoped it would be that easy.

***

"Being on a motorbike is just like flying," Kechi enthused. She'd been going on about being on a bike after she returned from the shops a few minutes ago. They were both in the kitchen preparing lunch.

Rita had tried to remain enthusiastic but her mind was still on what had happened this morning.

"It's a great feeling, having everything whizzing by at such speed," she said a little less enthusiastically.

"Are you okay, sweetie?" Kechi seemed to have finally picked up on her absent mind.

"No. I'm worried about Tony. Yesterday, he was calling me practically every two minutes. Today, he hasn't called me since he left."

"He's probably busy. He spent the night here. I'm sure he's trying to catch up on whatever he missed last night."

"Maybe. But I'm worried. So much happened yesterday and this morning. I think he's gone off me."

"You are kidding me, right?" Kechi put down the knife she'd been using to slice onions. "I saw the kiss between you too before we left. That man has the serious hots for you."

"I don't know, Kechi. As some say, 'Out of sight is out of mind'. Do you think I should call him?"

"I still think you're worrying for nothing, but if you are really worried, you should call him."

"Okay. I'll call him." She remembered she'd left her phone in the bedroom and Tony had taken the other one. When she came back out, Kechi was in the living room with two men. One of them was the driver that had taken her out yesterday.

"Rita, these men are looking for you."

"*Oga* driver," she said to the man she recognised. "I hope everything is okay."

"My name is Lanre and this is Chibby. We were sent to take you to *Oga* Tony's house."

"Oh." Rita looked from one to the other. Lanre was short and stout while Chibby was tall and lean. Both watched her with eagle eyes. "Did Tony ask you to come and get me?"

"No. His father did," Chibby said. "Are you ready to go?"

"Of course not," Kechi snapped. "You can't just walk in here and expect her to drop everything to go with you. How do we know you are from the Essiens, anyway?"

"It's okay, Kechi," Rita calmed her friend. She appreciated her coming to her defence. "Lanre is one of Tony's drivers. Moreover, I'm going to call Tony's number."

She found his contact details and dialled his number. The phone rang and she heard a click, then silence.

"Hello?" she said.

"Is this Rita?" a deep male voice that wasn't Tony's asked.

Taken aback, she replied tentatively, "Yes, it is. I need to speak to Tony."

"This is Kola. The Essiens' chief of security. Tony is unavailable right now. I sent two of my men to pick you up and bring you over here. You can see Tony when you get here."

For a brief moment, she imagined the worst and panicked. "Is he okay? Tell me Tony is fine. Please."

"Tony is fine. As I said, he is just not able to take your call at the moment. You can speak to him when you get here."

"Okay. I'm coming over right away."

"See you soon, then." He hung up.

"I have to go and see Tony," Rita said to Kechi and hurried to her room to grab her bag.

"Okay. But take care of yourself and call me as soon as you can so I know you are okay," Kechi said.

"I will." She nodded and followed the men out.

CHAPTER TWENTY-TWO

"I knew that girl was no good," Mrs. Essien said from where she sat next to her husband on the sofa.

Tony sucked in a deep breath, counted to five, and turned to his mother. "Mum, this really isn't helpful."

Whilst trying not to lose his temper, he didn't need a reminder that a girl he'd put on a pedestal had been playing him. He'd had to recount how he'd met Rita for the benefit of his family gathered in his father's den. He didn't like the feeling it stirred, knowing that when he'd been inviting Rita to auditions, she'd been more interested in wiggling a way into his life than being in his movies.

"But it's true," his mother carried on. "I nearly bought her innocent act when she turned down the money I offered her."

"What money?" Tony's dad asked, looking from Tony to his wife.

Mrs. Essien kept silent this time, looking uncomfortable.

"Mother here offered Rita twenty million Naira to stay away from me," Tony said.

"No way," Mark said and turned to his mother.

"Why would you do that?" his father asked.

Their mum pulled her face in a grimace. "To get rid of her. She was snooping around his things. I thought I could buy her off with money."

"But it didn't work, did it, Mum?" Tony's irritation filtered into his words. "You do this every time with any girl that shows a little interest in me."

"I'm trying to protect you. I don't want another girl to mess with your head and put you at risk the way Tamara did," his mother replied.

Tony growled and pressed his palms to his eyes, his elbows resting on his knees. It seemed he could never outlive his past. That no matter what he did, it would always haunt him.

A hand rested on his left shoulder. He looked up to meet Felix's gaze. His first brother was always so composed, as he was now.

"Stay calm," Felix said in a low tone to Tony before lifting his gaze to the room. "Mum, did you say you offered this girl twenty million and she turned it down?"

"Yes o. She claimed she wasn't interested in the money."

"Then Petersen must be paying her a whole lot more. Do we know anything at all about this girl apart from that she's an aspiring actress?" Felix asked.

"We haven't been able to dig up anything new yet," Kola said. "But I've sent a man to Owerri to find out about her family. And we are making enquiries here in Lagos, talking to neighbours about anyone she's been associated with. I'll let you know when I get some information."

"Good," their dad said. "I want to get to the bottom of this as soon as possible."

"So if this girl isn't motivated by money—" Felix said.

"Everybody is motivated by money," Mark interjected.

"Really?" Felix gave Mark a pointed look.

Mark shrugged. "Most people are. Just saying."

"Anyway," Felix continued. "If she can turn down twenty million, then she must have other reasons for doing what she did."

"She claims Apex Financial ruined her family," Tony said. "She said she wanted revenge for the death of her father."

"What?" Everyone around the room gasped.

"What has Apex Financials got to do with her family?" his father asked.

"Her father worked for a firm affected by the pension scheme debacle. He lost his job and his pension. Apparently, he died recently. She blames Apex Financials. She blames us. She wanted us to pay for her loss. And when Petersen offered the chance to exact revenge, she took it."

Tony's voice was flat and monotone as sadness drooped his shoulders. Rita had lost a lot because of his family and he wanted to make it right for her, even though he'd had no involvement with the business. "How are we going to make it right for her?"

"Are you out of your mind, Tony?" his mother snapped. "This girl put all our lives in danger, and you are concerned with how to make things right for her?"

"How can I not be concerned for her?" he retorted, his patience wearing thin. He sat bolt straight, shoulders tense. "How can we all sit here and be happy to make money out of other people's misery? People are losing everything out there, including their lives, and none of us gives a damn? Is that the kind of family we are?"

"Don't you raise your voice at me, Tony." His mother stiffened.

"Calm down, both of you," his father said.

Sucking in a breath, Tony turned to his brothers, staring from Felix to Mark, hoping they saw things the way he did. "I thought we were committed to running socially responsible businesses."

"We are," Felix said.

"So how can we do this to people?" Even though he wasn't involved with the finance businesses, he felt responsible.

"We don't," Mark said. "The pension losses were due to bad investments and the global banking crash. Apex Financials picked up a few firms in crisis during that period. We turned them around, invested in profitable long-term stocks, and guaranteed jobs and continuity. Unfortunately, the damage had already been done to some of their employees and the old useless pensions schemes had to be dumped and replaced by new ones."

Tony nodded. "So we're not responsible for the defunct pensions and the loss of jobs. But I feel responsible for Rita and I want to help her family—"

"No," his mother cut in.

"Let him speak," his father chided.

"Her father was the major income earner and his pension would have made a difference. Is it possible to set up a fund that pays out to them on a monthly basis? I don't mind giving up part of my allowance to cover it."

Everyone looked at him with a surprised expression. His mother opened her mouth to talk but his father shook his head. Kola stood up and excused himself from the room.

"Your allowance is already quite low, Tony," Mark said. He was responsible for monitoring his expenditure as part of the protocol set up with his addiction recovery. "Are you sure you are willing to lose some of it?"

Tony shrugged. Not like he was still sniffing fifty grand up his nose every weekend. Moreover, he didn't have to worry about paying rent or mortgage. His expenses were mainly around his movie business. For Rita, he would make the sacrifice.

"I don't mind. Can you set it up?"

"Sure. It can be done. But I'll wait until Kola gives his final report on her."

"Yeah. Sure." That way, he could be sure she wasn't still playing him.

The door opened as Kola returned and Tony looked up. His heart stopped. Behind the chief of security stood Rita. One arm clutched her shoulder bag, the other held her elbow.

Not expecting her to be here, he sprang to his feet. "What is she doing here?"

She swallowed, darting her gaze around the room before settling on him. She appeared anxious and he wanted to go to her. To reassure her. But his feelings were still all over the place. As he'd left her this morning, he hadn't been able to resist giving her one last kiss and telling her he loved her on her doorstep. Now, he wasn't ready to face her, although he'd defended her against his parents. Perhaps his pride still smarted.

"I sent for her."

Something about the way his father said the calm words made cold dread slither down Tony's spine.

"This must be Rita," Mark said as he stood and extended his arm towards her. "Come and sit down."

Rita took a step but halted when she saw the expression on Tony's face.

"Somebody tell me why she's here," Tony said, still rooted to the spot, hands balled to the sides.

"We need to talk to her," his father said.

"You are going to interrogate her?" Ready to explode, the muscles on his neck bunched, his veins straining against his skin. He strode across to where Rita stood and grabbed her arm.

"She has information we need," Kola said in a calm voice.

"There's no way I'm letting you lock her in a room and interrogate her like she's a criminal."

"She is," his father said, sounding annoyed for the first time that day. "She's been spying for Petersen. If she cooperates and gives us helpful information, we may not press charges against her."

"Press charges? I can't believe you are saying that."

"The video of her searching your house is enough to get her locked up in a police cell. We've got her on attempted burglary, at the very least," Kola said, arms crossed over his chest. "And she could be involved in a conspiracy to commit murder."

"Oh, God! What have I done?" Rita cried, pressing her hand over her mouth. "Please don't get the police involved. It'll kill my mother. I'll tell you whatever you want to know."

Her eyes looked feverish and her body shook as he held her arm. Tony hated to see her distressed.

"If you're going to question her, then I'm going to be there with her."

"No. It's not a good idea. It would hamper things. You are already invested in her welfare."

"Of course I'm invested. I'm in love with her," Tony bit out.

It seemed everyone in the room gasped, including Rita. He ignored them and carried on. "And this is my fault, anyway. If I hadn't messed up my life, there wouldn't be any need to keep any secrets and nothing for her or Petersen to dig up."

"This is beyond just you," Felix said in a hard voice. "Petersen blackmailed Ebony and tried to get her to divorce me."

"And he threatened Faith when she allowed me to buy her firm." Mark's tense voice matched their older brother's. "It seems using women to get at us is part of his modus operandi."

"Both of you would do whatever it took to protect your wives, wouldn't you?" Tony seized the opportunity.

"Yes," his brothers replied.

"I will do the same for Rita. I can't sit back and let anybody hurt her."

"But she's not your wife," his mother said.

"I'm hoping to change that soon." He knew this was probably the wrong time to bring this up. But he was already on a roll and would make the most of it. "I want to marry Rita, if she will let me."

Everyone fell silent. Rita's breath hitched and she glanced up at him, bewildered.

"You still want to marry me after everything that's happened?" she asked, staring at him as if he'd lost his head.

"We all make mistakes. I should know. And as you said, we need forgiveness. I want you to be my wife." He knelt on one knee. "I love you, Rita. Will you marry me?"

He was putting everything on the line proposing in front of his family. If she blew him off now, he'd probably never recover. Something told him he had to take the gamble so his family would understand how much she meant to him.

Tears glittered in her eyes. "Oh, Tony. I love you. But I don't think this is the right time for this."

His heart fell. She was rejecting his marriage proposal. "Are you saying no?"

"No," she said quickly. "I'm just saying this isn't a very good time. Your family members are rightfully angry with me for the things I did. I don't think they are ready to welcome me into their fold."

She was being reasonable, but he couldn't help the pain in his chest.

"My family do not bear grudges. I'm sure they will forgive you if you apologise and promise never to do it again." He turned around to look at his family. His brothers nodded. His father's expression was blank. But his mother still looked annoyed. She was going to be the most difficult to convince.

Rita went on her knees beside him. She gripped his hand tight as if needing his presence and strength.

"I really don't know how to express my deep regret for all the things I did against you all. I was stupid—"

"You can say that again," his mother interrupted.

Tony glared at her and she looked away. He squeezed Rita's hand so she could continue.

"And ignorant and angry. I wanted someone else to feel the pain I felt after my father died. When Petersen offered me a way of lashing out, I took it without thinking about the consequences of my actions. I trusted him when he told me it was part of investigative reporting. I thought I was doing the right things to progress my career. I'm really sorry and whatever you want me to do, I'll do it."

"You were offered money to walk away from Tony. Why didn't you take it?" Felix asked. There was no judgement in his voice, just curiosity.

Rita glanced at Tony and smiled shyly. "I fell in love with Tony. Taking the money would feel like I sold my soul, and walking away would feel like leaving a crucial part of me behind. I can't do that."

"She's got my vote," Felix said with a shrug.

"If you get involved with us and take our side, Petersen will consider you the enemy. Are you willing to take that risk?" Mark asked.

"Yes, I am. Knowing that I'm with Tony will make it worthwhile," Rita replied.

"If she's willing to face up to Petersen on our side, then she'd got my vote, too," Mark added.

"So will you marry me?" Tony looked at her, his heart practically in his mouth, his hand gripping hers as they knelt side by side. With his brothers' support, he knew he could convince his parents, eventually.

"Yes, I will," she said with a smile.

"Thank you," he breathed out in relief and squeezed her hand as he gave her a huge grin.

"You are still going to have to wait five years before you can get married," his mother said.

Rita glanced at him in surprise.

"I'll explain later," he said to her in a low voice. She nodded.

"Mum, we are going to get married as soon as it's possible," he said for the benefit of the rest of the room.

"That means you will lose your allowance and any access to Essien money. That's what you signed, Tony. Are you willing to risk that?"

He would do it if it came to it, but he had to bet his mother was bluffing, though. "For five years, I've been clean. I've done everything you asked by the book. Are you going to keep making me pay for what I did forever?"

"You agreed you would live according to the rules set out in the contract for ten years. If you did, then all your privileges would be reinstated. And if you didn't, you'd lose everything," his father said in a matter-of-fact tone.

"I know. But for the first time in my life, I feel as if I'm not merely surviving but actually living. I have a chance to be happy. And you want to take that away. If you cut off my money, I'll move out. Are you willing to take that risk, both of you?" He directed the question at his parents. They both glared at him.

He wasn't afraid of going out there to survive on his own. It would be tough but if he had Rita, they would make it together.

"Look," Felix cut into the impasse. "We have more urgent matters to deal with as a united family. We need to sort out Petersen once and for all. Tony, promise me you will hold off on any wedding plans until after that. Once we deal with Petersen, you have my consent to get married. And if Mum and Dad still refuse to come around, I'll cover your costs until you can get back on your feet."

"You can't do that," his mother said.

"Yes, he can, and I agree with him," Mark chipped in. "You guys are being way too hard on Tony. If he waits till Petersen is sorted out, he gets my vote to get married to Rita, too. I'll also contribute to whatever the two of them need to start a life together."

"Thank you," Tony said in a hoarse voice choked with emotion. His brothers had come to his rescue again.

"You're welcome to the family, Rita," Mark said with a smile as he helped her stand up. "This might all look strange to you but we all love each other dearly and will protect each other. So I'm glad you love Tony as it makes things easier all round. Be good to him and we'll all be good to you."

"Thank you," Rita said.

"If you come with me, we can get started," Kola said, directing Rita to the door.

"Wait a minute," Tony said before turning to the group again. "I'd like to take Rita to Beya for two days. Is that okay?"

"I don't have any objections," Mark said. "What about security?"

"I'll send a couple of men with them. Plus since it is remote, the risk is minimal," Kola said.

"Then that's settled," his dad said.

"Thank you," he said before taking Rita's hand and leading her out of the room.

CHAPTER TWENTY-THREE

Rita followed the man that had introduced himself as Kola down the hallway and outside through a side door. After the near-freezing temperature of the air-conditioned house, the heat from the blazing afternoon sun caused sweat beads to settle along her hairline as they walked past an ornate gazebo and a beautifully maintained garden. Pink bougainvillea hung on trellises while a row of lilac hibiscus shrubs demarcated the plants from the manicured green lawn that stretched for yards to what she realised was Tony's house.

He hadn't said anything since they'd left the rest of his family in the living room. But his presence stroked her skin even though he hadn't touched her, either. He walked a step behind her, almost like a sentry assigned to watch over her. Close and yet far. His demeanour had changed as soon they'd gotten into the hallway. Was he still angry at her?

Hyperaware of him, temptation made her want to stop walking just so he could bump into her and she could feel his heat on her back. Despite the anxiety knotting her stomach, she smiled at the thought. Was it strange that regardless of everything, she wanted to curl up and have Tony wrap himself around her like he'd done last night? She hadn't realised he could be so tender and loving. Such a contrast to the dark and tortured image he projected sometimes.

"In here."

Kola voice drew her from her musing. He opened the door to the two-storey gatehouse and ushered her into a room at the end of the hall.

Plain white walls, a large black desk, and chairs greeted her. It was a functional office with grey metal, locked file drawers, and grey carpet. Not the stripped-wall cell she'd assumed they would take her to in order to be questioned. She'd been watching too many crime dramas; her imagination had run away with her.

Kola waved at one of the seats in front of the table before going round to sit in the leather chair behind the desk. Rita sat down and turned around as Tony closed the door. He didn't move to take one of the available vacant chairs. Instead, he crossed his arms over his chest and leaned his shoulder against the door.

Heat rolled off his body in scorching waves, his pose animalistic and hypnotic. Mesmerised, she swept her gaze from his bulging arms to his lean, sturdy legs. Her core clenched, wept, and she struggled not to squirm under his intense scrutiny.

"Rita."

Kola's voice drew her attention once more.

She turned around to face him, her cheeks scorched with embarrassment. She'd been caught staring hungrily at Tony although neither man said anything about it.

"Are you ready?" he asked.

"Yes," she replied, her voice a little breathy.

"Our conversation is going to be recorded. It is for your protection as well as ours. If you want to have a break at any point, just let me know and we'll take five. Do you understand?"

She sucked in a breath and nodded. He was being so professional, like someone versed in the law. She hadn't really been expecting this...this consideration. It was probably designed to put her at ease. The enormity of how stupid she'd been by getting allied with Petersen still remained, making her body tremble. She had to thank her stars they hadn't called the police on her for what she'd done already.

"You have to speak for the benefit of the tape," he said.

She swallowed and cleared her throat. "Yes, I understand."

"Good. So tell me how you got involved with Kris Petersen."

She sucked in a deep breath and told him about her first visit to Mr. Petersen's office. She gave as much details as she could provide about what they'd done; places and times they'd met, people who'd been there. Kola was thorough, asking probing questions, even about her family life. She stayed honest for his benefit as well as for Tony's. She knew some of the things she revealed would only add to Tony's hurt, especially when she described her eagerness to entrap him.

Tony remained silent. It seemed to her he distanced himself on purpose, perhaps as a protective mechanism.

Sadness that she hurt him made her heart ache. But she couldn't regret meeting him. Surely, that was a good thing that came out of the whole ordeal. If she hadn't gotten involved with Petersen, she would never have met Tony Essien.

"Thank you, Rita," Kola said when he finally seemed satisfied she'd revealed everything. "You have been very helpful. If Mr. Petersen contacts you, do not let him know we are aware of his plans. However, do not go to see him again or contact him yourself."

"Okay. What if he sends someone to me?" she asked, remembering that Andy had come to her house this morning.

"I'm going to assign someone to be with you at all times—"

"She's staying with me over the next few days," Tony interrupted, the first time he'd spoken since they walked in here.

"I'll need to go home." She swung around and glared at him, annoyed that the first time he spoke was to give an order.

"To do what?"

"Stuff," she said stiffly.

He raised a brow. "We're going away tomorrow. Or didn't you hear me earlier?"

"I heard you, but you haven't asked me yet and I don't know if I want to go anywhere with you if this is the mood you're going to be in."

"It's best to stay here for a few days," Kola said in a placating voice. "There's no saying what Petersen will do when he finds out the game is up. You'll be safer here."

Rita gave Tony a final glare before turning back to Kola. "I'll stay here until you tell me it's safe to do otherwise."

"Good." Kola stood and walked around his desk. "I'm going to get Freddie to walk you back to Tony's place. I need to talk to Tony for a few minutes."

Tony strode into the room, past her. He didn't look at her as she followed Kola through the opened door. Freddie, who'd been talking to another man in an open-plan living space, walked up.

"Are you done?" Freddie asked.

"Yes. Take her back to the house. Tony will be there soon," Kola replied.

Thankfully, Freddie seemed less standoffish than his friend. He slowed down his pace and kept astride of her. He didn't talk and the silence felt awkward. When they got to the house, he opened the door and waited for her to go in.

She turned around in the living space.

"You know, I'm sorry for the things I did that hurt Tony," she said, hoping to clear the air between the two of them. The man had been good to her, especially when he'd helped Tony get rid of Anayo.

"I really hope you are." He stood feet apart and arms crossed. "I never took you for a game player. Tamara, his ex, was a player, and in the scheme of things, the worst thing you can do is screw with Tony's head."

She swallowed. "I'm not playing with Tony. I care about him."

"Then that's good for you because if I find out this is all an act and you end up screwing Tony up, Petersen will be the least of your worries."

Shocked, her mouth dropped wide open as she watched him stalk away. She hadn't thought her actions would engender such strong reactions from people. And it was obvious to her how everyone cared about Tony. Her eyes smarted and she lowered herself on the sofa and tried hard not to cry.

Somebody coughing made her look up. She greeted Tony's housekeeper.

"Good afternoon," Kudirat replied. "Can I get you something to eat or drink?"

"No, thanks. I'm fine."

The woman nodded and walked away, leaving her in peace. Rita dug her phone out and sent Kechi a message, letting her know she wouldn't be home tonight. She wasn't even sure when she'd be home. But she reassured her friend she and Tony were fine. At least, she hoped they were.

He'd proposed to her in front of his family. He still loved her despite what she'd done. He was just angry at her. She would have to find a way to make him less angry at her.

She curled up on the sofa, browsing statuses on social media. She didn't have many friends online, just old school mates. The closest friend she had now was Kechi. She sent a message to her sister for a quick catch up. Afterwards, she picked up the remote control and turned on the TV.

What did the future hold for them? How were they going to deal with Petersen? The Essiens obviously had a plan, though they hadn't revealed it to her. She didn't blame them. She'd been in the enemy camp and she wouldn't be so trusting of someone who had plotted against her, either. She just hoped the whole thing got resolved quickly so she and Tony could move on.

She stayed watching TV and fell asleep on the sofa. Tinkling of crockery woke her up. Kudirat was setting the table behind her. What time was it? She glanced outside and the sky glowed purplish-red, indicating the setting sun.

Had Tony returned and just left her to sleep all this while? Assuming he was upstairs, she went to look for him. She didn't find him but noticed a packed brown leather bag on his bed. She left the bedroom and a noise drew her to the gadget room. Freddie sat there playing a war game on the console and TV.

"Hi," she said tentatively. "I'm trying to find Tony. Do you know where he is?"

"Tony's gone to work."

"Work?"

"Yes, he's gone to Reams. This is Saturday night, the busiest of the week. He needed to go since he'd missed a few nights this week already."

Her face and heart fell. He hadn't even bothered to wake her and tell her he needed to go to work. The other night, she'd been here when he went and he'd come home very late.

Freddie switched off the TV and headed for the door.

"Tony had Kechi pack some things for you. The bag is on the bed. Are you coming to dinner?" he asked when she didn't move.

Tony had sent someone to her house, without informing her. So her stay here was really meant to be for more than one night.

She was too gobsmacked to speak so she nodded and followed Freddie downstairs. She hadn't eaten lunch. They'd been in the middle of preparing it when the Essien security team had arrived to bring her over here.

They ate mostly in silence and she enjoyed the yam potage with spinach and shrimps. Not having Tony eating with them plagued her mind.

"Why are you not with Tony?" she asked Freddie after a while.

He looked up at her. "He wanted me to stay here with you, so you wouldn't be alone when you woke up."

"But aren't you supposed to be minding him? You let him go alone?"

"No. He's not alone. Moreover, he didn't want someone you weren't already used to being here with you all night."

Despite her worry, her heart warmed. Tony had still been thinking about her welfare even when he wasn't one hundred percent happy with her.

"I want to see him. Please, will you take me to him?"

Freddie shook his head.

"Please. I know I messed up and that he's still upset with me. But I really love him and I want him to know I'll do whatever it takes to make it up to him," she begged. "If he wants me to just sit in a corner of the restaurant all night, I will. But I've got to see him. Please."

Freddie stared at her in silence for a few moments. Then he nodded. "Okay. I'll take you when we finish eating."

"Oh, thank you," she gushed, relief making her breath whoosh out.

"You are welcome." He grinned. "Just make sure you make it up to Tony. He needs you to be good to him."

"I will. I promise."

Excited, she cleared up the table, taking her plates into the kitchen. She placed them in the sink and wanted to wash them up but Kudirat shushed her away. Thanking the woman, she went upstairs to tidy up her appearance. She took a tank top and short skirt that looked suitable for a trendy top nosh restaurant like Reams out of her bag. The strappy sandals she wore didn't have too high a heel so she wouldn't trip over herself. She held her hair up with a hair band and put on some lip gloss. Happy with her appearance, she headed downstairs to meet Freddie.

"Do I look okay?" she asked Freddie.

"Of course you do." He smiled at her. "Come on, then."

Outside, the lights on the Mercedes G-Wagon flashed.

"Aren't we going on the bike?" she asked when he walked past his bike to the luxury SUV and opened the passenger door.

"Tony will kill me if you rode on my bike." He chuckled. "You're only permitted to ride with him."

She giggled as she climbed into the car, her cheeks heating up. Yes, that sounded like her Tony. Possessive as well as protective.

The drive to the restaurant didn't take long. Relaxed in the soft leather of the high expensive vehicle, she seemed far removed from the Lagos she usually encountered daily. The cool air-conditioned air she breathed lacked the fumes of exhausts and the sounds were muted. Even the pot-holes and bumps didn't affect her. Or perhaps there weren't any in this high-end part of Lagos. All the street lamps functioned and shone bright, the tree-lined roads quiet.

That was until they crossed Falomo Bridge into Victoria Island. This part of town felt more vibrant, with more traffic, both pedestrians and cars. Within ten minutes of leaving Tony's house, they parked in front of a white, two-level building. The front had no walls, just glass making the place look as if it extended beyond its boundaries. She could see inside through the window on the ground level, and the bar and restaurant seemed packed full already with revellers arriving and leaving. Upstairs, the glass had been darkened so she couldn't see inside, but she assumed they could see outside.

Inside, low Afro beats played from hidden speakers as they headed through a door with a 'Staff only' sign on it. Freddie pushed open a door and she recognised the office from the video Petersen had played for her.

"Wait in here and I'll find Tony," he said.

She shook her head as she remembered Lisa leaning on the table and Tony between her legs. Her stomach churned. "I can't wait here. Please don't make me."

He looked at her for a moment and puffed out breath. "Okay. Follow me. He is usually in the private lounge, especially if there is an event."

He took her up a flight of stairs and opened a door at the top. Packed with people, the music in this space was louder than downstairs, the sound mixed with people chatting and laughing with each other. Dim light showed low dark sofas on one end and an area cleared out for dancing at the other.

She spotted Tony and her stomach hardened into stone. He sat on a sofa with a fair-skinned girl next to him. The slut leaned into him as she whispered something into his ear and he laughed at whatever she said. The two of them looked so intimate.

Like old friends.

Like lovers.

As if sensing Rita's furious gaze, he looked in her direction, his amber eyes clashing with hers.

Chest burning, she pressed her lips flat and stiffened her back. Is this what he did when he came to the restaurant? Picking up girls? He'd promised her, dammit.

Propelled by jealous rage, she didn't know when she'd moved until she was grabbing the girl's arm and yanking her off Tony's body.

CHAPTER TWENTY-FOUR

"What the hell?"

One minute he was laughing and joking with Tari; the next, the girl had been flung across the sofa, in shock, and Rita stood over them both looking like she was ready to run him through with a knife.

It had felt good to switch off from his problems for a few minutes but he should've known he couldn't run from them.

"What is wrong with you, Rita?" he asked in a dismissive tone. He really wasn't in the mood for an argument. "And what are you doing here, anyway?"

"You want to know what's wrong with me? *You are,* Tony Essien." Her voice was loud enough for those standing around them to hear and turn their heads. "You leave me at home without even a goodbye and come here in the guise of working, only to pick up girls. You fucking promised me you wouldn't do that anymore!"

His nose flared at her use of the 'f' word. The first time he'd heard her use it, and he didn't like it. "Don't you fucking swear."

He grabbed her elbow and propelled her towards the back entrance she'd walked through.

"Why shouldn't I? You swear all the time."

He would've laughed out loud if he wasn't trying to be stern with her. He couldn't allow her to walk into a party and disrupt it the way she had. This was a business.

"That doesn't mean you have the permission to swear at me or in front of my guests." He stomped down the stairs and a waiter scurried out of sight as soon as he saw the boss.

Rita wriggled to get out of his grip but he didn't release her until they were in his office. She glared at him as she stepped away from him, her bum hitting the desk.

"You'll stay here and when you've calmed down, you'll go upstairs and apologise to Tari for your behaviour."

"No way. I'm not going to apologise to that girl, and if you think I'm going to stay here while you go back to your floozies, you have another think coming. What do they have that I don't?"

"You don't know what you're saying." He shook his head.

"I know exactly what I'm saying. What can they give you that I can't? I'm just like them."

"No, you're not."

"I am. I'm a woman."

"Do you want to be a groupie?" he growled angrily.

"What?" She appeared shocked.

"That's what they are. They are only followers, girls who flock around me just for what they can get out of me. Mainly for sex. With them, I don't care what I do as long as they are willing."

Her throat undulated as she swallowed. "Things like what?" Her voice came out breathy.

"Like something I've wanted to do to you since the first day I saw you. If you were a groupie, I would shove your face down onto that desk and make you grip the edge."

Her breath hitched and her eyes widened. He took another step toward her.

"I would spread your legs wide till your arse was sticking into the air and stick my fingers inside you while playing with your tits. Then I'd make you come and gush wetness all over my hand, before ramming my cock inside your pussy again and again until we're both sated."

Her breath came in short pants just like his. His dick had grown as hard as a rock and he really wished he could do everything he'd just described to her. But she wasn't one of his groupies and this lifestyle wasn't for her.

Or was it?

She closed her eyes briefly. Her pulse pounded on her neck and she licked her lips. She lifted onto the desk and parted her legs. Glistening curly hairs winked at him from under her skirt.

He groaned and nearly fell as his knees weakened. "You're not wearing underwear."

She gave him a slow smile. "I wanted to surprise you by coming here. I wanted to do whatever it took to make you stop being angry with me."

He reached her and pulled her off the desk, holding onto her sides, just under her breasts. She wasn't wearing a bra, either.

"I'm not angry with you anymore. I just needed some space so I didn't end up fucking you six ways till Sunday. I'm so close to giving up on my resolve to wait until we're married to fully claim you. It's physically painful."

"But I don't want you having sex with someone else, Tony. It'll kill me. I'm ready to give it to you now. It really doesn't matter to me when we have sex."

"It matters to me. My first time of being inside you won't be in my office." He led her to the sofa behind the door, kicking it so it swung but didn't shut fully. Since he'd disabled the camera in here, he wasn't allowed to be in the office with the door shut.

"Don't send me away, please," she said.

"I'm not sending you away. Not when I know you've got nothing under that skirt." He sat on the sofa and pulled her down on top. She straddled him and her skirt pushed up, exposing her pussy. He slid his hand between her parted thighs, meeting slick, silky hot flesh. Musk and sex filled the air along with her moans of pleasure as he stroked her pussy lips and swollen clit.

He used his other hand to hold onto her back as she arched, gyrating her hips with the movement of his fingers playing a tune of pleasure with her folds.

"Lift your top up for me. I want to suck your tits," he commanded.

Feverishly, she pulled her top over her head, exposing her breasts, her nipples already as hard as bullet tips.

He lapped one, swirled his tongue around it, before sucking it deep into his mouth. He repeated the action with the soft underside of her breast. She moaned again, rocking back and forth. He realised she was close to an orgasm and sucked hard as he pressed down on her clit with his thumb. She keened, writhing out of control as he held onto her.

His shaft felt like a brick in his trousers and he knew he was already leaking pre-cum. Watching and listening to Rita disintegrate into an orgasm was as addictive as having sex.

She lowered her sweat-slicked head onto his shoulder as she caught her breath. He was still trying to work out how he would get rid of his erection when her hand covered his stiff dick. She squeezed him and he couldn't suppress his groan as his body involuntarily rocked against her hand.

"Let me return the favour," she said in a husky voice.

"N—"

"I won't take no for an answer." She lifted her head. "Or would you rather go and fuck Tari?"

He coughed several times. "Are you crazy? Tari is my cousin. Blood. She is the closest thing I have to a sister. I don't do incest, thank you."

"Oh my God! She's your cousin? And I was such a bitch to her. I'm so sorry." She covered her head with her hands.

He chuckled. "It's okay. Tari is used to the crazy bitches that hang around me."

"Oh, no! That's even worse. Now I wish I could go and crawl into a hole."

"Just joking." He chuckled some more. "Don't worry about Tari. She'll get over it. I, however, am not going to get over you any time."

He kissed her then, seizing her mouth in a crushing kiss, his tongue fucking her mouth the way he longed to fuck her pussy but couldn't.

He took her hands and pushed them against his fly. "Open my fly."

She fumbled with his belt and zipper while he continued kissing her and kneading her breasts. He pressed kisses on her neck, sucking the delicate skin as she tilted her head to the side, giving him more access. She stilled her hand and moaned.

He really needed her to get to his throbbing dick soon, so he moved his lips down to her shoulder, nipping the skin.

Finally, he felt the zipper slide down. Only his stretchy boxers separated him from her touch.

"Baby, reach inside and grab me. Let me feel your hand wrapped around me."

She did, pulling his cock out, and he nearly came from the feel of her soft skin against his hot flesh. He sucked in a harsh breath and panted to control himself. He lifted his bum and shoved his trousers down until they tangled around his ankles.

"Hold onto my shoulders and slide down onto me."

She lowered her body and he slid his cock between her pussy lips.

"That's it. You're so wet. You feel so good." He wasn't inside her but he felt like he was touching Heaven as she glided back and forth, his hands grabbing onto her arse and pulling her down tight so there lay no gap.

For a man who'd often been inside women, he found he loved this new style of sex without penetration. Rita was the only woman he'd tried it with. And he couldn't really complain. Not with the wicked sensations flowing through him as her nipples grazed his chest and her pussy stroked his cock.

"*Oga*," a voice came through the open door.

Rita stiffened. Tony held her still as she made to rise.

"I'm busy," he called out before returning to nip the soft skin on Rita's shoulders.

"It's the party upstairs. They need you."

"Tell them I'll be there soon." He pressed Rita's hips down so her clit rubbed his dick.

"I'm so close," she moaned and arched for more.

The sound she made, she seemed to have forgotten there was someone at the door who could hear her.

He reached down her arse and trailed some of the juices from her pussy down her crease and pressed against her pucker.

She stiffened. "Tony?"

"Relax, baby. It'll feel good. I promise you." He pressed his left thumb against her clit and her body went limp and he pressed his index finger into her hole.

"Ohh," she cried out, her orgasm rocking her body, her pussy flooding his cock with liquid heat.

"Fuck," he shouted as he felt his balls tighten. He lifted Rita and crushed her down on his flesh as his cock jerked and hot cum shot up between them.

He kissed her, swallowing her panting breaths as both their bodies shuddered for moments on end. Completely sated, she slumped against him as he fell back onto the sofa, her cheek on his chest as his thundering heart tried to find its normal beat again.

CHAPTER TWENTY-FIVE

Rita sat in the helicopter as it rose high above Victoria Island, the Lagos landscape spread out below. Her first time in a helicopter, and her heart thumped loudly in her chest, her hands clammy.

"Are you okay?"

Tony's voice filtered through the headset she wore.

She glanced over to where he sat next to her and nodded.

"This takes a little bit of getting used to," she replied in a wobbly voice into her microphone extension attached to the headphones.

"A helicopter is a different flying experience from a plane," he said. "In a plane, you are quite removed and enclosed. But in a helicopter, you experience every aspect of the flight almost as if you were flying yourself. From the lift off, to the vibration of the rotors, to the turbulence and sounds you hear. Your body will adjust, eventually."

He squeezed her hand reassuringly and she gave him a small smile.

He was right—the flying experience was different from an airplane. She didn't fly often. The last time she flew in a plane had been when she went to Abuja with her boss. They'd flown in business class and spacious luxury. Prior to that the last time, she'd been in a plane when her father had been alive. On the times she'd recently travelled to Owerri, she'd taken the coach from Lagos. Cheaper but a longer journey, taking most of the day.

"Do you go to Beya often?" she asked, curious about the place he was taking her to.

"I go back once every year about the same time I was there five years ago as a pilgrimage," he said, his voice a little distant. "It's both a time of reflection and a reaffirmation of my commitment to continue on the path I've chosen."

"Okay." Conscious of the people around them, she chose not to ask more probing questions. Instead, she leaned her head against his shoulder and watched the scenes below the helicopter unfold. The landscape changed from sea to urban to rural as they headed north and east, concrete and overcrowded jungle transforming to greenery and leafy vegetation with sparse houses.

She sighed, grateful that she got to experience this with Tony. They'd not had much time to talk since last night's explosive lovemaking at the restaurant.

She'd lain on top of him, his arms around her on the sofa as the sweat on their skins cooled and their heartbeats returned to normal.

He'd pushed back damp hair from her face and whispered, "I promised you I'd never cheat on you for as long as we were together. You have to trust me. I'm not going to break it."

Ashamed of the jealous way she'd behaved in front of his cousin and friends, she'd burrowed into his arms, hiding her face. "I know. You've been faithful and good to me. But as soon as I saw the two of you together, I just remembered the image of you with Lisa and went mad. I really couldn't bear it if you'd had sex with anybody else. I just couldn't."

His hand had pushed her chin up. "I love you too much to do that to you. It's you I want morning, noon, and night. You don't know how much."

"I'm sorry," she said. "I promise to curb my temper."

"Also promise you won't go swearing in public like you did earlier. That is so unladylike. When we're in private, you can say those things to me, for my ears only. But never in public."

"Okay. I promise."

"Good girl." He'd brushed his lips against her forehead and then opened a hidden drawer under the small side table to withdraw some wet wipes which he'd used to clean both of them up.

She'd gotten dressed, making herself as tidy as possible, while he'd pulled up his trousers and made himself presentable again.

"We are going back upstairs and I'll introduce you to Tari," he'd said as he'd pulled a new t-shirt on from a fresh stack in a drawer. Lucky him that he had a spare. She couldn't change her now-creased skirt that had been bunched around her waist.

"No," she'd said, trying to wriggle out of facing all those people again, especially now she knew Tony hadn't been doing anything untoward. "Can't I just go back home with Freddie?"

"Oh, no, you don't." He'd given her a wicked grin as he'd pulled her into his chest. "You are going to take your punishment for thinking I was cheating on you and acting out. You will apologise to Tari and for the rest of the evening, you'll behave like the best girlfriend ever."

Something about the way he'd said those words had made her heart race. Not with fear. But with excitement. She loved the masculine, man-in-charge Tony.

"You'll be good, won't you?" He'd raised on brow as if daring her to disagree.

"Yes," she'd replied, giving him a shy smile.

He'd taken her hand then, leading her back upstairs to the party where he'd introduced her to Tari. Cheeks heated, Rita had apologised.

Tari had eyed her up and down before asking, "So you settled your lovers' quarrel, then. If I know my cousin here very well, then I know the make-up session must have been explosive."

Rita had gasped in shock at how direct the girl was.

"Tari," Tony had scolded jokingly. "Don't spoil my girl. She's not like you."

Tari had laughed. "I'm sure I can't spoil her the way you can. *Abi*, am I wrong? Rita," she'd teased.

Rita had been surprised and pleased that she'd been included in the light-hearted banter between the cousins. "No. You are right," she'd said. "Tony spoils me a lot more than anyone else can."

"Hey, cheeky." He'd pulled her into his side and leaned down to whisper into her ear. "I'm going to make you pay for that later."

Feeling more confident, she'd leaned into him and whispered, "I look forward to it."

The rest of the night had passed without much event. Tony hadn't left her side, introducing her to some of his friends that had been there, too. Before Tari had left, Rita had apologised again, hoping she could have a female friend in a family of very masculine brothers. At least, Tari was close to her age and perhaps they could get along.

"I'm really sorry for the way I behaved earlier when I got here. I shouldn't have done it."

"Don't worry about it," Tari had said and placed a hand on her arm. "I understand. Lagos is a jungle and some girls really don't care if a man is single or not. So I understand you trying to protect your territory. I would've done the same thing."

They'd chatted a bit more and swapped contact details. Afterwards, she'd waited in Tony's office with the other bodyguard, Chibby, who'd brought her over to Tony's house that morning while he dealt with the staff and closed up for the night. When they'd left, it had been past one A.M. on the clock on her phone. Tony, Freddie, and she got into the G-wagon and Chibby drove the other car. At Tony's house, they'd both showered and curled up in bed. He'd loved her one more time before they'd both fallen asleep.

***

"Rita, we're here."

Tony's voice roused her.

She stirred and opened her eyes, looking around her in confusion as she tried to remember how she'd gotten in a helicopter. She'd been dreaming about being in bed with Tony. She must have fallen asleep as she thought about last night.

Below the helicopter, mountains covered in emerald vegetation loomed ahead and stretched for miles as far as the eyes could see.

"How can we be here? This is the middle of nowhere," she said. People couldn't possibly live here. No houses or sign of life loomed beneath the trees and vegetation.

"It *is* the middle of nowhere. Watch carefully when I show you. If you don't know what you're looking for, you'll miss it." He pointed down to the side. "Between the trees, there's a clearing. If you look closely, you'll see some smoke."

She looked but all she could see was the trees. Eventually, they hovered above some huts in the settlements.

"Now, I see. Wow. If you didn't point it out, I wouldn't have known that people lived here. The place is hidden."

"This tribe was lost for a long time and only discovered in the eighties. They are still not fully integrated with the rest of Nigerian society."

"That's amazing," she gushed, staring at everything with wide eyes.

The helicopter landed in a clearing. The bodyguards who'd travelled with them alighted and off-loaded items. She hadn't realised how much stuff they'd travelled with until she saw the boxes and bags being moved.

Tony helped her out after he got down by lifting her and setting her feet down on the ground. A crowd gathered around them as young men and girls helped with carrying the bags. The smaller children chanted in excitement. Rita couldn't understand their language.

A woman dressed in a print cotton blouse and wrapper approached, a huge smile on her face. She spoke to Tony and they both embraced warmly. He said something to the woman in what seemed to be the local language and drew Rita close.

The woman turned to look at her, studying her from head to toe with assessing eyes.

"Rita, this is *Ma* Yise. She took me in and took care of me when I was in recovery. She treats me like one of her sons and I look at her as my adoptive mother."

"Good afternoon," Rita said and curtsied.

The woman smiled. It seemed she understood a little English. "Welcome," she said and made a gesture with her hand. "Come."

They followed her, the children milling around Tony as if welcoming a relative who'd come home for a visit. *Ma* Yise carried on chatting to Tony and he interpreted for Rita's benefit.

"She says she'd been expecting me for a while and wondered when I was going to visit. She says she's been having visions about me."

"Visions?" Rita nearly stumbled on the rocky footpath.

He grabbed her arm and steadied her. "Yes, she is a medicine woman. She can foretell some things." He shrugged.

Rita worried her lower lip with her teeth. "But she said she'd seen visions of you. What did she see?"

"She said she'll explain later."

The woman ushered them into a large hut. Compared to what Rita was used to, this proved very basic; yet, it was beautiful. The red mud walls were decorated with white chalks in tribal designs. In the corner sat a raised bamboo platform with a raffia matt and fabric on the top.

"This is our home for the next two nights," Tony said.

"Is this the hut you lived in when you were recovering?" she asked as she looked around the space. There wasn't much else in it. Two small stools sat on the floor. In the corner on a shelf sat wicker lamps.

"No. The hut I stayed in was smaller and separate from the settlement. I wasn't very well or sociable and she thought it was better I stayed isolated."

"So is this *Ma* Yise's hut?"

"No. This is my hut. I was given it when I was officially inducted into the tribe after I came back here. So this is my home away from home. This is where I come when I need a break from the rat race. This is the one place I know where I can be myself without judgement or comparisons. I don't have to be Tony, son of Aloysius Essien, brother to Felix and Mark Essien. I can just be Tony."

"Wow." Her eyes watered. So much humility in his words. For the first time since she'd met him, she saw a totally different man. She'd known he was special. But this...

She leaned in and kissed his lips. "I love you, Tony. So much."

Ma Yise returned and said something rapid-fire to Tony.

"We have to go and meet the chief of the clan," he said. He took Rita's hand and they walked outside. Freddie and Chibby were chatting and playing with the children.

"Where are the others going to sleep?" she asked.

Tony pointed to another hut next to his. "They'll stay in there."

After a few minutes of walking, they arrived at a fenced compound. A man in traditional woven attire sat on a hand-carved, heavy throne on a dais. He stood up and embraced Tony as if he was a close member of his family. Tony introduced Rita who curtsied in greeting. The man beamed a smile on her in response and indicated they should sit.

***

The men chatted as the chief asked about Tony's family and his business. He thanked Tony for coming to see them regularly like a good member of the clan. And then he turned his attention to Rita, telling Tony it was good of him to bring his bride to them. That every good member of the tribe always got married in the village. And tonight, they would be celebrating their traditional Beya wedding.

Tony tried to explain that he wasn't married to Rita yet. That they hadn't made plans, just gotten engaged.

The chief said it didn't matter. As a Beya tribe member, he had to perform the rites according to Beya custom.

Looking worried, Tony excused himself and went to talk to *Ma* Yise to explain that they couldn't get married. For one thing, his parents would cut him off if they found out he'd gotten married without their permission. And his brothers had wanted him to wait until after they'd sorted out Petersen.

They sat in *Ma* Yise's hut as he tried to explain his predicament.

"You have to marry her today or you will lose her," Ma Yise said.

"Why?"

"I have seen the vision. Pain and darkness is coming your way. If she is your wife, she will be your redemption. If she isn't your wife, you will both lose out. I see death."

Cold sweat broke out on Tony's skin. "Death? Whose death?" He tried to keep his voice calm. To not panic. But dread made him shudder. Thank God Rita couldn't understand the language.

"I cannot say. Except that it will affect both of you."

Fuck! He mouthed the curse and scrubbed his scalp with both hands.

"What's going on, Tony? What did she say?"

Rita's voice sounded agitated and he looked up.

"The chief said we have to get married tonight as part of Beya custom."

"Married? You're joking, right?"

"I'm not joking. I've tried to explain to *Ma* Yise why we can't get married tonight but she insists it has to be tonight or terrible things will happen. She thinks one of us will die."

"Die? This is crazy, Tony. I'm getting out of here." She pushed off the chair to get up but *Ma* Yise grabbed her hands, making her sit back down.

Ma Yise said to Tony while holding onto Rita's hands, "Translate this so she can understand me. If she doesn't marry you tonight, you will both lose each other permanently."

Tony nodded and translated.

"What?"

"Is that what you want?" *Ma* Yise asked, her voice stern.

"No. Of course not," Rita replied.

"Then sit down and listen to me," the woman continued.

Rita nodded and sat stiffly in the chair.

"As I said already, there is great pain and darkness coming Tony's way in the near future. His life is going to be turned upside down. In Beya custom, being married means sharing the good times as well as the bad times. If you marry Tony, you will share part of his great pain and darkness, not just physically but emotionally. The question I ask you is, do you love him enough to suffer his pain with him?"

"No," Tony said before he translated the last sentence. "I can't ask Rita to do that for me. If there's pain in my future, I don't want her to be part of it."

"You cannot change it. The path is already set. She is the cause of your pain. And yet, she will also be the salve that will heal it. You cannot make the choice for her. She needs to make it herself. Ask her the question the way I asked it."

Tony licked his lips as his heart thudded. He didn't want to ask Rita the question for several reasons. Mainly because he was afraid of what her answer would be.

"What is it?" Rita asked, scrutinising his face as if trying to read between the lines.

He puffed out a breath. "*Ma* Yise wants to know if you love me enough to suffer my pain with me both physically and emotionally," he said and held his breath as he waited for her answer.

CHAPTER TWENTY-SIX

Rita stared from Tony to *Ma* Yise and back to Tony. What was really going on here? Had she fallen asleep and dreamt all this?

"Tony, you have to know that this is superstition," she said as she shifted uncomfortably on her stool. Goosebumps covered the skin on her arms though the temperature remained warm.

"One man's superstition is another man's belief. Moreover, you go to church. Haven't you ever heard of prophecies before?"

"That's different. A man of God's prophecy is different from this."

"Really? So you think prophecies from some money-grabbing men who operate under the guise of being men of God are more authentic than what *Ma* Yise is saying?" He stood up abruptly and walked out.

Rita flinched. He sounded so convinced about *Ma* Yise. She wanted to believe it, too. But this was all a little too much to take in.

Ma Yise said something Rita couldn't understand and pointed at the door. It sounded as if she wanted her to go after Tony.

Rita nodded and muttered her apologies before going outside to look for him. She found Freddie, instead.

"Do you know where Tony went?" she asked him.

"I'll show you," he said.

They walked together down another footpath in the direction of some boulders and hills.

"Do you come here with Tony every year?" she asked, wanting to find out as much as she could about this place if she was ever to understand Tony.

"Yes. Coming here saved Tony's life and he acknowledges this by returning here every year. These people are his family as much as the one in Lagos."

She nodded. She could see the attachment Tony had to this place and people. But it didn't mean the things *Ma* Yise said were correct, did it?

They walked up a rocky incline and she saw Tony sitting on top of a boulder.

"He likes to come up here to think and reflect on his own," Freddie said. "Do you want me to help you up?"

"No. I think I can manage."

She climbed up on her hands. Stone and some rubble shifted beneath her feet. Good thing she wore jeans and trainers; otherwise, she wouldn't have made it to the top without being carried. Tony saw her climbing and reached out, gripping her arm and pulling her up. She panted as she sat beside him, her legs dangling over the edge of the boulder.

"Wow," she said, feeling almost light-headed sitting this high up. The scene that rolled out before her was breathtaking. Mountains stretched out for miles, the landscape green and brown and blue where she could see the expanse of cerulean sky. "This is beautiful."

"Now you know partly why I come here." His deep voice rumbled inside her as he spoke. "There are no skyscrapers obstructing the view. No exhaust fumes polluting the air. Wait until you eat the food. It is made fresh, with no additives or preservative. The water is pure volcanic mountain water that people pay a fortune to drink. Here, you get everything for free. The best detox ever. A cleansing of the body as well as the mind and spirit."

"I can see that," she said. They sat in silence for a while. "I'm sorry for upsetting you in *Ma* Yise's hut."

"You know..." He glanced at her. "I can accept it if you said you don't want to share my pain—"

She interrupted him. "Tony—"

He held up his hand, silencing her.

"I wouldn't want you to suffer for me," he continued. "But dismissing *Ma* Yise's vision because she's not standing in front of a pulpit? That is what I can't accept. Tell me what *Ma* Yise has to gain by telling you this. She hasn't asked you for any money. Hasn't asked you to sow a seed to receive prophecy or healing." Derision dripped from his words.

He turned and waved around him. "Look around you. Can you see any fast cars? Any private jets? Any mansions? These people live a pretty basic life. But they want nothing from me. They never ask for anything. Every time I come here, I have to make them take things from me. *Ma* Yise could live like a millionaire if she'd accepted the gift my father offered after I recovered. But she will not take even one kobo." His voice choked with emotion.

"Here is something that no one outside my family knows. Before I came here, I went to rehab in the USA. My parents spent a lot of money to get me clean. At rehab, people can be corrupted, bought. Find the right person and offer them the right price and you can get them to swap your urine sample for a clean one. Three months after I came back to Lagos, I was back to using drugs. As if nothing had changed until Freddie found me comatose from an overdose. It was the final straw for my parents. They knew I was going to die young unless something drastic happened. Kola made some enquiries and found out about this place. My parents agreed. It was the best decision they made as far as I'm concerned."

His muscles wound tight, his shoulders tense.

"I was only half aware the day I arrived here in a helicopter just like we did. I had to be sedated for the trip because I was too agitated from not having a hit. It would have been dangerous. I remember wondering where I was when I finally came to. I couldn't recognise anyone except Freddie. I did all I could to get out of here. I begged and bribed and threatened. Nothing worked. *Ma* Yise just cleaned me up when I was sick. Made sure I had water to drink. I ate food but didn't keep much down for a while. I was a wreck."

He shook his head. "When the craving got too much and I was delirious, I even tried walking to find the nearest town. They let me. Freddie and one of the men from the village were always nearby. I got lost. This place is just one mountain after another to a stranger. When I finally passed out, they brought me back to the hut. At that point, I was too sick to do much apart from shiver and groan in agony from the pain and fever. I never want to experience that again." He shuddered.

"One morning I woke up really hungry and *Ma* Yise gave me food. For the first time in weeks, perhaps months, I was lucid. I could talk without being doped. Then when I was strong enough, Freddie helped me to the waterfall and I had a bath for the first time in weeks. I spent a few more days recovering. Afterwards, I had to integrate with the village. *Ma* Yise said if I wanted to eat, I had to work. So I helped out in the farm and some days, I went out with the cattle herders. I learned the language and they accepted me as one of them."

He turned around to face her.

"*Ma* Yise saved my life. So when she says there's trouble coming to me, I believe her because I know she wants to help me. Not for what she can gain. But if you don't want to believe her, it's your prerogative. I can't force you."

He turned away.

Overwhelmed by his revelation and teary eyed, Rita leaned against him. The need to explain her earlier response made her body tremble and her voice quaked when she spoke.

"When my father died, I was consumed by so much anger. My parents were devout Christians, in church twice a week. We had family prayers every morning. We were brought up to believe in a God who cared for us and would always take care of us. So I couldn't understand why this same God would let so many bad things happen to us all at once. I'm in church every Sunday but it's a matter of rote rather than faith as I struggle to come to terms with what has happened."

She grabbed onto him and hugged him tight. His arms hung loose at the sides. Her heart hurt that he didn't return her hug, but she didn't let go. Couldn't let go. She loved him too much to give up.

"My response in the hut was just me showing my disdain for all things unexplainable. I would've had the same response if she stood at a pulpit. However, she seems a really nice woman and this place is wonderful. She is important to you. I get that." She sucked in a deep breath. "I trust you. So if you believe her, then I believe her."

His arms finally came up and wrapped around her. She sighed in gladness.

"What are we going to do? She wants us to get married. But your parents will go mad if they find out. They'll disinherit you."

He lifted her and sat her between his thighs so they were both facing the mountains and his arms engulfed her.

"I've been thinking about my parents' threat. I don't want to go against them or my brothers. But the alternative is that I'll lose you permanently and I can't live with that. I would rather lose my inheritance than lose you." His voice deepened with raw emotion and determination.

Tear pooled in her eyes and ran down her face. "Tony, it is a lot to give up for me. I don't even think I'm worth it."

"You are. My parents' money bought me good things but also brought me so much pain. I can survive without the money. After all, I lived in Beya for three months without money and I survived."

He tilted her head to the side so he could look at her face. His amber eyes blazed with intensity. Her breath caught in her throat and her heart thundered.

"With you, it is different. I am different. I know I'll survive whatever comes, if I have you with me."

His determination was all the encouragement she needed.

"Then, let's get married tonight," she said. She didn't know what the future held, and according to *Ma* Yise, it would be very bad at first. But together, they would overcome whatever lay ahead.

"You are an angel and I love you so much." He kissed her then, his lips soft and tender.

She tasted salty tears but wasn't sure if they were his or hers. Her skin tingled as her mind became fuzzy.

"I love you, too," she said when they broke apart and she put her head against his chest, listening to his heartbeat.

"Shall we go and tell *Ma* Yise? She'll be pleased." Tony grinned.

"I'm sure."

He stood and tugged her arm, helping her up. "I'm going to jump off and then help you down." With a two-step leap, he reached the base of the boulder. "Sit on the edge."

She did and he held onto her hips and lifted her off. Back on level ground, they both walked toward the settlement, Chibby and Freddie not far from them at any point.

They arrived at *Ma* Yise's hut to find a group of women gathered outside. Some were busy over cooking fires. Others were either chopping or crushing seeds or vegetables. They all beamed smiles at them.

Ma Yise waved them over to where she sat. Tony said something to her and she smiled when she replied.

"I asked her what all the fuss was about. She said they were preparing the wedding feast," he said.

Stunned, Rita asked, "How did she know we'd agreed to get married?"

"You want me to ask a woman who sees visions how she knew?" He chuckled.

"You've got a point," she conceded.

A young man came around the corner and started chatting with Tony. *Ma* Yise took Rita's hand and pointed to a stool.

"I'm supposed to go with the men," Tony said, looking a bit worried. "I don't want to leave you, but apparently, I'm not supposed to see you again until the actual rites are performed. Will you be okay with the women?"

"Of course." They were all women. Sure, she didn't understand a word they said. But how hard could it be sitting here with them? "I'll be fine."

Ma Yise said something and waved her hand as if shooing Tony off.

He squeezed her hand once and walked off with the man and the two bodyguards.

Rita settled in her stool and watched the women. Ma Yise was giving orders and people were scuttling around her, carrying out whatever she said. The delicious aroma from the foods they prepared made her mouth water.

She hadn't brought her phone and she didn't own a watch, so she couldn't tell the time, anyway. But the sun now hung low in the sky, and soon, it would be sunset.

Some young women turned up and joined in. After a while, one of them pulled her up. The girl could've been around her age.

"Come." She gestured with her hand for Rita to follow her. Rita glanced at *Ma* Yise who waved at her and nodded. She took that as approval that she could go with the girls.

This time, they took a different path from the one she'd gone on to find Tony earlier. The girls chatted and giggled along the way. One of them carried a basket while the other carried rolls of colour-dyed wrappers.

"You speak English," Rita said to the girl who'd first spoken to her.

"A little," she said. "I learn in school."

"Oh. You speak well. Where do you go to school?" Her skin flushed with excitement that she could have some conversation at least.

"In the village." The girl grinned. "Brother Tony give us teacher and school."

"He did? That's great." Tony hadn't even mentioned that he'd done that.

"Yes, he do good. He give us many thing. School. Water from pipes and even bus to take us to town once a month."

"My name is Rita. What's your name?"

"Yise."

Rita reared back. "*Ma* Yise is your mother?"

"Yes, Tony is my brother. So you be my sister when you marry."

Very soon, she heard the rush of water cascading over rocks. They rounded the corner and she saw the waterfall. Like everything else she'd seen, the sight was wonderful when it came into view. Droplets of water settled on her skin and clothes.

Some of the girls took their clothes off and dived into the pool of water.

"You go undress and clean." Yise waved at the water.

Rita felt a little uncomfortable undressing in front of strangers. But when Yise took off her clothes, she knew she couldn't stand in the sidelines. Tentatively, she removed her clothes and placed them where Yise indicated. She rushed into the water, and the cool drops on her hot skin felt glorious. The girls giggled and someone splashed her. Soon, they were all splashing each other.

Yise tugged Rita's arm and pointed to the shoreline. "Time you dress."

Rita nodded and followed the girl out of the water. But instead of letting her get back into her jeans and top, the girls pulled out hand-woven *leppe* fabric that looked similar to the traditional top and skirt she'd seen Fulani girls wear. As she sat on a rock, they braided her hair and inserted what looked like cowry beads into the intricate braids. Then, they decorated her skin in beautiful designs with something similar to henna. Someone pulled out a small, old chipped mirror and held it in front of her.

Rita's heart stopped. She couldn't even recognise herself. She looked... "Beautiful. You made me beautiful," she said in a breathy voice.

The girls giggled.

"My brother will have a beautiful wife," Yise said.

Rita's cheeks heated up and the girls giggled some more.

"Come. The sun is setting." Yise pointed at the sky where the sun was disappearing below the horizon.

They headed back to the settlement and the girls sang a song and clapped their hands. At *Ma* Yise's, they led her into the hut lit with a kerosene lamp.

"You sit inside until my brother comes," Yise said.

Her mother put a veil over Rita's head. They both left her in the hut. The singing outside continued, the women joining the girls. It seemed there were more people out there now.

Rita sat and listened, fidgeting nervously and trying not to put out all the threads from her beautiful attire as she fought to control her anxiety.

She was getting married. How did that happen? She'd dated Anayo for a year and they hadn't been any closer to marriage in all that time. They hadn't even discussed it after she'd told him she wanted to wait until she was married to have sex.

Now, she was only moments away from being traditionally wed. Yes, they would still have to travel to her hometown and do the marriage rites according to her custom. But this was still valid with regards to both of them. In Nigeria traditional marriages were as legitimate as civil ones. They would be man and wife after this.

And she'd only known Tony just over one week. *OMG.* She nearly hyperventilated at the thought. How did she go from wanting to make Tony and his family pay to marrying him in one week? Her mother would think she'd gone mad. Kechi would think she'd taken some drug. Nobody she knew ever did stuff like this. Yet, here she was, and she wouldn't change it for anything. All that mattered was her and Tony.

Ma and Yise came inside and her heart thudded. Was Tony outside?

"It's time." Yise helped her stand and she followed them.

Outside, the dark night was lit with lamps and it took a while for her eyes to adjust to the scene. Women stood in front of her, blocking her view of the crowd. *Ma* Yise made sure her veil stayed in place and Rita held onto it. The singing ladies parted and she could finally see the crowd. They led her to a chair. Her palms sweated and her hands trembled. This was actually happening.

Her skin prickled and she looked up and met Tony's gaze. Her breath hitched. He was dressed in a similar fabric to what she had on, in trousers and a tunic. He couldn't seem to take his hungry eyes off her. Her body flushed and she lowered her eyes.

The whole ceremony passed in a haze. She couldn't understand most of what was said in Beya, anyway. Music and dancing started. People ate and drank but she was still no closer to Tony.

Yise came to her. "You follow me."

She stood and followed her. They walked past *Ma* Yise's hut.

"Where are you going?" she asked.

"You will find out." The girl smiled at her. She stopped before the hut Tony had taken her to first and waved her on. "You go and wait for your new husband."

"Aren't you coming in?"

"No." Yise giggled. "You don't need me."

Rita wiped her palms on her skirt and walked into the hut. Her mouth dropped open. It had been transformed. Colourful fabric draped down the walls. The bed was spread out with beautiful blankets and the floor had woven mats covering it.

A lump formed in her throat. She couldn't believe how much trouble they'd gone to in order to make the place look so amazing. She was so enraptured with everything she didn't hear Tony come in. The skin on her back prickled with heat.

"How is the new Mrs. Essien?"

CHAPTER TWENTY-SEVEN

Rita swivelled around, heart thumping. Tony stood before her, masculine and magnificent in his attire. Shadows played on his facial features, capturing some of the dangerous magic that had drawn her to him that first night in Abuja in the splendour and glamour of the hotel ballroom.

In this basic yet beautiful hut lit only by flickering lamplight and decorated with fabrics and blankets, there was something primal about the way he studied her, his lips curling in a slow-building smile that had butterflies fluttering in her belly.

"You are the most beautiful bride I've ever seen."

The awe in his voice made it sound deeper than normal, the effect on her body even more pronounced as the temperature in the room seemed to rise.

Surely, he exaggerated. Surely, he'd seen brides more beautiful than her, dressed in expensive, sophisticated bridal gowns. She'd seen photos from his brothers' weddings. Ebony and Faith had looked divine in designer dresses with their hair and makeup done by award-winning stylists.

Rita, however, wore an outfit made by local tribesmen—she'd found out that the fabric weavers were men—and with her hair and makeup styled by local girls who'd barely left their teen years behind.

"Love must really be blind," she said in a croaky voice as a lump formed in her throat.

"Why do you say that?" he asked, still appraising her as if he couldn't keep his eyes off her. His hands, however, stayed hidden behind his back.

"Only love could make you say I was the most beautiful bride you've ever seen when I know you've seen other women dressed in lovelier attires."

Her heart warmed because she knew he loved her. Only a man in love would say such wonderful things, surely.

"Buttons, you are beautiful to me whether you are strutting around in a shimmering sexy red silk dress that looked painted on—" He winked at her and her cheeks heated, "—or lying in my bed wearing just my t-shirt or standing here dressed like a Beya bride."

"Really?" Her lips curled into a smile. He really knew how to make her feel good.

"Yes. It doesn't matter what you're wearing. Every time I see you, you take my breath away and make me want to rip your clothes off."

He closed his eyes and groaned, the deep rumble echoing off the mud walls.

"And right now, I have the father of all hard-ons. I'm afraid if I take a step, I'll be inside you within seconds and I'm really struggling to keep my control."

"Oh!" She covered her mouth with her hands. She'd forgotten about that. They were married so they could finally do the deed.

Have sex. Make love. *Fuck.*

He lifted his eyelids and a grin spread across his face, his darkened irises gleaming even as his pupils dilated. "You forgot the main event? The prize you made me wait for?"

She giggled as more butterflies took flight in her stomach. "Technically, I didn't make you wait. I would've given it up that first night."

He stepped forward and stood so close, his warm breath whispered on her skin. His shoulders tensed visibly and his hands balled by his sides.

"I'm glad you didn't. If I had fucked you that night, it would've been for all the wrong reasons. Tainted. That night, I'd wanted to fuck and toss you away. You would've been just another piece of ass, a means to an orgasm. Another high."

She'd known his reputation with women before she'd met him. He took playboy to a different level. Yet, her stomach twisted at his words and her eyes smarted. When Anayo had been mistreating her, she'd held onto the comfort of not giving her body to him. His power over her mind had been limited. However, if her plan for the night with Tony had worked, he would've used and then dumped her. *She* would've been tainted. Damaged goods. She wouldn't have recovered anytime soon. She lowered her head as tears pooled in her eyes.

He reached for her then, tilting her head up with his hand under her chin.

"Baby, I'm sorry. I didn't mean to upset you," he said as he thumbed her tears away and she leaned into his warm palm. "I wanted to explain to you why it was important to me that we waited. Since I became sexually active, I have never waited for a woman. If she offered, I took it. But with you, it was different. You are different. It's been tough walking the dicey line of control when I've been so close to being inside you. But I knew I couldn't treat you the way I treated the others. I care about you too much."

"Oh, Tony." She raised her hands up to his shoulders. "I'm not upset with you. You saved me from myself by sending me away that first night. At first, I was disappointed. But when I saw you at the auditions and the way you treated me afterward, I knew you'd been trying to protect me by sending me away. And I fell for you so hard, it hurts. I love you."

His lips covered hers, brushing softly from side to side.

"I love you, too," his hot breath whispered against her skin. "When you walked into that lift with me, you were mine. When you let me eat your pussy on the sofa, you were mine. Tonight, I'm going to make you mine for real."

He growled his words, the deep rumbles vibrating in her core, making her clench hard on empty space. She wanted him inside her.

"Make me yours," she managed to breathe out through a constricted throat.

"Now, here's an invitation I can't refuse."

He swept her up into his arms and she yelped as he carried her a few steps to the raised platform bed. Gently, he lowered her flat on the surface, the soft blankets cushioning her descent.

Tony covered her body with his and kissed her again. Hard, this time, his mouth claiming hers as his taut body pinned her down. She savoured this rough and tough aspect of him as his tongue ravaged her mouth, leaving her gasping for breath. He fed her, breathing life into her, setting her body alight with lust, with desire for him.

She moaned and he swallowed it. Her body writhed beneath his as his hands clasped hers above her head. Though she still had her clothes on, she felt exposed and needy.

He broke the kiss and they both panted for air. She sucked in oxygen in gulps, her lungs filled with the scent of him, spicy and masculine. She wanted to feel him all over.

Still gripping both of her hands above her head so she couldn't reach down for him, he nuzzled between her shoulder and her neck. The spot sensitised to the feel of the rough skin of his nose and then the soft brush of his lips, she moaned long and arched her body off the bed.

"Do you know what you do to me when you make all the sweet noises and move your body like that? You tell me how much you want me." He sucked the skin on her neck.

"I—I dooo," she keened and rubbed her hips against his, trying to find some friction for her clit. Her insides clenched so hard and without any panties on, her juices dripped down her thigh and left a wet patch on her skirt. He was turning her into an addict. An addict for him. "Tony, please..."

"I know, Baby." His hot palm covered her exposed midriff, scorched her skin as it travelled up before squeezing her left breast. More electricity zinged from her breast to her core. She closed her eyes and bit her lower lip, holding back a moan.

"You want me inside you and I want to be there, too. But this is your first time. *Our* first time. And I don't want to rush it. I want you to remember it for the right reasons. Moreover, I'm afraid of hurting you."

He pushed up her top and tugged it over her head, exposing her upper half. Lowering his head, he sucked her right breast into his mouth, rolled his tongue around the tip and then nipped it lightly, all the while squeezing and playing with her left breast. She got lost in sensation, heat and sparks wrecking her sense of self.

Gripping his head against her breast, she cried out again. As crazy as she was already feeling, she wanted more. More of everything.

As if sensing her need, he glided his palm over her contracting stomach muscles, pushed her skirt down, and exposed the V of her thighs.

"Raise your legs."

She did and he tugged the skirt off, leaving her bare and vulnerable.

Glinting eyes studied her, intense and heated. "You really are fucking beautiful. How did I get so lucky?"

Fingers parted her lower lips, slid down to her opening and smeared her juices over her folds as they stroked gently, as if coaxing her into submission.

Her thighs fell apart, opening up for him. Her hips rocked into his palm, seeking the delicious contact.

"That's it, Baby. Open up for me. Let me feel you tremble as I make you come."

He pressed the heel of his palm on her button. A fever spread from her toes, charged through her nerve endings, and she cried out in ecstasy even as she felt his fingers surge inside. They worked her tight opening as his mouth covered her clit and her hips rocked uncontrollably, another wave of orgasm passing over her.

He gripped her hips, held her down as he lapped with his tongue one minute, swirling circles around her clit another. Then he sucked her into his mouth. Feeling giddy, black spots formed around her eyes as she fell into her third orgasm.

When she came to, Tony stood at the edge of the bed with no clothes on. In the flickering lamplight, he looked like a dark angel, muscles honed and tense, eyes feverishly intense, his erection swollen and almost touching his navel. He looked magnificent. Her heart that had been returning to its normal pace beat faster.

"I need to be inside you," he said, his voice deep and rough with his hunger for her. "But I don't have a condom. Since we agreed it wasn't going to happen until we get married, I stopped carrying condoms. I didn't know we were going to be married today."

"Oh." She pursed her lips as the reality hit her. She hadn't been thinking about protection. She'd never really thought about it until now. He was doing that thing again. Protecting her. She really wanted to kiss him right now.

"I haven't had sex without a condom in five years. Every six months along with the drug testing, I have to be tested for HIV, among other things. It is part of the contract I signed with my parents. I'm clean, I promise you."

"I believe you." She shifted, sitting up and pulling her legs together.

"Don't do that," he growled. "Even if I can't be inside you right now, I still want to see all of you. Your sweet pussy is mine. Don't hide it from me."

Her body flushed with heat and her breath caught in her throat. This man was her undoing with his dirty talking and his possessive actions. No other man would ever make her respond the way she did to Tony. She moved her thighs apart, letting him see what he wanted. What belonged to him. She was his to do whatever he pleased. She didn't want their lovemaking to be disrupted but she had to be honest with him, too. "Tony, I've never been tested for HIV or anything else."

"You were not sexually active, so we can safely say you are clean." He gave her a huge grin and she relaxed as he knelt on the bed between her legs. The wood creaked. "But that also means you are probably not on any contraceptive pill, either."

"No, I'm not on the pill."

"Then I won't come inside you. Although, there's still a chance you'll get pregnant. Is that okay, Baby?"

Breathless, she didn't care at this point. Just wanted him inside her. To do something to soothe the ache in her core. "Yes."

He gripped her thighs and pulled her down, lining her up so the broad tip of his hard shaft nudged her wet entrance. He rocked his hips forward.

Her body tensed at the tight feeling. Sweat beaded her forehead.

"Relax, Baby," he said and leaned forward, kissing her. As he leaned on his elbow, his fingers worked her clit.

Delicious zings and tingles returned to her body, warming it, distracting her from the thick shaft trying to fill her up. She moaned, writhed as his fingers seemed to play a tune on her labia, driving her insane. Until she felt him slide out and surge back in. A twinge of pain spread out and she cried out.

He held still, his whole body rigid, sweat dripping down his face. "Do you want me to stop?"

"No." Not now that they'd gone past the hard part.

He kissed her again, and with excruciating slowness, started moving in and out of her.

Soon, the twinge of pain transformed into pleasure. As if a dam burst within her. Her whole body came alive, her channel clamping around him. She kissed him back without reservation, clinging onto his shoulders and loving him with her mouth and her body. Her nipples chaffed against the roughness of his chest, making them tingle. The sweat on their bodies made them slide against each other. She loved this connection with him, never knew their joining could be this way. That real sex would feel this good.

"You feel so good, Baby. So tight and hot and wet." He slid out of her and surged back in. "Fuck. I don't think I'm going to last long."

He seemed to swell and throb inside her. She clenched around him, gentle ripples sweeping through her. He slid his hand between their bodies, finding her swollen and throbbing clit. She moaned, grinding up against his palm as her pleasure rose.

The slapping sound of flesh against flesh filled the room along with their groans and moans. Soon, she became lost in bliss as they rocked together, the lubrication and sweat making them glide against each other.

"Oh, God. Tony, I'm going to..." Her body wound tight, every nerve, every piece of her on edge. Like a starburst, she exploded into a million pieces, delirium taking over her mind.

His pace quickened as he grabbed her thigh, angling it, his hips thrusting hard, slamming into her in a rhythmic motions. "Fuck. I'm coming, Baby."

Loving this raw, unrestrained wildness, she wrapped her legs around his hips, urging him farther inside her with each slam. She didn't want him pulling out. "Come inside me. I want all of you."

He broke rhythm. "Are you sure? You could get pregnant."

"I'm sure. I want our baby, if it happens." She couldn't explain the tightening in her chest except that her heart had expanded with her love for him. If they made a baby together, then they would both love him or her with the same relentless energy they loved each other.

His face brightened in a sexy smile that only made her feel even mushier as her breath became choppier.

"Then I better deliver, in this case." He pulled out and slammed in. "Essiens always deliver."

True. She smiled at his arrogant words. His first brother already had a son and his second brother had a child on the way. Would they make the third Essien grandchild tonight?

Tony returned to thrusting into her with powerful strokes that rocked her body and drove her pleasure up again. She tried to match his movement, surging her hips up to meet him. He lifted her legs, placing them on his shoulders, so that she was almost bent in half as he pistoned into her, practically nailing her into the bed.

"Come for me again," he said, bending forward and kissing her hard as he pressed down on her clit.

"O—oh—oh!" She detonated, her orgasm ripped from her before she knew it was there.

"Fuck!" His body rocked out of control.

She was barely aware of his grunt as he tensed and jerked his hips before collapsing and panting beside her as she tried to catch her own breath.

CHAPTER TWENTY-EIGHT

Tony lay on his side watching Rita sleep. He tucked the light sheet covering her naked body into the corner, her breathing lifting it gently.

Married. He was married to Rita, and they'd had sex. He'd been inside her and she'd blown his mind away. He'd been so out of breath afterwards, he'd collapsed beside her, panting to draw much-needed air into his lungs.

Watching her sleep, he wanted her all over again. Craved her so much his skin itched and his balls ached. But he loved her even more and he knew she had to be sore. He couldn't go back inside her so soon. This had been her first time and she'd been so tight, gripping around him like a slick vise. That he'd managed to hold off for so long had been damned miraculous.

Outside, the sounds of merriment carried on. But it wasn't as loud as it had been earlier. Perhaps some of the villagers had left.

Rita rolled over to her side, snuggling up to him. He tucked her into his side and threw an arm over her body, holding her close.

Married. The word scrolled through his mind again. She was now his responsibility. His to hold and to cherish. His to protect. Even more reason he couldn't screw up ever again. He couldn't let her down. He had to make a future for both of them.

His movie business was picking up. In the next few years, he knew he could make it a huge success. Great thing she loved acting. They could work on so many projects together. They could build a life together. Wouldn't it be great if her movie career took off just as his production company succeeded? They would be great working and playing together.

A tapping sound at the door had him turning his head. "I'm coming," he called out as he pulled his discarded trousers on.

He pushed the door aside. *Ma* Yise stood outside it. People sat around a campfire farther down her compound, laughing and chatting.

"Have you joined with your wife?" *Ma* Yise asked.

"Yes." He rubbed his hand over the back on his neck as unease passed through him. He knew what she'd come for, but it still unsettled him. He usually wasn't one to shy away from other people knowing about his sex life. But when it came to Rita, he wasn't keen to share her with others.

"Did you clean her with the white cloth just as you were instructed? Was she untouched?"

"Yes."

"Bring it to me."

"But *Ma*, why do you need it? I'm not comfortable with you showing her blood to the whole village."

"I know in your world, our practices seem primitive to you. But trust me, my child. There is a purpose to everything I do. I told you trouble is coming, and when it happens, everyone here will blame her for it. If I show them the proof of her purity now, it will help to soften their hearts against her, if they know she came to you pure of body."

"Whether she was a virgin or not shouldn't matter. I wasn't one." He lowered his voice, not wanting anyone else to overhear this ridiculous conversation.

"When you came here first, remember you had to earn our trust by living with us for a long time," she said in a matching low voice. "Your wife has not had the time for everyone to get to know her true nature. I'm afraid there will be no time for that. This—" she swept her arms to encompass their surroundings, "—should be a safe place for

both of you. I don't want that to change. So please, get me
the cloth."

He nodded and returned inside the hut. He was uneasy
about this but he trusted *Ma* Yise. Still, he had to convince
Rita. She stirred when he sat on the bed.

"Where did you go?" she asked as she rubbed her eyes.

"I was just speaking to *Ma* Yise," he replied, stroking
her arms up and down. Her skin felt so soft and he wanted
to climb back into bed with her.

"Is everything okay?" She leaned onto her elbow.

"Yes, but she wants me to give her something." He
picked up the piece of cloth he'd tossed on the floor when
he'd cleaned her up. "She wants this."

Rita's face screwed into a frown. "Why?"

"It is part of their tradition. It is presented to the family
as proof that you were a virgin."

"Oh. What if I wasn't?" She sat up, pulling the sheet to
cover her body in a defensive posture.

He didn't like that. He tossed the cloth down and stood.
"Don't worry about it. I'll tell her no. You are not Beya, so
it shouldn't matter."

"But it matters to them. It matters to *Ma* Yise. And if
you don't show them, what would they think?" she asked,
looking more worried.

"I don't know." He shrugged. "Don't worry about it."

She shook her head. "They will think I'm no good for
you. Please give it to her."

"Rita—"

"Tony, please. These people are important to you and as
such, they are important to me, too. I don't want them to
think badly of me. I don't mind, really. It's just a piece of
cloth with my blood stains on it. At least, there is something
to show them. I would've been more worried if there wasn't
anything on it."

"Okay." He picked up the cloth again and bent over to
kiss her on the lips. "For the record, if there was no blood
stain on it, I would have cut myself and put my blood on
it."

She leaned back as if surprised, staring at him intensely. "You would do that for me?"

"I would do anything for you, Buttons. Anything."

She grabbed his head, kissing him deeply. "I love you, Tony Essien. Hurry up and get back in here so I can show you how much."

"Yes, Mrs. Essien." He saluted with a wink before hurrying back to the door.

He passed the cloth to *Ma* Yise who promptly raised it so that all still gathered outside could see it in the bonfire light. A loud cheer rose into the night as he shut the door and returned to the bedside.

"Are you sure you're not sore, baby? We can wait."

"I can't wait. I'm now Mrs. Tony Essien, which means I'm entitled to take liberties on your body," she said as she sat up and straddled him, pushing him down on the bed.

"You can take all the liberties you want." He chuckled until she planted her lips on his left nipple and nipped him. He groaned as a bolt of electric current travelled to his balls.

Even though he wanted to flip her over and jam his dick between her thighs, he let her take her liberties. This was now his new reality. She was Mrs. Tony Essien. And what his wife wanted, his wife got.

***

After she'd gotten her fill of taking liberties, he'd been so strung he'd flipped her over and lost himself in her wet heat. Yise had woken them sometime mid-morning with breakfast before dragging Rita out to the river. Tony had used the makeshift shower he'd built at the back of his hut which was a simple pump that opened a valve and pumped water out of a bucket. After dressing, he was chatting with Freddie when he heard the sound of a helicopter. Surprised, they both cocked their heads and looked up at the sky. Sure enough, a helicopter approached.

"Are we going back today?" Freddie asked. He clearly sounded as astounded as Tony.

"No. We are not due back until tomorrow," Tony said. "Go and find out who it is. I'm going to look for Rita."

Freddie nodded and headed off in the direction of the clearing their helicopter used as a landing strip. Tony turned to head in the opposite direction but found *Ma* Yise coming his way.

"It has started," she said, pointing up at the helicopter hovering to land in the distance. "I sent for Yise and your wife to return quickly."

"What has started?" he asked, confused, his gaze still fixed in the distance.

"Your troubles." She gripped his arm, making him look down at her. She seemed really concerned, the first time he'd seen her worried since he'd first come to Beya five years ago. "Be strong, my son. You can overcome this."

"What—"

"Tony," Rita called out as she and Yise hurried toward them. Chibby followed behind. "We saw the helicopter and ran home. I thought we were going back to Lagos tomorrow." She stared from Tony to *Ma* Yise and back again.

Tony wanted to ask *Ma* Yise what exactly his troubles were supposed to be. But he turned his attention to Rita, instead.

"I don't know why the helicopter is here. I'm as surprised as you," he said. "Freddie has gone to find out who it is. I was waiting for you to come back."

"I'm glad she is here now, so you can both hear this," *Ma* Yise said. "Translate so your wife understands."

Tony nodded and told Rita, who grabbed his hand as she stood beside him and faced *Ma* Yise.

"You both need to be strong for each other." *Ma* Yise stared at both of them as Tony translated.

"No matter how bad things get, do not lose hope or faith in each other." She gripped Tony and Rita's hands in each of hers. "Do you understand me?"

"Yes, *ma*," they both said in response.

Tony turned as he heard approaching footsteps. Freddie walked beside Kola. A knot tightened in his stomach. Something bad had happened, although Kola's expression was unreadable. He knew they wouldn't send the big man to him unless it was something bad.

"What's happened?" he asked before he'd even greeted their security chief.

Kola greeted *Ma* Yise in the native language before turning to Tony. "Your father asked me to bring you home."

"Why? Is he ill?"

Kola shook his head.

"Is it Mum? Something happened to her?"

"No. Your parents are well. They just want you to come home."

"That's bullshit. My parents aren't going to ask me to come home unless something's happened. Tell me."

Kola grabbed his shoulder and pulled him aside. "Petersen came to see your parents yesterday. After their meeting, your father asked me to come here today to bring you home."

"What did Petersen say to them?"

"I don't know. I just know that your safety is at stake and your parents want you home."

Tony frowned. "Petersen threatened me?"

"Yes," Kola said. "I believe so."

"What the hell!" he raged. What was wrong with the Petersen man, anyway? There was a time he'd thought the guy was cool. But he was quickly turning into a pain in the butt.

"Okay," he said. "Give us a few minutes to pack up and then we can head out."

He turned and walked to Rita. "Something's come up. We have to go back to Lagos."

"Is everyone okay? Your parents? Family?" Her voice sounded panicky.

He stroked up and down her arms to reassure her. "Everyone is fine. Something came up with the Petersen investigation and my parents wanted me to come home for safety."

"Petersen?" Her eyes widened. "What has he done?"

"I don't know. We'll find out when we get to Lagos."

Luckily, there wasn't too much to pack, just an overnight bag. The boxes of supplies and bags of food he'd brought in the helicopter had already been distributed to the villagers.

After a tearful goodbye from Yise and her mother, they flew out that afternoon. The flight back proved quiet. Noticing Rita seemed unsettled, he held onto her hand throughout. *Ma* Yise's warning plagued his mind but he tried not to think about it. Yes, his parents had summoned him back. But if they'd met with Petersen in their home, then it couldn't be that bad. At the least, it shouldn't be life-threatening.

And if Petersen was upset that Tony's relationship with Rita had morphed into something stronger, then the man would have to get over it.

At the heliport, two cars waited to take them home.

"I'll take Rita to her house and you can go home with Freddie in the other car," Kola said as they strode to the cars.

"No." Tony shook his head. "Rita is coming home with me."

He couldn't even imagine being apart from her, especially so soon after getting married. Although Kola didn't know that.

Tony and Rita got into the back seat with Freddie up front with the driver. Kola sat in the other car with Chibby and the other driver. With Monday evening traffic, the drive home took a little long.

When they got home, Tony walked Rita into his house. "Welcome home, Buttons. Make yourself comfortable. I have to go and see my parents to find out what's going on. Will you be okay?"

"Sure." She smiled at him. "Are you going to tell them?"

"Not yet. Not until I find out what's going on," he replied. "When I get back, we'll sort out how we're going to move your things in here."

"Okay. Don't be long, husband." She stood on tiptoes and kissed him.

He pulled her in, holding her waist as he deepened the kiss. "You stay right here, wife. I won't be long." He tapped her butt and chuckled at the sound of her squeal as he headed over to the family house.

His parents were waiting for him in the living room. Kola must have informed them he was on his way. His mother looked quite apprehensive as she rapped her fingers on the arm of the sofa.

His father appeared more composed but he knew his parents well enough to know when something was seriously wrong. He greeted them but all he got back were nods in response.

"Sit down, Tony. We need to talk to you," his father said.

He lowered himself into the sofa opposite. "Is this about Petersen? Kola said he came here yesterday."

His father's sigh filled the air. "Yes, it is about Petersen. He contacted me and I invited him over to sort out this whole mess once and for all."

"And what did he want?" Tony clasped his hands together.

His mother shifted in her chair, her gaze not meeting his.

"You," his father said, his voice hard. "Petersen wants you. He claims you are his son."

CHAPTER TWENTY-NINE

Tony burst out laughing. He couldn't suppress the hysterical need to laugh out loud at the most ridiculous statement ever uttered by his father who delivered it in his most deadpan expression.

His father had to be joking, and this had to be one hell of a prank. He glanced up at his parents after his bout of laughter. Neither of them cracked a smile. In fact, his mother looked even more uncomfortable, his father's expression harder than before.

"That is craziest thing I've ever heard," he said when he'd finally calmed down. "I hope you suggested to Mr. Petersen that he needed to see a psychiatrist. Perhaps we can refer him to Dr. Uwaifo because the man has gone bat-shit crazy."

Dr. Uwaifo was considered one of the best psychiatrists in Nigeria and had treated Tony for his substance abuse. He would happily recommend Petersen as a patient.

"Of course I didn't believe him," his father said. "I wanted to throw him out of the house for making that statement."

"You should've done," Tony said. "The man has obviously lost his mind."

"But he insisted that he was correct, and he also brought this with him." His father picked up a brown envelope from the side table and held it in Tony's direction.

"What is it?" he asked.

"Take it," his father said. "This is the only reason I didn't kick Petersen out of here yesterday."

Something in his father's voice made him wary. The knot that had been in his stomach since Kola had turned up in Beya tightened. He took the envelope and gingerly pulled the contents out.

He tugged out a sheaf of papers with printed-out text. The title grabbed his attention immediately and his insides froze.

Exclusive Exposé: Druggie Tony Essien may not be an Essien, after all.

Heart thumping against his chest at an increasing rate, he scanned the rest of the page.

"What the hell is this?" he asked, this whole body tense as he sat on the edge of the sofa, feeling sickened. The article included details of his life and claimed they had insider information he wasn't an Essien. It also went on to outline his drug abuse with no obvious mention of his recovery.

"That article is going to be all over the internet and news media by tomorrow morning if we don't agree to Petersen's demand," his father said.

"Petersen? How the hell did he get this information?" He glanced from the paper to his father, his insides churning. What did he ever do to Petersen for the man to want to ruin his life?

"Didn't you see the name of the person who wrote the article?"

Tony glanced down at the paper in his hand. "R. Dike." His heart stopped and he dropped the paper as if it had bitten him. "Rita...wrote this?"

"It seems you brought a poisonous snake into our family." The vitriol in his father's voice made him glance up. "And you're not the only one to have made that mistake."

"Rita wouldn't do this." He sprang from his chair and paced the living room space. "She wouldn't betray me like this. She promised."

She was his heart and soul. He'd taken her to Beya and she'd married him, for fuck's sake. She just wouldn't do this, damn it!

"Who else knew about the drugs and why is it coming out now, if not her?" his father asked, his anger evident in his voice and clenched fists.

His mother looked ready to burst and he wondered why she hadn't said anything so far. She was usually more on his case than his father.

"No one else," Tony said, pausing to think about it. "Rita was the only one I told."

Only his close family members, Freddie, and Kola knew about his drug addiction. Dr. Uwaifo knew but he was a reputable doctor bound by client confidentiality. When he'd been treated for the drug overdose at hospital, he'd been taken to their family doctor's hospital. The staff that treated him had been made to sign confidentiality agreements and his room had been off-limits to anyone other than the nurse and doctor taking care of him. It made no sense for them to drag this up five years later when he'd been clean for so long.

"There you have it." His father waved in confirmation of his words. "I'm sorry she made a fool out of you, pretending to love you. But you are not the only one who's been duped."

Tony's chest felt weighted and the back of his throat hurt. He didn't want to listen to any more of this. *She promised me…She played me.*

His mind spun. His chest constricted and he couldn't get any air into his lungs. He doubled over in pain, gasping for air.

"Tony!" his mother exclaimed.

His father's hand settled on his shoulder. "Are you okay, son?"

"I'm okay." Sucking in a breath, he straightened and stepped away from his father who didn't return to his seat. "I can't believe Rita wrote such nasty things about me. I need to talk to her."

"There's more you need to know," his father said. "Petersen wants a DNA test."

Fury swept through Tony and he swivelled around to face his parents. "Why the hell are you even entertaining this, Dad? Did you adopt me?"

If they had, then surely, they would have told him before now. But they had baby pictures of him with his mother in hospital when he was born, so it couldn't be that. The alternative was too bad to even think about.

"No. You are not adopted." His father looked as if he'd suddenly aged, worry lines appearing on his face, his skin losing some of its brightness.

"Then why?" He glared at them now, tired of this bullshit. He needed to confront Rita.

"It is best if your mother explains. I'm going to leave the two of you to talk." His father stood up and walked out of the room, his steps a little slower than usual.

Tony crossed his arms over his chest and waited. He was close to tapping his feet with impatience.

"Sit down, Tony, and I'll explain."

For the first time in as long as he could remember, his mother sounded cowered.

He stepped back and sat with a thump on the sofa, raised one eyebrow.

His mother cleared his throat and began. "Many years ago, before you were born, your father and I were having an affair. At the time, he was married to Felix's mother. I had thought he would leave her and marry me. But he didn't, and then Mark was born."

He knew this already. "How does Petersen feature in all this?"

"When Felix's mother died, your father mourned her loss. He neglected me as a result. Yes, he moved me in here after a year of mourning her and we lived together as husband and wife. But things were not the same any more. For months, years, he immersed himself in work and ignored me. We barely talked to each other, let alone touched each other. I felt lonely."

Her throat undulated as she swallowed and tugged at the collar of her blouse.

"I met Kris Petersen about that time. He was young, carefree, and charming. He paid me the attention I needed. I fell for him and we began an affair. After a while, Kris wanted me to leave your father. I couldn't. Your father finally started noticing me again and I thought we could mend things between us."

Fuck! Tony sprang from the sofa, restless energy coursing through him as he paced. "You had an affair with Petersen." He said it more as a statement than a question. "You cheated on Dad."

He thought his life was pretty screwed up, but this? *Fuck!* He froze. "Dad is not my father. Is that what you're saying?"

"No. Chief is your father."

"How can you be sure? You were sleeping with both men!" he accused.

"It was months after I broke up with Kris Petersen before I found out I was pregnant with you. You are Chief's son," she insisted.

He shook his head. "So why is Petersen claiming I'm his?"

"I don't know." She waved her hands in seeming exasperation. "He was angry when I told him it was over between us. He's held a grudge ever since. He's tried several times over the years to get me back. But I won't return to him. I guess this is his way of getting back at me and your father."

This was all kinds of fucked up. What would Petersen have to gain by claiming him as his son, if the man didn't think there was a chance? It made no sense. The only plausible explanation was that Petersen could be his father.

The flip side? There was a possibility he wasn't an Essien. He'd spent most of his life trying to fit in and be identified as an Essien. Trying to live up to the Essien name and failing. Now, there was a chance he wasn't even one. He was a nobody. His father wasn't his. He only had one blood brother instead of two.

Gut tightened and with bile in his throat, his head swam, making him feel faint. He needed some air.

"I need to get out of here," he said and strode toward the door.

"Tony, wait." Her voice sounded panicky.

He stopped but didn't turn around.

"What do you want to do about the DNA test? Petersen wants a response tonight or he'll release the exposé about you."

He swivelled around so fast, his head spun. His mother stood a few steps from him, wringing her hands.

"Do you think I give a shit about the article apart from the fact that the woman I love wrote such hateful things about me? Do you think I give a damn about Petersen's threat except for the fact that it means the world I knew— the things I thought were stable in my life—was all a load of bullshit? Hmmm?"

For the first time since he could remember, he became so angry at his mother that he leaned forward, towering over her.

She took a step back and fear registered in her eyes. "I'm just thinking about you. What this news will do to your future if it gets out."

"This is you, isn't it? All about the society and your status. All you ever worry about is what the people out there will think." He clenched and unclenched his fists by his sides. "Well, here is a newsflash. You better start thinking about the people around you. Like your husband and your children. What do we think about what you've done? Do you even care what I think, or is it just about keeping up appearances?"

She stiffened, standing taller. "Of course I care about you. You are my son. I did all this to protect you."

Leaning back, he gave a harsh bark of cold laughter. "To protect me? That's a laugh. You wanted to protect yourself. You wanted to eat your cake and have it. I bet Petersen was not as rich as he is now in those days, and when he asked you to be with him, you thought 'No way. I can't give up a wealthy man for a poor man when I can have all the money and the trimmings that come with it.' Isn't that what happened?"

Smack. His mother's hard slap made his head whip to the side.

"Don't you dare talk to me like that. No matter what's happened, I'm still your mother!"

He clutched his smarting cheek and glared at her. "Well, here's another newsflash. I wish you were not my mother."

He turned and stalked out of the room.

CHAPTER THIRTY

Tony paced the courtyard in front of his house. As much as he'd been eager to find out what Rita had done from her own lips, he dreaded uncovering the truth. The ache on his neck increased and he scrubbed his head.

Facing up to Rita would be facing up to the fact that he'd been taken for a ride. He'd made a total fool of himself. He'd laid out himself as an easy target. A *mugu*. And she'd taken him to the cleaners.

He doubled over, hands braced on his knees, and gulped in air to ease the tightening in his chest.

"Tony?"

Rita's soft voice had him squeezing his eyes shut. She sounded so concerned.

Yet, he knew it was all pretence. She didn't care about him. Back stiffened, he straightened just as she reached him.

"Are you okay?" she asked as she extended her hand toward him.

"Don't you fucking touch me!" he snapped, his entire body rigid. He didn't know what he'd do if she did. But it wouldn't be good for either of them.

She recoiled as if he'd slapped her, her eyes and lips wide open. She stared at him as if he had two heads. "What's wrong?"

"Oh, you'd like to know, wouldn't you? You'd like to know if you managed to ruin my life. Well, go ahead and start celebrating. You got your revenge."

"Huh?" She leaned back, the surprised expression remaining on her face. "Tony, what are you talking about?"

"Oh, you are good. You are very good. Oscar-fucking-material." He shook his head. No point in trying to talk to her. She would continue telling lies like she'd been doing. He had to get the proof somehow.

"Tony, please talk to me. What's going on?" She touched his arm.

It was a light, tentative touch as soft as the breeze. But he felt its tingle straight to his bones. He wanted to pull her into his arms and crush his lips against hers. He wanted to sink into her wet heat and forget that his world was beginning to crumble apart all around him.

And it annoyed him that he still craved her—still responded to her touch with such intensity—despite her betrayal.

Shaking her hand away, he sidestepped her and stalked into the house. He needed to be as far away from her as possible. Looking at her wore at his resolve and reminded him of all the passion they'd shared. Well, at least on his part. She had been pretending all this while, hadn't she? The content and tone of that article spelt out the way she truly felt about him. Hate and revenge were all she was interested in.

Mind churning, he took the steps two at a time upstairs and slammed the bedroom door.

He just needed some space to think. But his head was everywhere. So much information to assimilate in a short period of time. He pulled his t-shirt off, thinking a shower would help him gather his thoughts.

He knew he needed to deal with Petersen's threat. He needed to talk to somebody. Freddie would usually help him sound out his thoughts. But right now, he couldn't bear to face anyone. Didn't want to talk to anyone. How could he express the defeat crushing his shoulders that he couldn't even build a sincere relationship? Or the disgust eating away at his stomach like acid that he had allowed himself to be duped? Or the hurt shredding his heart into ribbons at being betrayed? Or the anger simmering in his veins that made him want to punch something?

He stepped into the closet and saw Rita's bag on the drawer. Her laptop sat at the top.

If she'd written that article, then a copy of it would be on her laptop. He could give it to Kola to search. He lifted it and walked into the room and sat on the bed. Then he lifted the lid and turned it on. No password was required and without much effort, he opened her file explorer. A quick search didn't bring up anything that looked like what he was looking for. Then he spotted her mailbox application and clicked on it. He searched through it and found a file in the sent folder.

He opened the document and scanned it quickly. It seemed to be a bare-boned, less vitriolic copy of the same article he'd left in his father's house. Perhaps the revised copy had been edited elsewhere.

"What are you doing with my laptop?"

He glanced up. Rita strode across the room, her eyes blazing.

"You were being abrasive outside," she continued. "Now I catch you with my laptop. What is going on, Tony?" She stood with her hands akimbo.

"I was searching for this." He turned the screen around so she could see it.

"You are snooping on me?" she shouted. "I thought that was something the rest of your family did."

Balling his fists, he ignored her dig at his family. With his luck, he didn't have a family anymore, anyway. "Is that really all you can say after what you've done?"

"I don't know what's gotten into you." She came around and snatched up the laptop, staring at the screen. She covered her mouth with her hand when she saw the document. "Oh my God. How did you find this? I thought I deleted it."

He stumbled back a step, hand clutching his stomach. "You didn't want me to see it."

"Of course I didn't want you to see it. I don't know what I was thinking when I wrote it." She fiddled with her laptop, closing it down.

She might as well have plunged a serrated knife into his heart. He hurt all over. "So it's true. You wrote it," he muttered to himself and stared at her as if just seeing her for the first time. How could someone wrapped up in such an innocent exterior be so cruel?

"Yes, I did. But—"

"I don't want to hear it," he cut her off, grabbed his t-shirt, and pulled it over his head as he walked to the door.

He needed to get away from her before he did something he would regret. He'd already lost his temper with his mother. The hurt he felt at Rita's betrayal was a lot worse. He didn't know what he would do to her if he stayed in the same room. His head felt as if it was going to explode. He wanted to smash his fist through a wall.

Gripping the door frame, he turned around, his gaze fixed on her face, disgust making him sneer. "Was anything that happened between us real for you, or was it all an act?"

"Tony, I love you. Of course everything between us is real." As she spoke, all he could see was his mother's image standing in her place.

Revulsion turned his stomach, bile rising in his throat.

"Liar!" He spat out and turned away from her, walking down the stairs and out of the house.

He got on his bike and rode to the main gates. The gateman didn't move from the spot to open the gates.

"Hussein, open the fucking gates!" he snapped at the man.

The man shifted from one leg to the other. "*Oga* Tony, I no fit."

Tony's mind exploded into red mist. He kicked out the stand on his bike and ran at the man. He grabbed Hussein by the collar, yanked him up, and kicked his legs in a sweeping motion. Next, he was on top of the man on the hard ground, pounding into him.

Someone yanked him up and he lashed out. A band of arms caged him.

"Tony, take a deep breath. Calm down."

Panting, he recognised Kola's deep voice. Slowly, the mist cleared and he saw Chibby and Freddie helping Hussein up. Blood ran down the man's nose and Freddie pulled out a handkerchief from his pocket and gave it to the gatekeeper.

"Let me go," Tony said, hating being restrained.

"Not until I know you've calmed down," Kola said. "What happened?"

"He wouldn't open the gates for me when I asked him to." He sucked in a deep breath and blew it out. "I'm calm now."

Kola released him and stepped back. "You know the rules, Tony. You're not allowed out on your own."

"Fuck the rules," he said as he strode to his bike and turned on the ignition.

Freddie ran over to him. "Tony, hold on. You haven't even got your helmet on. Look. I'll take you wherever you want to go." He ran into the gate house and came out a minute later with the keys to the G-Wagon. "Come on."

Tony knew Freddie was doing the sensible thing. In his current state of mind, riding a power bike was a bad idea, especially without a helmet. In any case, none of them were going to let him leave the premises unless he was willing to fight them all. Perhaps he could fight Freddie or Chibby. But Kola was ex-military and the way he had restrained him, Tony couldn't get out of his grip.

He glared at the men surrounding him and with a grunt, switched off the ignition on the bike. He tossed the keys at Chibby. "Make sure there's no scratch on my bike. And I don't want Rita getting out of here tonight."

"I'll take care of you bike and your wife, boss." Chibby gave a mock salute.

Tony gave him another glare before heading to the car port. He didn't care that the man referred to Rita as his wife. He'd been there during the wedding ceremony in Beya and he was sure they had already given Kola the report. But Kola would hold off telling his parents unless it came to a life-threatening situation. That was one reason he respected the man.

Freddie got into the driver's seat and Tony sat in the passenger seat, throwing it into a reclining position before closing his eyes as they headed out.

Hours later, he was in a darkly lit bar trying to numb his roving thoughts with shots of whisky. Several women had already tried to chat him up. He'd sent them away not very nicely, either. He wasn't in the mood for any woman tonight. Not after finding out that the two closest to him had stabbed him in the back.

He waved at the barman for another shot of whisky.

"Are you still drinking lemonade?" he asked Freddie who still nursed the same glass of drink while Tony had had about three doubles. "You are no fun at all, Freddie."

"Is that what you're doing? Having fun?" Freddie said in an annoyed tone matching the sour expression on his face. "I thought you were drowning your sorrows."

"Well, we would be having fun if you joined me and had something stronger than lemonade."

"Someone's got to make sure you get home in one piece," Freddie said and took a sip of his drink. "Well, well, well. Look who just walked in."

Tony looked up. Petersen strode towards him with a young woman probably about Tony's age on his arm and a man walking behind him.

"Fancy meeting you here," Petersen said.

Tony leaned back into his seat, spreading out his arm at the back of the sofa. "Are you stalking me?"

The man laughed, full head back. The sound annoyed Tony but he just gritted his teeth.

"Hardly," Petersen said when he stopped chuckling. "I'm out with some friends, as you can see. This is Bridget and Andy."

The girl smiled at Tony in a seductive manner and the man nodded in acknowledgement. Petersen waved them over to another table. "Can I join you for a moment?"

Tony eyed him for a few seconds and nodded. "Sure."

Freddie stood up and stepped away but didn't go far. He joined Andy and Bridget on the other table.

"Did you get my message?" Petersen asked after a waiter had brought him a glass of whisky.

"Yes, I got your message loud and clear." Tony took a sip of his drink and leaned forward with one arm on the table. There was enough noise and music in the venue to mask their conversation. "What I don't get is, if you think I'm your son, why would you want to blackmail me?"

Petersen's face tensed up for a minute. "The threat is for Chief and Angela. For years, they have denied me access to you and pretended that I never existed. Well, I want to sort this out once and for all. This is the only way I could force their hands."

"Really?" Tony cocked his brow sardonically.

"Of course." Petersen leaned forward, his voice low as he jabbed his hand through the air. "If I hadn't threatened, they wouldn't have told you. Don't you want to know the truth?"

Tony leaned back into his seat and thought about it. Yes, knowing the truth about his birth would be good. But at what price? The disintegration of his family? "Truth has many shades. It's not always black or white."

"Touché." Petersen mirrored his pose and leaned back, too.

Tony took the moment of silence between them to study the man. He'd never really paid much attention to Kris on a personal level except that he was a good client of Reams. Now, he watched the man as a potential father figure. But he just couldn't picture himself addressing Petersen as "Father." Perhaps if he'd never had a father figure in his life, it would've been easier.

Despite all their ups and downs, Chief Essien had raised him and done his best for him. He was the only man he could refer to as "Dad." Partly why he didn't want to take part in the DNA test. He couldn't bear the thought that the man he'd called "Dad" wasn't his father.

"I already have a father," Tony said. "What if I don't want you as one?"

Petersen sighed. For the first time, Tony saw a softening around his mouth.

"We don't get to choose our birth families. I would rather know definitely if I have a son or not. What you do with that information afterward is up to you."

"You know I won't give in." He shrugged. "I will call your bluff."

"Then you leave me with little choice. Your family will suffer as a result."

"If you print that article, I will never be your son."

The hardness returned to Petersen's face as he stood up. "So be it." He turned to his friends at the other table. "We have to go."

They scuttled off after Petersen. Freddie returned to sit beside Tony. "I take it that didn't go very well."

"Not for him." Tony returned to his drinking.

CHAPTER THIRTY-ONE

Rita knew when her world started falling apart. She'd been in Beya with Tony. They'd had a blissful wedding night and had still been basking in its glow until Kola had arrived to take them back to Lagos unexpectedly.

She'd sensed something bad could have happened. Since no one had said anything, she'd been waiting for the outcome of Tony's meeting with his parents. However, she hadn't been expecting his behaviour when he'd returned home. He'd been rude and downright mean to her. Calling her a liar because he'd seen the article she'd written. So she hadn't meant him to see it. She'd thought she'd deleted it. Somehow, he'd managed to dig it out.

Why had he gone to snoop on her laptop in the first place? She sat alone that evening, wondering what had happened. She didn't even have Freddie to talk to as it seemed he'd gone out with Tony. Although Chibby was in the gadget room upstairs, she couldn't talk to him. She didn't have the same rapport with him as she did with Freddie.

She couldn't even call Kechi to tell her because she didn't even know what to say. She'd agreed with Tony they wouldn't tell anyone yet about the wedding until he'd told his parents. She still wasn't sure if he'd told his parents or not.

Bored of flicking channels and tired of waiting for Tony to get back, she went upstairs. After getting ready, she pulled on a t-shirt and got into bed. She fell asleep thinking of Tony and how wonderful things had been between them in Beya.

The creaking sound of an opening door roused her. She peeled her eyelids apart to the dim light of the lamp and found Tony walking across the room with unsteady footsteps. Was he drunk? She'd never seen him drunk before. Something terrible must have happened.

"Tony, are you okay?" She bolted upright, heart thumping.

He staggered over to the settee at the foot of the bed and tugged off his boots. "Stop asking stupid questions. Do I look like I'm okay to you?"

His words came out slurred.

His harsh tone cut through her like a knife and she blinked back tears. "What is wrong with you? You've had an attitude since we returned to Lagos. Why are you being such a bastard?"

"I am a bastard," he snapped at her. "Or haven't you heard I don't have a father? Unless you're counting Petersen. But you know that already."

He threw his boots at the wall. The loud thud made her flinch. He stormed out, slamming the door behind him.

Oh, God. What was going on? Why were they fighting? Should she go after him? In the mood he was in, they would only end up fighting more.

Growling, she pounded her frustrations into the pillow. Getting back to sleep proved near impossible as she tossed and turned. Tony was so angry with her; he was refusing to sleep in the same bed with her. Why would he say he didn't have a father when Chief Essien was alive and well? And what did he mean by his reference to Petersen? She could swear her boss had a hand in whatever had gone wrong. If Tony wouldn't tell her, then she would have to confront Petersen in the morning.

She eventually drifted off to sleep close to dawn. The sound of her phone ringing had her jolting out of bed. She reached across to the bedside table and saw that it was Kechi calling her.

"Morning, Kechi," she said in a groggy voice.

"Ha, Rita," her friend said. "Where are you?"

"I'm over at Tony's house. We got back earlier than planned yesterday so I just stayed at his. What's up? Are you at work?"

"You are still at Tony's. Ha. Is he there with you?"

"I'm in the bedroom. He's not here at the moment."

"Take my advice and get out of there before he logs onto the internet and sees what you've written."

"Huh? What are you talking about?"

"Your article about Tony and his family is trending on social media this morning. Everyone in my office is talking about it."

"What article?" She clutched her hand to her chest, dreading the answer.

"The one you wrote about Tony Essien. All the major online news media are running with it."

"Oh my—" she cut off her exclamation with a hand over her mouth. That's what Tony was angry about last night. She scrambled out of bed and rushed to pick up her laptop. "Hang on a minute."

She logged on and did a search for Tony Essien on the internet. The first ten sites listed were news channels and they had more or less the same headlines. *Tony Essien, drug addict and illegitimate son.* She clicked on the first link and saw her name as the news reporter.

She cringed. "Oh, God! What have I done?"

"Girl, I never knew you had it in you to write something like that. I thought you were in love with the guy. But some of the stuff you wrote is just horrible. When Tony sees it, he's going to flip. You need to get out of there unless you have a death wish."

Tony had already seen it and he had already flipped.

"I have to find Tony. I have to explain."

"I don't know how you're going to explain this."

"I promise you it's more complicated that it looks. I'll explain everything to you later." She reached for Tony's robe and covered herself before heading for the door.

"Okay. But be safe, please. And call me."

"I will," she said as she ran down the stairs. She looked outside and Tony's and Freddie's bikes were still out there. She walked into the sitting room and found Freddie pacing.

"'Morning, Freddie," she said tentatively. "Do you know where Tony is?"

"Out," he said in a low voice with his back to her.

"Out where? I need to talk to him."

Freddie whirled around. "He doesn't want to talk to you."

She bent her head forward as her heart sank. "Has everyone seen the article?"

"The whole world has seen your piece of journalism, Miss Reporter. Congratulations. You got what you wanted."

Her stomach twisted. "It's not what I wanted. You've got to believe me. I didn't want that to get out."

"Yeah. Like I'm going to believe that."

"You have to. Why would I get it published and still be here? Why would I marry Tony if that was how I still felt?"

"I don't know. I don't know what kind of sick mind games you can conjure up. Perhaps watching Tony's world implode around him is what you really want. Because that's what you're going to get."

"What?"

"Tony is this close to relapsing." Freddie pinched his thumb and forefinger together. "All he needs is the opportunity and he might take a sniff of something just to make the nightmare go away for a moment. And then he'll be lost. Because this time, there won't be a family to hold him together when they've all fallen apart. Thanks to you."

"No. No." Rita shook her head as the enormity of what she'd done hit her. "I don't want that to happen. I swear to you. I need to see Tony. Please help me."

"Why should I help you? I should be out there with Tony making sure he is safe. Instead, I'm stuck here with you." He turned his back to her again.

"Fine. If you won't help me, I'll go and look for him myself."

"You won't get very far since you're not allowed out of this estate."

"What? Who said that?"

"Who else?"

Tony said she couldn't be let out? If he was so mad at her, shouldn't he be getting rid of her instead of keeping her locked in?

"We'll see about that."

She dialled Tony's phone number. It rang for several seconds but he didn't pick up. Annoyed, she huffed and went upstairs to shower and get dressed. She'd see if anyone would actually stop her from walking out of the gates.

Dressed and ready to go out, she ignored Freddie and walked the distance down the long drive to the gates. Both the pedestrian gates and the double gates were locked. She walked over to the gate house and peered into the window of the foyer. The gate man lay on the long sofa.

She pulled the door. "*Oga* gateman, please open the gate for me. I need to go out."

He sat up and she noticed large plasters on his cheek and over the bridge of his nose.

"Aunty, abeg sorry o. But I no fit. *Oga* Tony talk say make I not let you comot for house."

So it was true. Tony had instructed them not to let her out. She puffed out a breath and tried a different approach. "It's okay. I'm just popping out quickly. I'll be back in no time."

"Sorry, ma. I no gree. I no get *Oga* Tony chance. He been put me for hospital last night. I no want him wahala."

"Tony did that to you?" She pointed at his face.

The gateman nodded.

Freddie had been right. Tony was really on the edge if he could beat up the gateman and cause injuries. As much as she wanted to get out, she didn't want to get the man in any more trouble with Tony.

"Okay. Don't worry."

She headed back to the house. Perhaps she could persuade Freddie to take her to see Tony.

She found Freddie on the phone. He looked at her when she came in.

"Yes, she's here," Freddie said. "Tony wants to talk to you."

That surprised her. He passed the phone over to her.

"Tony, I—"

Tony cut her off. "Freddie will bring you over to Rebel Studios. There are some papers I need you to sign."

His voice was so cold and distant, it was as if something had died inside of him. Her gut twisted and her heart ached. She'd done this to him. At least, he wasn't kicking her out. There was hope.

"Okay," she said in a deflated voice and handed the phone back to Freddie who switched it off and pocketed it.

"Are you ready to go?"

"Yes."

The drive out to Rebel Studios was silent in the SUV. Freddie couldn't seem to stand her presence and she didn't seem to know what to say to him. He'd warned her that if she ever hurt Tony, she would have him to deal with. The fact that he even kept civil with her spoke of his professionalism.

Tony, however, was a different kettle of fish. As soon as she walked into one of the studios Dapo had ushered her into, his anger was apparent even if it was muted.

"Here she is," Tony announced as he stood and approached her, taking her arm and pulling her to where Joel and another man she didn't recognise sat. "The woman of the hour. Gentlemen, I don't know if you've met my wife, Rita. She is a potential award winning actress and I just found out last night that she is also in line for awards as an investigative journalist. Fancy that, hmmm."

Rita cringed and shifted from one foot to the other trying to get out of Tony's grip. She wished the ground would open up and swallow her. She managed to give a tight smile.

"Some of us can't even find one thing we're good at. Yet, she's been blessed with two talents." He turned to look at her, his expression grim. "This is Rotimi, my lawyer, and of course, you know Joel already.

"Nice to meet you," Rotimi said but he didn't stand up or extend his hand.

Joel just nodded at her. Neither of them said congratulations. Rita knew instantly these two were not in her corner.

"Thank you," she muttered.

"Rotimi has the contract for the role in the new movie," Tony said.

Rearing back with surprise, she turned to face her husband. "I got the part?"

"Of course you did. Didn't I just say you were a great actress?"

Rotimi lifted a brown A4 envelope from the pile on the table. "Your contract is here. Read through it and sign all the sections I've highlighted."

"Okay. Thank you," she said before biting her lips as she took the folder. "Tony, can I talk to you privately for a moment, please?"

"Gents, excuse me," Tony said and strode out of the room down the hall to his office.

She pushed the door to shut it when she got in after him.

"Leave the door open," he barked.

"Tony, I know I deserve your behaviour. But that article wasn't me."

He swirled around and pointed a finger at her. "You see, this here is why I'm fucking furious. I know I'm screwed up. I know I'm a failure. But you know what? I fucking own it. I take responsibility for the things I've done, good and bad. But you—" he waved his hand up and down at her, "—you came to me looking all innocent, making me believe you were genuine. Making me believe I could make something out of my life. Making me believe I'd found the one person who would accept me as I was. Not knowing you would become the mother of all my nightmares."

"Tony—"

"No. I don't want any fucking excuses. Stop hiding behind Petersen. The man is fucked up and yes, I blame him for a few things. But he doesn't hide who he is." He jabbed his finger at her. "You need to take responsibility for your actions. Petersen published that article. But you wrote it. Admit it. Take responsibility. Own it. I will have a whole lot more respect for you than with all the fucking excuses."

She swallowed hard. He was right. If they were going to move past this, she needed to accept responsibility and beg for his forgiveness. If she hadn't written the article, Petersen wouldn't have had any ammunition over Tony or his family. It didn't matter that she hadn't written about the drugs. Petersen must have found out somehow. Perhaps he'd put a listening device in her room.

She remembered Andy. He'd been in her house. He could've sent the file to Petersen on her laptop. Her computer hadn't been sleeping when she'd brought him water to drink. Had he planted a listening device in her house?

She sucked in a deep breath. "Tony, you are right. I am responsible. If I hadn't written that article, Petersen wouldn't have had anything to publish. I'm sorry for what I've done. Please forgive me."

Tears misted her eyes and she lowered to her knees.

"Get up. Get up," he said curtly. "It's good of you to apologise but it's too late now."

"Tony, please," she sobbed, her body racking, her gut twisting.

"Enough." He dragged her onto her feet. "I don't want your tears."

"What do you want from me? Take whatever you want. Just forgive me, please." She clung onto his arms.

"If you're looking for absolution, you've come to the wrong person. I have no forgiveness in me right now."

"If you won't forgive me, then I have to go. I can't bear to have you hate me so much." She turned away.

He grabbed her and turned her around.

"You think this is hate?" He gave a harsh laugh. "The only person I hate is myself for still wanting you even when you've crushed me to dust. For not having the strength to let you go as everyone keeps telling me to do."

He scrubbed his head with the other hand.

"But you know what, I'm not going to let you go. We are husband and wife, after all. In Beya tradition, there is no divorce. The only thing that will part us is death. So if you want to leave me, be prepared to shoot me down or drive a knife into my heart."

"Tony, please."

"No. You took an oath for better or for worse. You are not going to drop me into a nightmare and walk away. You will live it every day with me no matter how bad it gets."

"Okay," she said. She'd done this to him and as Freddie had warned, there was a real chance he would relapse. She couldn't leave him to cope alone. She had to face this with him. She loved him too much.

"Do not give up hope or faith in each other."

Ma Yise's words came back to her. She couldn't give up on him. Hopefully with time, his anger would fade away and he would forgive her.

"I'll stay. I love you, Tony."

"I'll believe that when I see it." He sidestepped her and stalked out of the office.

CHAPTER THIRTY-TWO

The nightmare didn't go away. Over the days and weeks, it grew, engulfing every member of the Essien family. It was obvious the relationship between Tony's parents was strained as Petersen gave press releases and interviews about his past affair with Tony's mother and Tony being their love child. He kept up his challenge for a DNA test to be carried out to dispute his claim.

The Essien family issued no public statements. Privately, their weekly get-togethers continued but Tony didn't make any appearances and he didn't take Rita to them, either.

Tony and Rita's relationship didn't fare well, either. They lived in the same house. But Rita slept in the bed alone every night, crying her eyes out. He hadn't touched her or made love with her since they'd returned from Beya. Tony remained cold. In other people's presence, he maintained civility. When they were alone, he ignored her. He rarely kept her company, always finding an excuse to get away.

He spent long hours at the studio or the restaurant. Every time they went out to an event, they were hounded by paparazzi. She lived in a gilded cage. She couldn't go anywhere without company. Her phone conversations were listened to; her movements were watched. She tottered on the edge of madness. She thought she could cope because she hoped Tony would eventually forgive her. But his behaviour towards her didn't change.

The movie production continued although some of the sponsors pulled out citing Tony's addiction. Rita's misery continued as he kept his word by keeping her on the cast. There were moments when she wished he'd let her go and perhaps his life would get better.

About two months after the trouble started, Chief Essien was rushed into hospital, suffering from high blood pressure. The doctor prescribed plenty of rest and no stress. Tony's mood spiralled from there and Rita knew she had to do something. If Tony's father died, Tony would never forgive her, as he would see his father's death as payback for her father's death.

She would have to get to Petersen. But she couldn't get there without anyone knowing. So she decided to recruit Kechi to help her out. She didn't tell her on the phone but arranged for them to go shopping. In the shopping mall, she managed to convince her friend in the ladies, out of Lanre's earshot, to help her.

Kechi distracted Lanre as Rita slipped out of the shopping mall. She used Kechi's phone to call a taxi and headed to Petersen's house.

At Petersen's house, the gateman seemed to recognise her and let her in. She walked toward the front door but overheard Petersen's voice coming from the side of the house. She stood by the corner and listened as he spoke to someone on the phone.

"Now that he's finally agreed to take the DNA test, we need to make sure everything goes as planned. I'm paying you a lot of money to get this done." There was a pause as he seemed to listen to the other person. "Yes, if I get the result I'm expecting tonight, you'll get the balance in the morning." He paused again. "Good. I look forward to it."

She heard approaching footsteps and straightened, pretending she was walking to the house.

"Ah, Miss Dike. What do I owe this surprise?" Petersen asked as she rounded the corner.

"Good afternoon, sir," she greeted him. "I came to ask for your help."

"My help?" He looked at her sceptically. "Shouldn't you be asking the Essiens for help since you seem to have taken their side?"

"Things haven't worked out between Tony and me. I've had to practically escape captivity from him. He watches everything I do. My phone is tapped. I can't go anywhere without his permission."

"So how did you get here?"

"I had to get my friend to help me. I took her phone with me so they couldn't track where I was going."

"Are you sure? You know I'm not one you should cross. I will make you pay for it if you do."

"I'm sure. I wouldn't dare."

"So what do you want me to help you with?"

"I wondered if it's okay to come back to work at Zen Media. When I leave Tony, I won't be able to work in the movie industry any more. I want to continue with my career as a journalist."

"Fine. You can have your old job back." He scratched the stubble on his jaw. "But you have to do something for me."

"What is it?"

"Convince Tony to take the Petersen name. He doesn't have to call me Dad. But I want him to accept my name."

"Sir. I'm not sure Tony will ever change his surname. He is an Essien if not in blood but in attitude."

"Well, it is your job to convince him that being an Essien only brings him trouble. And his past history is only proof of that. Do whatever it takes. You duped him before. You can dupe him again. Do this for me and I'll give you whatever you want."

"Okay, sir. I'll do it."

"Good. Do you want to come inside?"

"No. I have to head back. I don't want anyone to get suspicious."

"Remember what I told you."

"Yes, sir." She headed out and got into the taxi she'd hired that had been waiting for her. She'd booked him for the day.

They headed back to her old house. She'd wanted to pick up some things and it would give her a good cover in case Petersen had her followed. When she got to her old house, she called Freddie's phone because Tony didn't answer her calls anymore.

"Rita, where are you?" he said when he answered.

"I'm in my house. I—"

"Stay there. I'm coming over."

"Freddie, listen. I have information about Petersen than can help Tony."

"You can tell me all about it when I get there." He hung up.

Hyped up, Rita paced the living room until there was a knock on the door.

"That was fast." She pulled the door open. "Anayo!"

She tried to push the door shut but he pushed it back and she fell backward as he stomped into the house and locked the door behind him.

"Anayo, what are you doing here?" She cringed back. The look in his eyes terrified her.

He sneered at her and stalked towards her. "I've come to take what you denied me. I dated you for a year, gave you money for your family, and even promised to marry you. But you refused to open your legs for me." He yanked her up and tossed her on the sofa.

"Anayo, no!" she shouted and he backhanded her. Her head spun and she struggled to see anything for a moment.

"And that drug addict comes along and within a few days, you spread yourself out for him like a slut to do whatever he wanted. Now I hear you are married to him."

He shoved her down with one hand and she kicked out, hitting him with hands and limbs. He slapped her over and over again until her ears were ringing and the room was spinning. She struggled to breathe and she realised he'd gagged her with some cloth that covered part of her nose and her mouth. Her eyes smarted and tears fell as she tried to suck in air and fight him but his weight on her body made both impossible. He tugged her jeans off and it hung around her ankles, restraining her legs as he shoved her thighs apart. Pain seared through her and she blanked out.

***

Tony paced the hospital waiting room, the image of how he'd found Rita unconscious and bleeding with Anayo over her replaying over and over in his mind. He'd nearly lost his mind after walking into her house and seeing that.

Lanre had brought Kechi to him when he couldn't find Rita during her shopping trip and Kechi had confessed that she'd left. Since neither of them knew where she'd gone, Lanre had brought Kechi to Rebel Studios and they'd been there when Rita had called. They'd hopped on the bikes and ridden straight to her house only to find the awful scene.

The way he'd kicked and pounded into Anayo, only God knew if the man was still alive. If he was, Tony wanted to kill him. Only Freddie's reminder that they needed to get Rita to hospital had saved the man's life.

They'd brought Rita to hospital in the taxi she'd hired. She'd been rushed into emergency surgery and Tony had been pacing outside ever since. For the first time since he could remember, he prayed to any deity out there that was listening. He would swap everything he had for Rita's life. He would swap his life for hers. It didn't matter what she'd done to him. He would forgive all as long as she was well. He didn't want to lose her.

He couldn't lose her...

"Tony!"

He turned around to find his mother, Mark, and Kola walking over. His eyes smarted that they'd come.

"We heard what happened. Are you okay?" his mother asked.

"I'm fine," he said.

"What about Rita? How is she doing?" his brother asked.

"She is in surgery. She was unconscious when we got there. The animal had covered her mouth and nose."

"Oh, no!" his mother exclaimed in shock.

"I don't know what I'll do if she doesn't make it." For the first time in his life, he grew genuinely scared.

Mark put a hand on his shoulder. "She's in capable hands. I'm sure they are doing their best." He turned to Kola. "I hope we are making that asshole pay."

"Oh, he'll pay, all right," Kola said. "When the boys finish with him, they are tossing him into a police cell with some of the hardest criminals in there. He'll get to experience what rape feels like on the receiving end every day for a very long time."

"Mr. Essien."

Tony swivelled around and one of the doctors dressed in blue scrubs stood in front of him.

"How is she? How is my wife?" Tony asked, heart thumping.

"We can talk in my office," the doctor said.

"Tell me here. This is my mother and brothers."

The doctor nodded. "We had to rush your wife into emergency surgery as she was bleeding heavily internally and suffering from asphyxiation. We stemmed the bleeding and revived her."

"Thank God," Tony's mum said.

"Does that mean she's okay?"

"She will make a full recovery. But unfortunately, we were unable to save the baby."

Tony gasped. The baby? "She was pregnant?"

"Yes. I'm sorry for your loss," the doctor said.

Tony's head hung forward.

"I'm so sorry, Tony," his brother said.

He nodded, blinking back tears. "Can I see her now?"

"Sure. But she's only allowed one visitor at a time. She needs to rest. The nurse will take you to her when you're ready."

Tony nodded as the doctor walked away. He turned to his family that looked as devastated as he felt. "Thank you for coming. I really appreciate your support."

"Of course we had to come as soon as we heard. Dad would've been here but he's under strict doctor's order for bed rest and Felix is in New York with Ebony and Alex. Faith will be here later."

Tony's eyes watered some more. He really couldn't do without this family, no matter how dysfunctional they were.

Kola pulled him into a hug. "Remember what Chief always says. Blood or not—"

"Family is family," Tony finished, the corner of his lips lifting in a smile. His father had adopted Kola who shared no blood into his family. There was no reason Tony couldn't be a part of it, even if he was half-blood. "Thank you."

"You are welcome. Now go and see your wife."

The walk down the hospital corridor to Rita's room had to be the longest he'd ever taken. Apprehension knotted his stomach as to what state she would be in. But the doctor had said she was alive and that meant there was hope she would make a full recovery. He pushed open the door to her room and his heart stopped.

She was hooked up to a drip and heart rate monitor as well as other machines. Tears misted his eyes and fell down his cheeks. He closed his eyes shut, trying to stop himself for doubling over.

"Tony."

Her voice sounded so weak.

He opened his eyes and was beside her bed in two strides, holding onto her free hand. Her face was covered in cuts and stitches. He leaned over and pressed his lips all her face. "I'm so sorry."

"This is not your fault. I shouldn't have gone out without somebody with me. But I was trying to bring you proof that Petersen was planning something really bad."

"It's okay, Buttons. I don't care about Petersen. I just care about you. If I hadn't been so angry...if I had forgiven you earlier, this wouldn't have happened."

"This was going to happen, one way or the other. It was the price I had to pay for betraying you. Your suffering is my suffering. I took the oath."

Tears ran down her face and his tears mingled with hers as he kissed her. "Do you forgive me, Buttons? Please! I promise that for the rest of my life, I will never let you go through anything like this."

"I forgive you, Tony. I'm just sad I lost the baby."

"You knew you were pregnant?" He leaned back in shock.

She bit her lip. "Yes, I'm sorry I didn't tell you. I took the test a few days ago. It was partly why I had to do something about Petersen. I wanted us to stop fighting."

He sighed. "It's okay. I'm just glad we're not fighting anymore."

She gave him a beautiful smile even through her pain. "Promise me we'll try again soon."

"Try what again?"

"For a baby."

"You bet we'll try again soon, when the doctor reassures me you're well enough for it."

She giggled. "I love you when you're being so macho."

"And I love you. Period."

He kissed her again to emphasise his words.

CHAPTER THIRTY-THREE

Freddie drove the SUV down the short drive after the gateman had let them in. The car pulled up underneath the portico of the modern, stucco-fronted three-level mansion.

Tony sat in the car reluctant to get out although the engine had been killed. "So this is my father's house."

His bodyguard nodded. "You know nothing changes between us. I've got your back regardless of the DNA result."

He took a deep breath and puffed it out. "Freddie, I don't think I've thanked you for your support, especially in the last few months. You are my brother as much as Mark and Felix and Kola."

Freddie's hand rested on his shoulder and squeezed. "And you are my brother. You don't need to thank me."

"In any case, thank you. I don't think I could've done this without you. Are you ready?"

"Ready when you are."

Tony pushed open the door to the passenger side as his bodyguard strode around to the entrance and pressed the bell. The red slab pulled back and Andy ushered them inside, leading them into a reception room where Petersen stood to welcome them.

"Tony, it is good to see you here."

Thankfully, the man didn't try to embrace him or even shake his hand.

"Kris," he said unable to address him any other way although he had proof the man sired him. "You know Freddie."

"Yes. Andy, show him around the place while I talk with Tony," Petersen said before waving for Tony to sit down.

Tony nodded to Freddie who followed Andy out and then he sank into the red sofa, leaned back and crossed one leg over the other at the knee, projecting outward calm he didn't feel.

Finding out Petersen had sired him had been devastating news, aggravated by everything he and Rita had suffered at the hand of the same man. But he'd had no other choice but to go through with the DNA test when his ill father had begged him to undertake the procedure and end the stalemate between him and Petersen. So here he sat, sucking up the fact that he had a different parent from the one who had raised him.

The man in question strode across to the bar section. "How about some scotch to celebrate, or would you rather have champagne?"

"Whisky is fine." He certainly didn't feel in a celebratory mood, not with his wife at home still recovering from the brutal attack by her ex. Lucky for the man, he sat locked in police custody. Otherwise, Tony would've killed him. Last he'd heard, Anayo had been assaulted by his cellmates and ended in the prison medical ward with injuries.

Petersen returned with the drinks and gave him a glass. "Here's to a new family."

"To families," Tony toasted before taking a sip and savouring the burn down his throat.

They sat in silence for a minute before Kris said, "I'm going to arrange for another bodyguard for you."

Tony's nose flared and he tilted his chin up. "Freddie stays with me or I don't stay."

"I understand you are attached to him. But there's no need keeping an Essien employee."

"This is not negotiable. He doesn't work for my father."

Petersen's smile died. "You're right about that. He doesn't work for me."

"You know what I mean. He doesn't work for Chief Essien and I don't see him as an employee." He took a calming breath. There was no need to lose his temper. It wouldn't change the situation. Only make it worse. "He is my friend. The closest thing I have to a brother right now."

"Look..." Petersen's voice softened. "I know it must be hard for you to come to terms with the whole situation. You are my son and I want to make you happy. So I'll let Freddie stay if it pleases you."

"It does. Thank you."

"You're welcome. I want to get the practicalities sorted out. My lawyer is coming over later to sort out the paperwork. Once you sign the affidavit confirming you as my son, I will arrange for him to name you on my will as my sole heir. He'll also show you details of the Petersen estate including the apartment in Victoria Island I bought recently as a gift to you."

"Really? You are naming me in your will?"

"Yes, of course. You are the only child I have and my closest relative. I've waited a long time to have you in my life and having you legally acknowledge me as your father will make me very happy, indeed."

Jaw tightened, Tony lowered his gaze. If things had been different, perhaps this news would've pleased him. But after everything that had happened, he couldn't help the rise of bile in his throat at taking anything from Petersen. He swallowed down the bitterness in his mouth and looked up at a grinning Kris.

"It'll be good to finally know where I belong. But I can't help wondering why it took you so long to finally want to claim me as your son."

Kris's expression sobered. "I tried. I loved your mother and it broke my heart when she dumped me for Chief. I knew it was because I wasn't as wealthy as he was." His lips flattened and his eyes hardened. "When I found out she was pregnant, I knew it was mine. But she cut off all communication. There wasn't much I could do but work hard to make money, and plot my revenge. If I couldn't have her, I would definitely fight to get you."

"How far would you have gone to claim me?"

He shrugged. "You know what I did already."

Tony nodded. "The threats, blackmails. What if none of that had worked?"

"I would've kept up the heat until Chief Essien's family disintegrated around him. It was already working. I know Angela is miserable and Chief is very ill. I had every intention of getting what I wanted one way or another."

"Even murder?"

"I'll be honest with you because you are my son and this stays between us, right?"

"Right."

"I had planned an assassination as a back-up, if everything else didn't work. Lucky for Chief, there's no need for that now."

"You were even going to have the DNA result doctored, weren't you?" Tony asked. Rita had revealed what she'd found out the day she'd been attacked. As a result they'd employed the services of other independent labs, three times. The outcome had remained the same each time.

Petersen shrugged. "I didn't have to. I'm glad the results vindicated my actions."

"But why did you pick Rita? You could've accomplished your plan without her." This was the one thing which bugged Tony no end. And he needed to know the answer.

"She was just a pawn. A pretty face I wanted to use to get closer to you. I let her believe Apex Financials had been involved in her father's demise and she lapped it up."

Tony couldn't help the growl the rumbled through him and the tightening of his jaw. "She is my wife."

"That news came as a shocker, I can tell you. You were supposed to fuck her and dump her."

"I love her." He stood, hands balled.

"After everything she did to you, you still love her? Wake up, son. She screwed you over. Women cannot be trusted. Fuck them by all means but never, ever fall in love with them."

Tony flinched as he made the realisation. "This hatred you have for women is because of my mother, isn't it? You're still not over her."

"Oh, I'm well over her. I don't need one woman when I can have as many as I want. Think of all the fun we're going to have, you and me. You can have the pick of any woman you want."

"I don't want other women. Rita is the only one for me."

"Don't tell me you are still interested in her. She is damaged goods after what Anayo did with her."

"What?" Dread slithered down Tony's spine. Only members of his immediate family knew, and Anayo's arrest hadn't been made public yet. "How did you know what happened?"

"The man is my employee. He was assigned to keep an eye on the girl. To keep her in line. The last time she came here, I suspected she was up to something, so I sent him to shut her up."

Tony didn't know when he leapt over the low table separating them. The next thing he knew, his hands were wrapped around the man's neck, his right knee bearing down Kris's chest as he made a gurgling sound.

"You sent that asshole to rape my wife. She nearly died and we lost our baby," he snarled at the bastard.

Commotion exploded around him, heavy footsteps resounded in the room and hands tugged him as people attempted to pull him off the choking Petersen. Even as they got him off, he fought to return and strangle the man for what he'd done.

"Tony, calm down." Kola's voice penetrated the fury of his mind.

Two men in police uniforms helped Petersen up. A third held onto a handcuffed Andy.

"Officers, arrest him." Tony pointed at Petersen. "He arranged the attack on my wife."

"Officers, there's been a misunderstanding."

"Mr. Petersen, I am Detective Sadiku," a man who wasn't in uniform said. "You are under arrest for conspiracy to murder, attempted murder, and battery and assault. You need to come with us to the police station."

"What? This is a family matter. No need for the police. Moreover, you saw him attacking me. But I don't want to press charges. Anyway, how did you guys get here?"

"There's been a sting operation. We have you confessing on tape to blackmail, attempted murder, and other crimes."

"What? Tony?" Kris asked in an uncertain tone, his eyes narrowing. "What did you do?"

"I played your game." He curled his lips in a smug smile as he pulled up his shirt, exposing the wire and microphone taped to his skin. "I played your fucking game and beat you at it. Check-fucking-mate."

"You can't do this. You are my son."

"I told you months ago that if you printed that article, I would never be your son. You printed it."

"I—I...It was a mistake."

Just then, Mark and Felix strode in with more men wearing uniforms bearing the Economic and Financial Crimes Commission logo.

"Mr. Petersen, we are from the EFCC and your assets have been frozen pending investigations of insider trading and money laundering. You are requested to vacate these premises immediately."

The men handcuffed him.

"You can't do this. I need to call my lawyer."

"You can do that from the police station," Mr. Sadiku said.

"Due to the EFCC investigations, your shares in Apex Holdings are forfeit. But just to make things fair for you, they have been sold and this is the check for the value," Felix said as he dropped a cheque slip on the table.

"You can't do that," Kris protested.

"Yes, we can. It's part of the contract. If any Apex Holdings shareholder is investigated for fraudulent transactions, their shares are nullified or sold if a buyer is found at the earliest opportunity."

One of the EFCC men picked up the slip. "We have to seize this, too."

Tony couldn't help smiling. Petersen would lose everything he'd worked hard for during the past few years. He would know what it felt like to be desperate.

The man kept protesting as the officers dragged him out of the building. The gatekeeper got dismissed and they secured the property.

Felix, Mark, Kola, and Freddie stood around Tony while Petersen was taken to one of the police cars.

"Don't let them do this to me," Kris begged, his handcuffed hands raised towards Tony. "I'm your father, your family. Your blood."

"You are nothing to me," Tony spat out. "My name is Tony Essien, Chief is my father, and these men beside me are my brothers. My family. Blood or no blood."

Tony turned his back and faced his brothers as his birth father was taken away to face up to the crimes he'd committed. "We did it." His lips curled in a slow smile. "We fucking did it."

When Kola had devised the plan to entrap Petersen, to snare him in his own trap, Tony had been unsure. He'd been certain he would've strangled Petersen on sight if he'd come close to the man. But his brothers had believed he could pull it off and Kola had trained him on how to control his emotions and keep them hidden. And it had worked.

"You did it," Mark said, sporting a huge grin as he clutched his shoulders. "You took down Petersen."

"Yes, you did," Felix said, grabbing his other shoulder.

"I couldn't have done it without you guys. I couldn't have survived the past three months without you all. I couldn't have wished for better brothers than all of you. I love you guys." His voice was choked with emotions.

And it was all thanks to his father, Chief Essien, who had raised them. Despite his faults, his father had done one thing right. He'd taught them to love each other. His brothers had stood by him no matter how much he'd screwed up, even recently bailing out his movie when the sponsors had walked away after news of his addiction broke. Felix had made sure the finance didn't get pulled and Mark had helped him sign up new sponsors.

"We love you too, Tony," they chanted.

"Group hug, people."

They laughed as they huddled together out there on a quiet tree-lined street on this early evening, all five of them, billionaires and bodyguards, Essien or not, shoulder to shoulder and chanted, "Blood or not, family is family."

OUT NOW!
KOLA, THE ESSIEN SERIES, BOOK 4

BLURB:

When sassy heiress Tari Essien needs a place to escape the pressures of the hounding press, she turns to Kola Banks, a deeply scarred ex-soldier who's also the Essien chief of security. Kola can't offer Tari anything more than his protection. She's family, for goodness sake, even if they share no blood ties.

It's a weekend of lessons for both of them. Together, they can't avoid the explosive heat that sizzles between them, nor help pushing each others' boundaries physically as well as emotionally.

But when the weekend ends and Tari's life is in danger, will Kola put his body as well as his heart in the line of fire to keep her safe?

OTHER BOOKS BY LOVE AFRICA PRESS

Healing His Medic by Nana Prah

Queer and Sexy Collection Volume 1

His Defiant Princess by Nana Prah

His Inherited Princess by Empi Baryeh

His Captive Princess by Kiru Taye

CONNECT WITH US

Facebook.com/LoveAfricaPress

Twitter.com/LoveAfricaPress

Instagram.com/LoveAfricaPress

www.loveafricapress.com